"I know you can do it, Daddy."

With a heavy sigh, Rafe lifted his head and locked eyes with Dani. He clearly wanted rescuing.

Dani lifted her brows as if to say, *Sorry, you're on your own*. Really, what harm would it do to look a little foolish if it made Frannie happy?

But she suspected Rafe wasn't the kind of man to let himself be caught at a disadvantage. Not for anyone. Not even a five-year-old child who just happened to be his daughter.

And then the frown lines across his forehead disappeared. He nodded slowly, even as he muttered a curse under his breath. "All right," he told them, "I'll enter the contest. Bring on the pies."

"Go, Daddy!" Frannie squealed. She bounced in place as if she had springs on the bottom of her sneakers.

Over his shoulder he gave them a look of such seriousness that he might have been a soldier going off to war. "If I end up being sick, don't say I didn't warn you."

Dani stared after him in disbelief. Maybe Rafe wasn't complete‿ he was learning

Available in September 2008 from Mills & Boon® Superromance

For His Daughter by Ann Evans
Rafe is learning how to be a parent. He can't afford to be distracted. Still, he's finding it harder and harder to ignore Dani – the woman from his past who may be his future!

Her Sister's Keeper by Julia Penney
When her sister goes missing, Melanie realises that she needs to let go of the past. To save Ariel, she'll have to trust Kent, the man who's shown her how to love again.

A Time To Come Home by Darlene Gardner
Tyler is a straight-arrow prosecutor and her secret could ruin him. Diana will risk everything to protect him – but Tyler's determined to raise his daughter with the woman he loves.

Small Town Cinderella by Caron Todd
Innocent Emily is suspicious of the handsome newcomer – but as he pays her more and more attention, she begins to blossom. It's time for Emily to seize her moment and start living.

For His Daughter

ANN EVANS

MILLS & BOON

Pure reading pleasure™

*This edition published in Great Britain September 2008
by Harlequin Mills & Boon Limited,
Eton House, 18-24 Paradise Road, Richmond, Surrey TW9 1SR*

*First published in 2006 by Harlequin Enterprises Limited
under the title Misfit Father.*

© Ann Bair 2006

ISBN: 978 0 263 86172 3

38-0908

Harlequin Mills & Boon policy is to use papers that are natural, renewable and recyclable products and made from wood grown in sustainable forests. The logging and manufacturing processes conform to the legal environmental regulations of the country of origin.

*Printed and bound in Spain
by Litografia Rosés S.A., Barcelona*

For the wonderful women of Toronto –
Kathleen, Zilla, Laura and Paula.
If I could bottle your understanding,
patience and expertise, I'd be a millionaire.

PROLOGUE

RAFE D'ANGELO KNEW THE GUY at table four was cheating. He just didn't know how.

Yet.

Over the past two hours, play at that table in the blackjack pit had heated up significantly. The dealer, a long-time Native Sun employee, was someone Rafe trusted. The table shoe had gone through half a dozen fresh decks. Even the security guys in the Eye-in-the-Sky booth upstairs had reported nothing unusual.

And still this jerk was up two hundred grand.

As pit boss, one of Rafe's jobs was to spot the cheats. He was good at it. But this guy didn't fit any profile.

And he was winning, damn him.

Rafe didn't like losing. Sure, it wasn't his money, but when he was working he felt as if it were. For all the casino's fake Native American heritage, Native Sun had been good to him. Sometimes, when he allowed himself to invent a future for himself, he thought he could work here forever.

He'd always moved around a lot but he'd held this

job longer than most—almost a year—and people respected him. He had a decent place to live, a good income and enough women to keep his ego happy. At twenty-four, he was probably the youngest pit boss on the Vegas strip, but he knew most people thought he was older. Hell, inside he *was* older.

Not bad for a runaway from the backwater Colorado town of Broken Yoke.

The sound of feminine laughter made him turn to the left.

She was still there. DeeDee Whitefeather—now *there* was a stage name if ever there was one—was fawning over a loudmouthed suit at the number twelve craps table.

She was one of the best-looking mannequins who worked for the casino. She wasn't dressed in her showgirl outfit, of course, since the theater was dark on Mondays, but she still stood out in a crowd. All that long dark hair and those pretty gray eyes.

She wore a miniskirt and a blouse that did amazing things to her breasts. When she bent close to her companion, you could see plenty of skin. Rafe watched her trail long fingernails through the man's hair and whisper in his ear.

She'd shown up two months ago, passing herself off as part Apache to get the job. If there was one drop of genuine Apache blood in her veins, Rafe would have bet it was there by accident. Still, she held up her end of the G-rated Native American show the casino put on for the stroller-and-convention crowd five nights a week. Kept to herself. Never complained. Never seemed overly eager to find a sugar daddy like some of the other girls. So what was she doing, attaching herself to this guy with a pizza gut and bad hair plugs?

Of course, he was a high roller. Big incentive for a working girl to find something in him to like.

But still, Rafe was disappointed. Of all the women shopping it around the strip, DeeDee Whitefeather was the last one he would have expected that from.

He swore under his breath. Rafe wasn't supposed to be following her progress, he was supposed to bring the hammer down on the card mechanic at table four.

Mickey Norris, one of his protégés who was only a couple of years younger but about a thousand years behind Rafe in life experience, sidled up to him.

"No face book," Mickey reported, referring to the file of pictures security kept on hand to help them spot cheaters. "Maybe he's a hit-and-run artist."

"Maybe," Rafe said, unconvinced. "I think he's got someone spotting for him. I just can't figure out who."

Mickey huffed out a sigh of disappointment. "You're off your game tonight." The young man scratched his chin. "Maybe you're distracted, huh?" Mickey jerked his head toward the craps table where DeeDee was allowing Hair Plugs's hand to roam freely over her tight rear end. "I notice you watching the action on table twelve. Pretty lady. I don't blame you for— Hey! Don't I know her? Isn't that one of our own little Indian princesses?"

Rafe shrugged, struggling for a blank, disinterested look. "She's about as much a real Indian as the wooden one outside the lobby gift shop."

Mickey practically smacked his lips. Tonight he seemed dedicated to the business of pissing Rafe off. "Who cares? I'd like to spend time in *her* wigwam."

"Go check for a back-spotter, Romeo," Rafe told him.

Before long Rafe found his eyes turning back to DeeDee. Just his eyes, not his head. Hair Plugs was trying to catch the attention of one of the cash-cart girls.

Rafe couldn't resist the opportunity. Quickly he slid up next to DeeDee on the other side. She blinked at him, looking surprised. She knew as well as he did that management discouraged the girls from going after players at the tables.

He leaned near, so that only she could hear him. "You think this is a smart idea, Pocahontas?" He jerked his chin to indicate her companion on the other side of her.

Her eyes went flinty hard. "Butt out, Oz. No one's asking your opinion."

Everyone in the casino knew him as Oz. It was a nickname one of the girls had given him, and it had stuck. Something to do with a talent he had in bed, he thought, but he'd never cared enough to find out exactly. God knew, he'd been called worse.

For a guy lucky enough to have snagged someone like DeeDee, her companion was busy flirting outrageously with both the cocktail waitress and the cash-cart girl. Rafe ran his hand down the length of DeeDee's bare arm and pulled her aside.

"I didn't realize you were partial to sweaty, big-mouthed asses with bad hair."

She scowled at him. "I'm sure you can't imagine why any woman would be interested in any man that isn't you."

"He looks like trouble, DeeDee. Be careful."

"Jealous?"

"Hell, no. Just wondering how a bright girl like you can end up being just another dumb hairdo on heels."

He saw something flash in her eyes that might have been discomfort, but it was gone in an instant.

She shrugged. "Maybe I just got tired of missing out on what some of the other girls have."

He couldn't resist a tight laugh. "If it's a little fun in bed you're after, I can try to squeeze you in."

"Tell me something, Oz," she said softly. "Is there anyone you admire as much as yourself?"

"No," he admitted. He let her see his gaze travel over her. "Want to find out why?"

"No, thanks. Your reputation precedes you, and I'd rather eat ground glass."

She was a tough one, all right. He tried a different angle. "You realize that working the guests is strictly against casino policy?"

"Suddenly you're a rule follower?"

"I guess I just don't want to see you get hurt."

That wasn't what he'd intended to say, but he realized he meant it.

"Aww…what a sweetie," she said in a voice that sounded like syrup sliding out of a pitcher. Then her brows lowered. "Now get lost. Go chase the card manipulators and leave me alone." Hair Plugs's hand settled on her shoulder, and she turned with a big smile. "Gil, honey! What took you so long? Should I be jealous?"

Rafe stepped away and left her to her conquest. There was something about the guy he didn't like— some small meanness around the eyes—but what else could he do? He had bigger worries.

He spent another ten minutes watching the shark on table four continue to rake in chips. The guy seemed completely at ease. No nervous hand movements. No darting glances. Just steady, methodical betting that might eventually leave Native Sun bleeding green big time.

Annoyed, Rafe cut a glance in DeeDee's direction to see how she was making out. Her date offered her a highball glass full of amber liquid that Rafe assumed was whiskey. Neat, he noticed. No ice.

DeeDee swallowed it down. He suspected she wasn't really much of a drinker. In Vegas, you got to where you could spot the problem drinkers on sight, and she wasn't the type.

But in another few minutes, Rafe's suspicious nature went into overdrive.

Up until now, DeeDee had been friendly to her

date—little touches here, a whispered laugh in the guy's ear there—but suddenly she seemed completely out of control.

She was loose limbed enough to slide under the craps table, and her date had to keep her upright, fastened against him with a hammy hand against her rib cage. She rubbed against him. There was nothing coordinated about her actions. They weren't natural. They weren't normal.

Had Hair Plugs added something to her drink?

Just when Rafe thought the guy would lose his hold on DeeDee, another man approached to add his support. The men seemed to know one another. DeeDee's head flopped back, and the two guys laughed over her, as though sharing the same stupid joke.

Mickey was suddenly at his side again. "No spotters, boss. What now?" He frowned, realizing that Rafe's attention had wandered. "What's the matter?"

Rafe turned his attention back to Mickey. *Concentrate on what you get paid to do.*

And then suddenly everything clicked. "Ah, hell," he swore under his breath. "He's counting cards."

Mickey scowled. "Nah. He's not even watching the shoe half the time."

"He doesn't have to watch the cards coming out of the shoe. He can see them in the whiskey glass by his left elbow. His buddy has been nursing that drink for over an hour. Our friend is reading the cards in the reflection of the glass."

Mickey nodded. "Nice catch," he said. Rafe was clearly his hero once more. "We gonna escort him out?"

With that mystery solved, Rafe looked back to see the two men moving DeeDee away from the craps table. She looked more and more like a puppet who'd had her strings cut, hanging limply between them and smiling vacantly.

They were headed toward the bank of elevators. Once they got upstairs, DeeDee was going to find herself flat on her back in one of their hotel rooms.

Go after her.

Shut up, he told his brain. *I'm not getting paid to save the world.*

"You ready?" Mickey said beside him.

He nodded, heading toward their cheater. "Let's do it."

"I love this part."

Rafe couldn't resist one final look back. Hair Plugs had DeeDee propped up against the wall by the elevator. Giggling, she reached out with a finger and played it down the guy's cheek. Beside him, his friend laughed and kissed her. She frowned, as though suddenly realizing that she had herself two asses to deal with instead of one. The card mechanic on four wasn't the only one in for a surprise tonight.

Rafe pulled up short, yanking Mickey back as well. "Mickey, go do the honors with our cheat, would you? Make sure he gets the spiel about us filing trespassing charges if he ever shows his face in here again."

"*Me?*" Mickey's eyes went huge. "All by myself?"

"You know the drill. Consider it on-the-job training."

The elevator had arrived. DeeDee was getting man-handled onto it. Just another drunk who needed to be put to bed, people would think.

Mickey looked stunned. "Oldman ain't gonna like that. Wait a minute! Where are you going?" he said in a low voice as Rafe took off in the direction of the elevators.

"Business," Rafe called over one shoulder. *I'm going to lose my job because one idiot female doesn't know when she's playing with fire.*

But he didn't stop.

CHAPTER ONE

THERE WERE TIMES IN LIFE that called for begging.

This was one of those times.

Danielle Bridgeton looked across her desk at the state editor of the *Denver Daily Telegraph*, the newspaper she worked for. She lowered her head, sighed dramatically and pasted on her best wounded-puppy look. "Please, Gary," she said, softly pleading with him to understand. "Get me out of here. I'll do anything you want. *Anything.*"

Gary Newsome shook his head sadly. "You know, when I was young I used to dream about a beautiful woman saying that to me."

Gary was fifty-something, bald and complained frequently of acid reflux. He was the most honest newspaperman Dani knew. He was also torturing her.

Dani steepled her fingers. A nun couldn't have seemed more penitent. "Look at me, Gary. This is me, begging."

Gary pushed air between his lips in a disgruntled rush. "I came up here to see how you were getting along, not to make you beg. I can't do it, Dani. You piss off the pope, you get excommunicated. It's as simple as that."

But it wasn't simple, it was unfair. Cruel. Even the pope believed in forgiving people, didn't he?

"It was one lousy article," Dani pointed out. "*One.* And I've learned my lesson."

"No, you haven't. You're the most unrepentant journalist I know. Honest. Sincere. But definitely not repentant. Didn't I try to tell you what would happen if we ran your story? You're not the only one who's got the publisher on his back, so take your lumps like a good girl. Work the I-70 corridor for a while and enjoy being a bureau chief. I'll let you know when it's safe for you to come back to Denver."

Bureau chief. Gary made the job sound like a promotion. And it might have been if the bureau she'd been assigned to had been one of the state's hottest news spots. But what kind of reporting could you expect when all you covered were the small towns that ran along the highway between Denver and Grand Junction? Those mountain towns were cute, scenic… and dull as dishwater.

"It's been *two years,*" Dani pleaded. "I'm dying out here."

Gary laughed. "It's been two months."

"Well, it feels like years."

A lot more than two, in fact. Living in Broken Yoke could leave her brain-dead. There weren't any interesting stories here, or in any of the other one-horse towns she was supposed to cover for the *Telegraph*. It was humiliating that she'd been reduced to this.

How was she supposed to continue building a respectable career in journalism? The most exciting thing she'd written in two months had been about some tourist who'd slipped off a ledge in the Arapaho National Forest and broken his arm.

Yes, officially she was the region's bureau chief. But what a place to be in charge! And what a miserable end to a story that should have won her a bucket load of awards and national recognition.

Last year Dani had been resourceful and lucky enough to make a very important contact at Humanity Haven—one of the most prominent, respected and lucrative charity organizations in Colorado. By the time she'd finished months of digging, she'd uncovered all the inside dirt. Questionable expenditures made by key executives. Murky business deals. Fraudulent balance sheets.

Her five-part article hadn't brought Humanity Haven down—its own culture of ambition, greed and arrogance had done that—but she'd certainly started the ball rolling.

Unfortunately, Dani had also unearthed that her publisher's mother-in-law had been secretly dating Humanity Haven's good-looking, much younger chairman of the board.

To say that Lorraine Jennings Mandeville had turned into a bitter, vindictive woman over the death of her now embarrassingly public love affair would have been stating things too mildly. Lorraine had had Dani exiled to the boonies. Dani couldn't prove it, of course, but only an idiot would fail to see the connection.

"Pretend you're on vacation," Gary suggested. He looked out the tiny window that was the only source of light in the enlarged closet Dani was forced to call an office. "This is definitely a prettier part of the state than brown-cloud Denver."

That might be true, but who needed pretty when you had a career to build? "They don't even have a decent bagel shop. Do you know how many times I've had to listen to 'Welcome to Broken Yoke, ma'am. Yoke—like the harness, not the egg. Ha, ha, ha.'"

Gary looked out the open office door toward the reception area. "Your office help seems nice."

Dani scowled. Cissy Pendergrass, the receptionist/ secretary/ad salesperson sat just a few feet away at her desk, polishing off a salad from the little restaurant down the street.

"She hates me," Dani said in a near whisper.

All right, that wasn't true. But if it made Gary reconsider this punishment, she'd be willing to look as though she feared for her life.

"Then she'll have to get in line behind Lorraine Mandeville," Gary replied.

He rose, hitched up his pants and walked over to the map that adorned one pine-board wall. It showed the entire western half of the state, every county a different color. This was Dani's turf now, and Broken Yoke her home base. If anything of interest happened in any of those mountain towns, Dani would make sure it found a spot in the regional weekend supplement of the *Telegraph*. So far, there had been darn little.

Slapping his hand against the map, Gary said, "Come on, Dani. There have to be dozens of stories out here just waiting to be unearthed. The people who settled in these mountains are sons of pioneers. These canyons are filled with tales of stolen treasure, unsavory characters, heroes who weren't afraid to take chances."

"This town is so small that their McDonald's only has one arch."

"So you think Broken Yoke is too insignificant, filled with boring people leading boring lives?"

Afraid that Cissy might have heard, Dani got up, gave her receptionist a smile and shut the door for privacy.

"It's not just the size of this place," she said. "It's the whole area. Most of the people I've met have been very friendly, very eager to make me feel at home. Some of them are…eccentric. A couple are downright weird, but you'd get that in any town. It's just that… there's nothing here for me to sink my teeth into. The biggest thing coming up is the summer festival, which I hear bombed last year. It's so boring around these parts that I might as well be writing obits."

Gary gave her an impatient look. She could tell he

was either in need of his antacid tablets or heading into lecture mode.

"What will destroy a journalist's career, Dani?" He shot the sudden question at her. "What can destroy you fastest?"

"Lorraine Jennings Mandeville?" she ventured.

"No! It's the unwillingness to open your mind to possibilities. Keep your ear to the ground and your eyes open. You'll find something you can use." Her boss took her arms between his hands, looking her straight in the eyes. "Just keep a positive attitude." He reached out and placed his fingers on either side of her lips, forcing them into the semblance of a gruesome smile. "That's my girl."

Dani's lips might have been fixed in a grin, but her eyes were sending him the kind of warmth that blows in off a glacier. She was whipped and she knew it.

Numbly she followed Gary outside while he said goodbye to Cissy and then walked out into the afternoon sun. His car sat at the curb. This late in the day, the street was thick with shadows, a pleasant, nondescript spring afternoon to fit a pleasant, nondescript town.

A young woman climbing up the outside steps of the bureau office smiled at Dani as she and Gary made their way out.

"Who's that?" Gary asked. "She could be bringing you the next big story."

"Becky from Becky's House of Hair," Dani said

in a lackluster tone. "Stop the presses. She's probably just discovered that the Farrah Fawcett shag is on its way out."

Gary looked disappointed. "I always liked that hairstyle on Pauline," he said, referring to his wife of thirty years. When even that didn't get a smile from Dani, he gave her a regretful but determined glance. "Come on, Dani. I hate leaving you like this."

"Then don't. Take me with you."

He took an exaggerated interest in his surroundings to keep from starting this one-way argument again.

She watched his eyes roll past Landquist Computers next door, the drugstore, the café where Cissy had bought her lunch, the hardware store that only yesterday had begun advertising Easter baskets. She stood in a warm pool of sunshine and waited. She'd made that mental trip down Main Street so many times, she knew the exact sequence of stores and just how many sections of sidewalk lay between here and the post office at the opposite end of the block.

"Somewhere on this street could be a story just waiting to be written," Gary said in his best sleuthing voice. "Somewhere. You just have to look."

"Uh-huh."

"Or maybe it's *someone*."

The question in his voice made her follow the direction of his gaze.

The best-looking man in three counties was coming out of a shop halfway down the block. Your typical tall, dark and handsome guy, with an extra edge of male virility that a girl couldn't help but notice. When he saw Dani watching, he lifted his hand in a wave and smiled.

Gary was quick to pounce. "Well! I see you're not completely oblivious to the people around here. You've scoped out one of the more…interesting Yokers."

"They like to call themselves Yokels. Get it?" Dani inclined her head back toward the sidewalk. "That's Matt D'Angelo. He's one of the local doctors."

"A doctor!" Gary's enthusiasm was only slightly less than that of a Jewish mother in search of her daughter's future husband.

"He's getting married to his nurse at the end of this month. I'm covering the wedding. Childhood sweethearts reunited. Friendship turns to love…blah, blah, blah."

Dani could see she had left Gary speechless at last. In all fairness, she knew he sympathized with her exile.

Giving him a genuine smile this time, she went to the driver's side of his car, reached up on tiptoe and planted a kiss on the side of his cheek. He went beet-red.

"I know you're trying," she told him. "Just don't forget about me up here."

"I won't," Gary promised. "I have a voodoo doll with Lorraine's picture on it, and the moment it works, I'll be on the phone to you."

"Great. My fate lies in the hands of a man who believes in the power of black magic but can't balance his checkbook."

He gave her a hopeful smile. "Lorraine's fate lies with the voodoo doll, Dani. *Your* fate lies with you. Make this time work for you."

She nodded and stepped back from the car. She watched him pull away, turn at the corner and go over the bridge that crossed Lightning River, the creek that bisected the town. He'd be in Denver in less than an hour, but it might as well be the end of the universe. It was all she could do to finally turn away and go back to the bureau office.

Becky was still there, sitting on the corner of Cissy's desk, playing with a pen between two brightly polished nails. She didn't even look up when Dani entered.

She lifted one hand as though preparing to swear on a stack of bibles. "If I'm lying, I'm dying," she said to Cissy. "Althea Bendix saw him through the window of the real-estate office yesterday making eyes at that slutty Nina Jordan, who just about fell at his feet. *Of course.*"

Cissy didn't look all that impressed. "Could have been business."

"*Monkey* business, if you want my guess," Becky said with a sharp nod of her head. "He's up to no good, I'll just bet you, and you know Nina. The woman can speak six languages but doesn't know how to say no in any of them."

Dani had been making her way back to her office, but suddenly swung around to join the women's conversation. People who were "up to no good" were of considerable interest to her. Rule followers seldom did anything worthy of the front pages of the newspaper.

"Who's up to no good?" she asked the two women.

"Rafe D'Angelo," Becky supplied. "He's back in town."

The name meant nothing to her, although she knew that the D'Angelo family ran the Lightning River Lodge resort up Windy Mountain Road. The upcoming marriage of their son, Matt, was the talk around town. "And that's a bad thing?"

Becky pursed her lips. "That remains to be seen. Lots of folks around here were glad to see the last of Rafe when he left."

"When was that?"

"Straight out of high school. At least twelve years ago. Hasn't been back since."

"And people are still holding a grudge?" Some of Dani's enthusiasm dissipated. This was starting to sound like stale news to her. Besides, she'd heard the D'Angelos were some of Broken Yoke's town leaders. She didn't need to make any more enemies.

"Not holding a grudge, exactly. Just hoping that his stay here is temporary."

Cissy laughed. "Considering the way Rafe and his dad got along, I'm sure it will be." She whistled through her teeth. "Just being around the two of them during one of their disagreements was like spending an hour in a blender."

"Never dull, that's for sure," Becky agreed. For Dani's benefit she added, "But what could you expect, really? His parents had their hands full trying to keep up with him. Rafe was such a daredevil. And the women—he was like the Pied Piper."

Dani waited for more, but Cissy had discovered a final black olive in her salad and was busy chasing it down with her fork, a feat that Becky seemed to find fascinating.

"I can't wait to see him," Becky said at last. "He was so great looking as a teenager. Imagine what the man must look like."

Dani could think of several boys from high school who had not aged well at all. "A lot can happen to change a person in that amount of time," she said. "Are you sure he's still worthy of all this anticipation?"

Becky rolled her eyes. "Honey, I went to school with him. You didn't. Trust me, he's worth it no matter what age he is. Besides, he's one of the D'Angelos. They've all got that mysterious Italian blood. They age like fine wine."

Cissy had found her olive and now sat happily munching it. She nodded agreement to Becky's claim.

Dani frowned down at her. "You couldn't have been more than ten when he left."

"I was nine. But I remember my older sister being nuts for him. She snuck out of the house once to meet him. Ended up getting grounded for two weeks. Even after our parents had yelled at her, she just looked at me all dreamy-eyed and said with a goofy smile, 'Cissy, it was all worth it.'"

Becky's head bobbed. "You can find stories like that all over this town."

Dani sniffed. "I wonder if that's not all you can find all over this town because of Rafe D'Angelo."

Becky looked confused, but Cissy arched one blond brow. "You mean little kiddies? Naw. Any woman who hung around with Rafe will tell you he was always a gentleman, even when you were getting dumped by him. Sexy, powerful…"

"How can an eighteen-year-old have any power?" Dani asked, truly skeptical now.

"You'd have to have been here to understand. Demanding, daring—but according to my sister, he always took good care of you."

That made Dani laugh. "Ah. A *thoughtful* cad."

Becky tilted her head at Dani. "I'm sensing you have some hostility toward men."

"Really?" Dani replied. "Because if they rounded up every man on earth right now and sent them all to the moon, they would still be too close to suit me."

She sounded so bitter that she wished she hadn't said anything. But the truth was she knew all about devilishly attractive men who didn't have it in them to be faithful or trustworthy. She'd just broken off with a first-class rat. Two years ago, she'd come close to moving in with one. Even as far back as when she'd been working in Vegas she could remember one particular playboy whose favorite hobby seemed to be breaking hearts. Oz had been his name—the Wizard of Women.

Her mother had been right. Men never failed to let you down.

Becky gave her a sad-eyed glance. "Divorced, sweetie?"

Oh, well. Might as well admit the truth. Besides, she was well over Kirk. "No. But I just dumped a rich, powerful jerk who sounds just like your Rafe D'Angelo."

Becky perked up considerably. Even Dani had heard that Becky was looking for husband number three. "Does he live around here by any chance?"

"No. Denver. And you're welcome to his address if you think you can make him concentrate on anyone but himself for more than ten minutes at a time. The louse has a Ph.D. in arrogance and a master's degree in snake-oil salesmanship."

"You'll get over him."

"Already am. But you were saying…"

"Oh, yes." Becky settled in, heading back to gossipy basics. "Just that I heard from Althea Bendix who heard it from Polly Swinburne that Rafe has bought up half a block of old buildings on the town's main street. *Including* the old Three Bs Social Club."

Very few of the buildings in Broken Yoke were noteworthy, but Dani had already learned that one of the genuine historic sites in town was the Three Bs, a rambling, deserted old hotel and watering hole of questionable origin. Given the right designer and a huge infusion of cash, it might make an interesting salute to the town's silver-mining days.

"What's wrong with fixing up the Three Bs?" Cissy asked Becky. "It's been an eyesore long enough."

"Well, where would he get that kind of money, for one thing? When he and his daddy had their big falling out, he ran off without a nickel to his name. Of course, he could have won the lottery. He always was a lucky devil."

Dani tapped her chin, thinking of the business possibilities for the old place. "He could cut it up, I suppose. Turn it into shops and restaurants and maybe even condominiums."

Becky shivered visibly. "You'd never catch me going anywhere near there. People say it's haunted."

Cissy made a derogatory sound and dumped her empty salad bowl into the trash can beside her desk. "Oh, for heaven's sake. People say Elvis is still alive and you don't hear any new songs on the radio, do you? I think it would make a wonderful focal point for the town. A way to revitalize downtown."

Becky wasn't about to be sidetracked by logic. "Why would Rafe care about revitalizing downtown? He wasn't all that fond of Broken Yoke when he lived here before."

"Maybe things have changed," Cissy said. "Everyone changes. You long to put down roots eventually."

"Rafe D'Angelo, putting down roots?" Becky said in a horrified tone. "My Lord, what's the world coming to?"

CHAPTER TWO

THE SILVER SADDLE BAR and Grill, which was more bar than grill, boasted a sizable back room where private parties could be held. This morning, more than forty people had crammed into the space, and there wasn't the slimmest hope that a party was in the making.

The planning session for Broken Yoke's summer festival was in full swing, and so far, there was only one thing that everyone at the town meeting could agree on. That no one could agree on *anything*.

Rafe D'Angelo sat toward the back of the room, next to his older brother Nick. Over the tops of people's heads—mostly gray, he noticed—he could make out his father seated near the front.

Just like Pop, he thought. Because of his stroke, Sam D'Angelo still relied on his wheelchair occasionally instead of crutches to get around, but that didn't keep him from seeking out the center of the action. And right now, the center of the action was up front, between those two old geezers Mort Calloway and Howard Hackett.

Over the years, Rafe had developed a pretty keen

nose for trouble. He could usually tell just when fists were going to replace words. Right now, he was fairly certain that Mort was thirty seconds away from decking Howard.

The fact that Mort was in his eighties and needed a shot of oxygen with almost every breath, or the realization that Howard's eyesight was so poor he couldn't have seen Mort's fist coming, much less prevented it, didn't have a thing to do with it. The two men were furious with one another, and no one could get them to calm down. Not even Sheriff Bendix, who stood between them like a referee at a prizefight.

"It was just an idea," Mort said for the third time. The lifelong naturalist had proposed a botanical theme for this year's festival—complete with a wildflower exhibition, guest lectures and an orchid contest.

"Well, it was a stupid one," Howard replied tersely. "Are you out of your wood-pecked, termite-infested mind? How many people in this state do you think will give a rat's rear end about seeing a slide show on how to identify a bunch of poseys?"

Mayor Wickham spoke up from the sidelines. "It doesn't seem in keeping with the history of the festival, Mort."

Mort swung on the mayor, an action that left him more than a little breathless. "Since this is only our *second* festival, and the first was such a god-awful failure, I don't see how it can mess much with the *history* of the danged thing." He took a sip of oxygen, then whipped his mask away so he could turn back to Howard. "And my idea has as much merit as a harmonica contest or watching a bunch of morons being used as human bowling balls."

"At least people won't fall asleep in the street!"

Evidently, some of the other Broken Yoke citizens thought Howard had a point. There were murmurs of agreement from the crowd.

Rafe slid down in his chair, wondering why he'd let Nick talk him into coming here. He'd been back in Broken Yoke for two weeks, but it already felt like a lot longer.

A reed-thin older woman at the front of the room stood up. Beside Rafe, his brother inhaled sharply. "Uh-oh," Nick said under his breath. "Here comes trouble."

The woman said in a crisp voice, "I have an idea."

The years since Rafe had lived here suddenly swept away. He remembered this woman—those small, sharp eyes, the posture that made her look as though she'd snap in two if someone tried to bend her. Polly Swinburne. Paranoid Polly, the kids had called her. Rich. Widowed. A bit "off."

"Why don't we have a naked festival?" she suggested.

Okay. Make that a lot "off." Rafe groaned, wishing he had stayed back at the lodge.

The room went deathly silent for a long moment. Finally, Sheriff Bendix cleared his throat and asked the question on everyone's mind. "Polly, what exactly is a naked festival?"

Polly practically went pink with enthusiasm. "Well, you all remember that I went to Japan for vacation last year?" Several gray heads bobbed. "They celebrate something there called Hadaka Matsuri. All the participants wear loincloths, and one man is chosen to run naked through the streets. Everyone tries to touch him."

"Touch him where?" someone asked.

"And what for?" Mort Calloway added, looking like all the oxygen in the world wasn't going to be enough to keep him from passing out.

"Just to touch him," Polly said. "He's supposed to bring good luck and absorb evil. The custom's over twelve hundred years old in Japan."

"Well, it isn't gonna last twelve *seconds* here in the good old U. S. of A.," someone else said, and everyone laughed.

Polly looked annoyed. "This year there were ten thousand participants and over three hundred thousand spectators. Excuse me, but I thought the idea of having a festival was to make money."

"Where would people in loincloths keep their wallets?" Howard asked.

A few people giggled, and after that, the discussion deteriorated even more as several ribald comments were made. Polly subsided with a scowl.

A few more ideas were trotted out. Not surprisingly, the owner of the Silver Saddle voted for a beer festival. Someone suggested they repaint all the store-fronts to look like bare wood, throw down two feet of dirt on the streets and pretend to have returned to the 1850s. Wesley Macgruder, the owner of the local Feed and Seed, recommended they convert one of the abandoned mine shafts into a thrill ride. The ideas went steadily downhill from there.

Nick leaned close to Rafe. "Wesley may look like an idiot and talk like an idiot," he whispered, "but don't let that fool you. He really *is* an idiot."

Rafe shook his head. "Tell me again. Why exactly did you think I should come to this thing?"

Nick grinned. "Because Matt refused, and I needed a buffer between me and everyone else."

Rafe knew better than to believe that excuse, but he nodded anyway and settled back in his seat, tuning out the sound of angry voices.

When he'd first come back to town, he'd known that it would be difficult to reestablish a relationship with his father. After all the harsh things that had been said between them during that final argument, after all the years of noncommunication, there was no way he could waltz back into Sam D'Angelo's world and expect a warm welcome.

In that, he hadn't been disappointed. He knew that if his father tried at all to meet him halfway, it was strictly for the sake of Rafe's mother. Pop would do anything to please Rose. Even make nice occasionally with a son he probably considered a first-class bastard.

But Rafe had also anticipated a cool reception from his brother Nick. He'd never had a problem with his brother Matt and younger sister Addy, but Nick—the two of them had seldom gotten along as kids. Nick was a stickler for order and obeying the rules, and Rafe, well…Rafe had always figured rules were for other people.

So he was surprised that Nick didn't seem to hold much of a grudge against him. Time seemed to have mellowed his big brother. It could be because he was a married man with kids of his own now. A brand-new baby son, in fact, in addition to a teenage daughter who had discovered boys big time.

Did Nick finally understand what it was like to find yourself on the opposite side of a chasm from someone you loved, with no clear way to make the leap that would bring you back together?

Rafe felt a nudge against his arm. Nick was drawing his attention back to the front of the room, where his father seemed to have won the floor.

"…can argue this from now until Christmas," Sam D'Angelo was telling them all.

In spite of the wheelchair, his father still had a commanding way about him. He'd turned sixty just a few months ago, but he was as powerful a presence in the room as he'd been years ago, when he'd stood by Rafe's hospital bed and told him that he was no longer welcome in his house.

"So what do you suggest, Sam?" Sheriff Bendix asked.

"I suggest we form a committee to investigate the

best theme ideas we've been able to come up with here. Explore all possibilities. Eliminate the most problematic of them, then bring the two most viable ones back to the group for a vote."

"There have been an awful lot of ideas pitched tonight," someone behind Rafe pointed out.

"Very few that have actually been thought out," Sam said, waving away the comment. With his chin he indicated the man seated across the aisle from him. "We could start with the Founder's Day Celebration Bill suggested. He's done his homework about the beginnings of Broken Yoke. Let's find out if any of it would be interesting to anyone outside of the people in this room."

Phil Pasternak, a fifty-something guy with a great tan who owned Alpine All Weather, the only sports store in town, stood up. "I think my idea of a Christmas in July celebration bears serious consideration. It's quirky enough to draw outsiders, and over the past few months I've spent quite a bit of time and money planning out sample venues of the games and entertainment we could offer."

Everyone knew Phil wanted to unload a surplus of winter sports equipment he'd been saddled with after several winters of modest snowfall, but no one had hooted down his idea for the festival. Most were intrigued by the idea of how he intended to pull off snowball fights and sleigh rides in the middle of summer.

Sam nodded. "Fine. Let the committee decide if it's workable."

"And profitable," Phil couldn't resist adding.

"I'll volunteer to be on the committee," Mort Calloway said from around his oxygen mask.

"Me, too," Howard Hackett piped up.

Polly Swinburne sniffed loudly. "I certainly think I should be part of any committee that makes those decisions."

Sam wasn't a good enough actor to keep his disappointment from showing. These three were obviously not who he'd had in mind when he'd made the suggestion.

He tossed a glance around the room, finally settling on a mild-looking fellow whose face would live in no one's memory. "What about you, Burt? You're calm and logical. You'd make a good candidate for the committee."

The old guy blinked a couple of times, then creaked upward from his seat as though he'd just been asked to recite the Pledge of Allegiance. "I'll do it if everyone insists," he said politely. "But I'd prefer to stay out of it."

"Why?"

"Because I'm not even sure Broken Yoke should have a summer festival. What's wrong with just keeping things the way they are?" The elderly man frowned. "No. I'm not your man."

Nick expelled a sigh. "Good call, Burt," he said under his breath. To Rafe he added, "Working with Howard and Polly and Mort would send him to the loony bin. Poor Aunt Sof would go nuts worrying."

Rafe gave his brother a puzzled look. "Aunt Sof" was one of their mother's Italian sisters. Sofia and Renata were both widowed. After his father's stroke a few years ago, the two women had arrived to help out. They'd never returned to Italy and now seemed firmly entrenched in helping to run the family lodge. Rafe had never met either one of them until he'd come home. They seemed nice enough, but he still didn't really know them.

"Why poor Aunt Sof?" he asked his brother.

"She's sweet on Burt," Nick said. "But don't ask either one of them, because they'll just deny it."

Rafe looked back at Burt with renewed interest. Still some life left in the old boy, it seemed. Nice to think of two older people finding love, even at this late date. He wished them well, because as near as Rafe could figure, love was a pretty slippery slope to try to climb. One reason why he'd stayed firmly away from it.

Another half hour was spent determining just how the newly formed committee should proceed and when the deciding vote for a festival theme would be taken. Just when Rafe thought they had a hope of getting out of the Silver Saddle before his backside went completely numb, his father spoke up again.

"Independent of the festival committee, I think we should elect a Publicity chair. Once a decision is made, we can't afford to waste time trying to decide how to get the word out. We need someone to start exploring what kind of publicity we can get for this thing. How much it's going to cost, and just what we need to say. Anyone want to volunteer?"

No one spoke up.

"Then I'd like to suggest my son," Sam said, looking toward the back of the room. "Nicholas."

Beside Rafe, Nick went upright in his seat. *Poor bastard.* Rafe was barely able to hide an amused smile. *Roped into service and stuck with trying to please all these people.*

Nick stood up. "Pop, I don't think I'm the right person for the job. This really calls for someone with PR skills, and everyone knows that isn't something I'm good at."

Sam looked annoyed when there was mumbled agreement from a few others.

"Besides," Nick went on, "it shouldn't be someone who has a particular personal agenda. You know I'd like to pick up some business for the lodge and our helicopter tours. We need a person who can be fairly unbiased."

"Like who?" Polly Swinburne asked skeptically.

Nick tossed a desperate look around the room, and in the same moment when Rafe could hear his own inner voice saying *No, no, no,* his brother's gaze landed on him like a load of concrete. "Like Rafe, for instance," Nick said.

There were several moments of silence. Rafe knew that most of the people here, while perhaps not having an actual ax to grind with him, might find him an interloper in their midst. No, maybe more than that. He let his eyes do a quick circuit around the room. How many of these people had he had run-ins with as a teenager?

Short of killing his brother very slowly, Rafe couldn't think of a suitable revenge. He shook his head. "Nick," he said at last, clearing his throat. "I don't think—"

"Not Rafe," Sam said with a dismissive wave of his hand.

For just one moment, Rafe's eyes met with his father's. They had lightning in them.

Rafe's heart gave a kick of annoyance so faint he hardly felt it. He knew what the old man was thinking. Mustering all of his self control, Rafe said, "I'll do it."

"No," Sam said.

Rafe felt his jaw setting in anger. If there had been a collective gasp in the room at that moment, it couldn't have been more obvious that everyone knew more was going on here than just a simple difference of opinion.

"Why not him?" Sheriff Bendix had the guts to ask.

In spite of his surface poise and bland ease, Sam's eyes hinted a warning toward the man. "My son hasn't lived in this town for years. He cannot know what would work best for Broken Yoke. He has no interest in it."

Polly Swinburne swung a glance in Rafe's direction. "I heard you bought up part of First Street downtown. Is that true? Because that doesn't sound like someone who has no interest to me."

"It's true. I've come back to Broken Yoke with the intention of making it my home." Rafe's eyes locked again with his father's in a light challenge. "Permanently."

He waited, refusing to look away.

Sam settled back in his wheelchair. "You have landed here for now. But a home is more than just an address."

Before Rafe could say anything, Nick jumped in. "That's beside the point. As an outsider, Rafe has no preconceived notions about what would serve us best. What he does have is plenty of PR experience. All those years in Vegas and L.A. He'll know what will catch people's interest. How to massage the media to get the best coverage."

Someone laughed. "Way I hear it, you were always good at massages, Rafe."

"This is a serious discussion," Howard Hackett complained, and Rafe tried to remember if the man had a daughter. Truthfully, he couldn't recall many of the local girls he'd romanced and left behind.

"I know how to handle the press," Rafe acknowledged. "If you want me to do this, I will. Otherwise, I'm perfectly happy going about my own business."

"I nominate Rafe D'Angelo for publicity chairman," Nick said quickly. "All those in favor say aye."

There was a surprisingly supportive vote of confidence in favor of the motion. There were no opposing votes, though Rafe suspected his father's silence cost him dearly. He could tell from the older man's posture in his chair that he wasn't liking this turn of events. Not liking it at all.

A short time later, the meeting broke up. Rafe was trapped in a round of congratulatory handshakes and slaps on the back, so that he couldn't immediately join his father and brother on the sidewalk in front of the Silver Saddle. Calloway, Hackett and Swinburne, who he'd already begun to think of as the Unholy Trio, cornered him with promises to be in touch soon.

When he finally emerged from the bar, he found his father and Nick waiting near the lodge's van in the weak sunshine. From the matching set of their hardened jaws, Rafe could tell there had been harsh words exchanged. He could make a safe bet on the topic.

He decided to ignore the ice forming between them. Before Rafe and his father were through with one another, he suspected there were going to be plenty more worthwhile arguments between them. He didn't need to run interference for Nick, who had always been able to take care of himself.

He tucked his hands into his jacket pockets, wishing he'd remembered to bring gloves. Easter might be right around the corner, but there was still snow on the mountaintops and the air was chilly.

Yanking his collar up, he said, "I'd forgotten how cold it can be up here, even in spring."

His father's expression was a mixture of annoyance and something more petulant. "Easy to forget," he snapped, "when you don't come back to a place for twelve years." He banged on the side of the van near the sliding door and looked at Nick. "We gonna stand around talking all day so I can freeze to death, or can we go home now?"

Nick just grinned and shook his head, and in no time he had helped Sam to the backseat and stowed the wheelchair in the cargo hold. As Rafe closed the back doors, he nudged Nick's arm to grab his attention.

"Why did you do it?" he asked in a low voice so that Sam couldn't hear. "You know you just made the old man mad."

"He'll get over it."

"I'm serious. One son on his hit list is more than enough."

Nick shrugged. "The way I figure it, you'll never get *off* his list if you don't throw yourself into what matters to this family. Pop's right about one thing, Rafe. Your home has to be more than just an address. Whatever you have planned for a future here, it will work better if you make your family a part of it."

"I'm not used to involving other people in my business. My private life stays private."

"Then you made a mistake coming back. Trust me, there's very little in this family that isn't a group effort. Whether you like it or not."

There was a muffled rap on one of the side windows. Pop, trying to hurry them along.

They wove up the winding mountain road in silence. The sky was cloudless, a bright, clear, uncomplicated blue that the postcard companies must love.

Every so often, Sam sighed heavily from the backseat, but neither Rafe nor Nick remarked on it.

When the quiet reached an uncomfortable level, Rafe looked over at his brother. "So how's the local rag of a paper? Is it still only fit for lining the bottom of a birdcage? I suppose if I'm going to drum up interest in this festival thing, I should start there."

"We have a new person in from Denver working the area," Nick replied. He shrugged. "We do all right. Nothing much earth-shattering to write about around here."

Rafe couldn't help a derisive laugh. "Oh, how well I remember that. A night on the town around here takes about ten minutes."

"You would know," his father commented from the back-seat.

There was another long, ugly moment of silence. Rafe stopped the impulse to turn in his seat to look at Sam. *Don't say anything. Don't feed the temptation to strike back. You open that dialogue, and there's no telling where it will go.*

He took a couple of calming breaths. "So this reporter…what's he like?"

Nick tossed him a grin. "*She.* Danielle Bridgeton. And from what I've heard around town, she's not all that excited about being stuck up here. But I'm sure you can win her over. It's part of the reason I suggested you. The old Rafe D'Angelo charm might come in handy."

Sam muttered something under his breath.

Since he'd been gone, Rafe had become quite an expert in a lot of things. He knew how to break a horse, how to spot a cheat at the blackjack table, how to survive thirty days on a week's worth of rations. He had learned patience and the art of compromise. So how could his father get to him?

He can't. Not if you don't let him.

Ignoring the annoyed, grumbling sound from the back of the van, Rafe said to Nick, "You realize that these people will never agree on anything, don't you? This festival is going to be a mess no matter how many committees get formed."

Nick frowned. "I hope you're wrong about that. It needs to be a success."

"Why do you care? If I remember correctly, you were never much of a townie, either."

"What's good for Broken Yoke is good for the lodge. Every year we lose a few businesses. A few more young people move down to Denver where they can find work doing what they want instead of what their fathers want. It's a trend I'd like to see stopped, and if a festival can help that, then I'm in favor of it."

Rafe rubbed his jaw thoughtfully. "I don't know, Nick. That's a tall order. There's no focus for this thing, no focal point."

Nick gave him a quick look. "That's why I threw your name up for publicity chair. If anyone can find a way to make something mediocre sound exciting, it's you."

Rafe knew Nick was referring to all the times he'd

talked his brother into some harebrained scheme as kids, the girls Rafe had convinced to sneak out of their bedrooms for a clandestine meeting at Lightning Lake. Or the goose bump– producing trips he'd got them to make to the boarded-up Three Bs Social Club, which everyone said was haunted but was still one of the most perfect make-out places in the world.

"It will take more than that," Rafe said, pursing his lips. "Journalists don't like to be manipulated. The town wants this thing to make money, but this Bridgeton woman won't be interested in a festival that's motivated by greed. She'll want some charitable or civic angle. They don't like to feel like puppets for some commercial venture."

Nick nodded thoughtfully. "I see your point. But the festival isn't just to line the pockets of every businessman in town. This all started last year because we want to add on to the library, create a kid's playground at the city park and clean up Lightning River Overlook."

Worthwhile causes, every one of them. But what kind of spin could Rafe put on it for this newspaper woman to catch her interest? The whole thing was so disorganized at this point. How much money was the city willing to spend? And even if they could get people to come, how could they handle the influx?

He shook his head and laughed. "This is ridiculous. I'm not a PR person. I never have been."

"What about when you worked for that Crews guy? I got the impression you did some of that for him."

"I did a lot of things for Wendall Crews for several of his development projects. But I wouldn't say it was PR work."

He wasn't sure what he would have called the years he had worked for Wendall. They'd had an interesting relationship. More mentor and student than anything else.

Shortly after leaving Las Vegas, Rafe had latched on to a job as a river raft guide on the Colorado. Wendall, an overweight and out-of-shape real-estate developer from Los Angeles, had signed up for one of the trips. It was clear none of the other tourists wanted the businessman for their raft partner. He was friendly enough, but clearly, they thought he couldn't hold up his end of the overnight trip down the river.

They were right; he couldn't. On the second day, on the next-to-the-last rapid, his raft had gone careening down one of the chutes, and Wendall had gone over the side and into the churning river. Caught in a whirlpool, the guy had sunk like a boat anchor. Rafe had gone in after him, hauling the panicked guy onto some flat rocks, even pumping water out of him before it could do him any serious harm.

Later, everyone had said Rafe had gone beyond the call of duty to save Wendall. At the time, he would have said all he was trying to do was keep from losing a customer on his watch.

But Wendall had been convinced that he would have died without Rafe coming to the rescue. He was so grateful that the next day he'd made Rafe a business offer to come work for him. One no one in their right mind would have refused, especially not an opportunist like Rafe. He'd quit his job and moved to L.A., where he'd worked by Wendall's side for four years, until last fall when the big guy's heart had finally done him in.

"You'll think of something," Nick reassured him. "You always had the power of persuasion."

"What am I going to say?" Rafe spread his hands out as though framing a sign. "Come to Broken Yoke's second annual festival…unless the high-school gym floor is being varnished."

His father slid forward on his seat so he could catch Rafe's eye. He looked thunderous. "This is exactly why I didn't want you for the job. Take it seriously, or resign. We need someone who can appreciate Broken Yoke for what it is, not for how many jokes can be made about it."

"I'm not going to resign," Rafe said quietly. His father was getting on that buried nerve that was not quite dead yet. "In fact, I'm going to see this reporter at the paper as soon as possible."

He could almost see Sam's back stiffen for battle. "I'm sure you'll have the woman dancing to your tune in no time. Just make sure it's legal."

The insinuation burrowed and found a home under Rafe's patience. His father's capacity for being strong-willed and unreasonable really rose to sublime heights at times. Rafe turned a little in his seat, and their anger met head-on. "Do we need to talk, Pop?"

If this was a quarrel at last, then let's have it.

Nick took his hand off the steering wheel and chopped the air, cutting through the unpleasantness. "I think the two of you have talked enough for now."

Sam settled back in his seat. "There's nothing more that needs to be said anyway."

His mild, colorless voice diluted some of Rafe's irritation, and the knowledge that they had just made the turn-off to Lightning River Lodge did the rest. Sooner or later he supposed they'd have it out, just like the old days, but not today. Not with the rest of the family waiting for them, and the sky so blue that anything seemed possible. Even peace.

The lodge was busy and noisy. There were several noon checkouts keeping Brandon O'Dell, the front desk manager, busy. He barely managed a wave in their direction before he was pulled back to attend to another guest.

The small dining room was still doing a brisk business, too. As the three D'Angelo men wove their way around the tables toward the kitchen, Aunt Renata looked up from where she was trying to make sense of an Easter decoration she had strung out along one of the banquet tables. Fake green grass lay everywhere. Rafe knew that they would have a full house on Easter for Sunday brunch.

The kitchen had always been the heart of the lodge.

Even twelve years ago, Rafe had spent more time here than in any other room in the family's private quarters, which lay just beyond the double doors. Around the big wooden island table rested so many memories. This was where his father had chaired family council meetings, and his mother had taught all four of her children—Nick, Matt, Rafe and Addy—with gentle persuasion and stern looks.

Every surface in the room was covered with gaily wrapped pieces of candy and more eggs than Rafe had seen in years—all of them in various stages of coloration and preparation. He knew that each one of the lodge's guests would find a small basket waiting outside their room door on Easter morning. As Nick and Rafe swung through the double doors, with Sam bringing up the rear in his wheelchair, Rose D'Angelo looked up.

"About time you were back," she told them. "Come eat lunch."

His mother presided over a quaint collection of copper pots, garlands of herbs and spices, and all the latest gadgets with the command of a general. In Rose D'Angelo's life, the preparation of food had the same importance as the eating of it, and if you entered her kitchen, you often got drafted into helping out.

She dished up bowls of steaming minestrone from the stove and began setting them on the wooden table while all around her waiters and waitresses bustled about to make sure every wish of the diners in the dining room was heeded.

"I'm not hungry," Sam said shortly. "I'll get something later."

He wheeled through the kitchen, then settled near the back door where earlier that morning he'd been working on replacing a broken handle.

Rose D'Angelo gave him a narrowed glance, then turned a questioning look toward Rafe. "I take it things didn't go well?"

"You could say that," Nick answered for them both.

Rafe went over to the prep sink to wash his hands. He thought of all the years he'd lost with this family. Sometimes he sat in this very room and thought about the love he had given up twelve years before. Sometimes he wanted to rush back through those years and change everything.

Was he being foolish to think he could ever recapture any of it? Sam was stubborn. Unforgiving. Why the hell did Rafe think he could ever make things right with his father?

Why, in God's name, am I bothering?

The double doors from the family quarters burst wide, and five-year-old Frannie marched through them, picked up something from the top of the big wooden table, then made her way straight for him. Her solemn little features were fixed on him like a laser.

She didn't plow into his legs like some kids might. She approached him calmly, quietly, and when she reached him, she held out her hand. On one multicolored, dyed palm lay the brightest blue Easter egg Rafe had ever seen.

She looked up at him, her hair falling down her back like strands of black pearls. The light from the windows near the back door caught her full face. It was beautiful on her, clean and sweet, strong and loving.

"Aunt Addy said I should make Easter eggs for everyone," she said simply. "I made this one for you."

He lifted the egg, prepared to offer compliments. Hell, what else could you do when a kid gifted you with something like that?

He rolled it in his hand, and etched clumsily across the egg, one word had been stenciled with a wax crayon. His heart turned over and a fluttering sensation spread out from his abdomen.

DADDY.

He raised his head, making the instant connection—eye to eye with the little girl. And the moment crystallized, as some moments do. In that half blink of time, he remembered.

This is why I came back here. She's the reason.

This child who barely knew him.

Frannie, his daughter.

CHAPTER THREE

HIS MOTHER WOULD HAVE SWORN the odd feeling in Rafe's gut when he held the egg Frannie had decorated was love. Rose would have claimed the feeling was one any father would have toward their child.

But the problem was he couldn't be sure it wasn't plain old, ordinary fear.

Truthfully, he could count on the fingers of one hand the number of conversations he'd had with children in his lifetime. He still couldn't believe he was a father. The father of a five-year-old. A little girl, at that.

But Frannie was his now, and had been since December, the most unexpected, unsettling Christmas present he had ever received.

He looked down at her upturned face. She had the feminine version of D'Angelo features that had been part of the family's legacy for generations—the firmly cut mouth, dark hair and bold eyes, those very long lashes that drew your attention and held it. She was his daughter, all right. The infinitesimal splinters of chance that went into making up a person's DNA had left no question of that fact.

He knelt down to her level, examining the blue egg as though it were a Russian Fabergé. He was aware of everyone's eyes on him. Only his father seemed disinterested in watching the interaction between Rafe and his daughter.

"This is very pretty," he told her.

Frannie seemed unimpressed by the compliment. "Can I eat it?"

"No."

"Why not?" she asked, her dark brows drawing together. Rafe had already discovered her stubborn streak.

"Because these aren't for eating. Not yet."

"They're just eggs. I like eggs. I got to eat lots of them with Mommy."

They were in dangerous territory all of a sudden. This was a situation they'd yet to discuss much. *Mommy.* He dreaded when that name came up. Someday they'd have to have a deeper discussion of why Mommy was no longer in the picture—something more than the awkward explanation Frannie had been given so far. But not today.

He rose, walked over to the table and placed the blue egg alongside the others on the drying racks. "Not this time," he said.

Frannie had never seemed to be afraid of him, but neither had she come to terms with the idea that he was calling the shots in her life now. She came right over, gazing up with stormy eyes and a hard jaw that reminded Rafe eerily of his father.

"Why not?" she demanded to know again.

"Because I…" He broke off, uncertain where to go from there. *Because I told you so?* Hell if he'd fall back on that tired parental cliché.

As though sensing he needed help, his mother came to the rescue. She approached the little girl and turned her around to face her. "Francesca, remember the job I gave you and Aunt Addy this morning? I want you two to make as many pretty eggs for Easter baskets as you can. These are not for eating."

"But I like hard eggs."

"Then I'll give you some to eat for lunch. Not that one. That one goes in the family basket, like a present. That's your job today—to help me get ready for Easter." She smiled down at the child, chucking her under the chin. "All right?"

Frannie considered this explanation for a long moment. Then her brow cleared and she nodded. "I guess so."

"Good. Our guests will be very happy on Easter morning."

Frannie turned back to Rafe. She waggled her hand over the eggs on the table. "I made all these."

He pretended to give them serious consideration. Pretended, at least, until he noticed that all the eggs Frannie had colored were two-toned with spots. Red on yellow.

Purple on pink. A sickly looking green on orange. Not a solid-colored egg among them. Except his.

Deliberate or subconscious, he wondered? A not-so-subtle attempt to show him that he didn't fit into the world she liked? Or maybe just an accident?

Deciding to ignore the implications, he cocked his head at the eggs, then gave her an enthusiastic look. "I see you like spots."

Did her jaw harden again? Just a little? "Spots are my favorite," she said clearly. "Don't you like spots?"

His sister Addy jumped in to save him this time. She touched Frannie's sleeve and drew her attention toward Sam seated near the back door, still working on the handle. "You aren't the only one. Your grandfather thinks polka dots should be a color in the crayon box."

All their lives, the D'Angelo kids had known that their father loved polka dots. Every tie at Christmas had been dotted, every pair of socks. One year there had been a weeklong silence in the house when Rose had vetoed Sam's intent to have all the curtains in the lodge redone in a dotted Swiss pattern.

Rafe didn't know whether his father had been paying attention to the conversation or not, but Sam suddenly looked over at them and pointed with his screwdriver. "There's nothing wrong with spots," he said in a no-nonsense tone. "They're bold and make life interesting. And why stick with one color when you can have two?"

Frannie nodded as though this logic made perfect

sense, though she didn't make eye contact with her grandfather. From the moment they'd met, she'd seemed shy of him, and unexpectedly, considering how much Sam loved children, he hadn't been overly friendly to the girl, either. But it was somehow annoying to Rafe that even his father seemed able to make a small connection with Frannie, when he had not.

"Francesca," his mother spoke up. "Will you go tell Mr. O'Dell at the front desk that we need more baskets from the storage shed?"

The child ran out the double doors to do as she'd been asked.

Rafe gave his mother a grateful look. "Thanks. I was starting to flounder there, wasn't I?"

His mother smiled up at him, touching the back of her hand to his cheek. "You'll get the hang of it. You just haven't had enough practice."

"I haven't had *any* practice."

"You were always quick to learn. I have faith that you can handle whatever Francesca throws your way."

He shook his head, unable to share his mother's confidence.

Of all the things he had envisioned for his life, a future built around kids had never been one of them. They were inconvenient. Noisy. Sticky. They liked to yank a person out of sleep and leave your nerves twitching until noon. Most of all, they needed you, and he didn't like that. He'd liked the image of himself as unencumbered, and nothing messed up a man's plans more than the responsibility of kids and family.

Last Christmas in Los Angeles when Ellen Stanton had called, letting him know she was in town and asking him to come by her hotel, he'd never suspected that the promise of a few hours of reliving old times would turn into a declaration of fatherhood.

He hadn't seen Ellen for years, not since they'd been river raft guides together on the Colorado. He remembered her as a woman who had liked sex fast, hard and slightly earthy. Their one evening together had not been a summer night filled with soft breezes and the glow of a full moon overhead. That night had ignited some chemistry that was all sex and excitement, but very little else. They'd coupled wildly, then said goodbye to one another at the end of the week without a single regret.

Going to Ellen's hotel suite, they'd barely passed the routine civilities of renewed acquaintance before she had trotted Frannie out of one of the bedrooms, pushed her in Rafe's direction and stated flatly, "Frannie, this is your daddy."

She'd waited for the words to sink in. They'd sunk.

He could still remember the ripple of shock that had run through his body. For a moment or two, he'd fought it, ready with denials. But he'd canceled that impulse when he'd looked down at the child. She had features alive with intelligence and the potential for sweetness. Her precise little mouth had been sullen and tight, but with little tremors in the muscles around it. He'd known instantly that she was scared to death.

He'd also known this was no outrageous lie of Ellen's. Frannie *was* his. Even as badly as he'd wanted to refute the claim, he could see it in her face and feel the truth of it in his bones.

The meeting between him and Frannie had been awkward, and when Ellen had sent the girl back to her room, Rafe couldn't feel anything but relieved.

That relief had soon turned to anger when Ellen had announced that she wanted Rafe to raise Frannie from now on. She had struggled financially for years, she'd said, but had finally found a great man to marry. An older man, who'd brought up his own kids and didn't want to have any more in the house. This was her only chance for real happiness, and it was time Rafe shouldered his responsibility.

He had wanted to run. He had wanted to tell her it was too late to expect scruples from him. A long time too late. The way he'd lived his life, he figured he had sacrificed them years ago.

He might have been able to pull it off if he'd never seen the kid. But from that moment on, Rafe knew that within him there lay a very fragile thread of scruples after all, a basic sense of fairness that told him that no matter what, he could not simply walk away from this little girl the way Ellen could. Whatever his daughter needed from him, he'd make happen.

Which was why he was home now, trying to make

peace with a father who had no use for him and a family that didn't know what to expect from him. He needed to settle down, make a stable home for Frannie. Give her as much time as possible with this extended family so that she could feel as though she belonged someplace at last. Most of all, figure out how a father-daughter relationship ought to work.

It wouldn't be easy. It wouldn't be quick. But there were bigger things at stake now, like his daughter's well-being.

A daughter who didn't really know him at all.

SAM D'ANGELO RARELY SLEPT through the night anymore and often slipped from bed unnoticed. After forty years of sleeping beside the same woman, he knew Rosa's sleep patterns, and that night, when he struggled into the metal cuffs of his crutches, he had no fear of waking her.

He made his way slowly out of the bedroom, through the family's private quarters and past the lodge kitchen toward the lobby. It was after 3:00 a.m. and no one was about. The lodge's sixteen rooms and two suites were full, but quiet.

Before his illness, Sam would have slipped on a jacket and gone outdoors to the side patio, a place where during the day visitors could pull up one of the hand-carved rocking chairs to enjoy a view of the mountains and Lightning Lake. It would have taken their breath away. The Rockies were giant monoliths watching over them, and even on the darkest night, the lake—now melting in the spring thaw—sparkled through the trees like diamond dust, a hidden treasure that never ceased to enchant.

But the flagstone surface of the patio played havoc with Sam's balance on the crutches, and even the view was not worth yet another trip to the hospital down at Idaho Springs.

He settled instead on the library, though without a fire in the grate and people to enjoy it, it seemed cold and unwelcoming. Disappointed, he slid into the deep leather chair in front of the chess set his father had brought all the way from Italy so long ago.

Odd to think that he would have found comfort in coming across a fellow insomniac at this hour, even a stranger. Usually, when he was this restless, he preferred his own company, but it might have been nice to share the peace and tranquility of this place, this black velvet night, with someone else who appreciated it the way he did.

Someone whose presence might help quiet his disordered frame of mind.

Maybe that was too tall an order from anyone. After all, he'd been on edge for a few weeks now. Ever since Rafe had come home.

What real hope was there that fences between them could be mended?

Perhaps it was impossible. Sam knew that Rosa was irritated with him often these days, feeling that he wasn't trying hard enough to find a way to bridge the gap between himself and Rafe, if only for the sake of the child.

But how could he when the past was so clearly etched in his brain?

He vividly remembered those last days before he and Rafe had had their final argument at the hospital. It had been springtime—just like now—but there'd been nothing hopeful and green about it back then. A tardy, disappointing season, muddy underfoot. The lodge's winter receipts had been weak, too many empty rooms on the weekends due to a lack of fresh snowfall.

Most of all, the edgy discord between every member of the family had been palpable. Little irritations. Petty warfare between the children. And always, always, too many moments of cold, silent disapproval and heated words that could not be taken back between Sam and his youngest son.

Rafe had always been their most difficult child. Never as focused and steady as Nicholas, as easygoing as Matthew, or as sweet-natured as Adriana. But Sam had not expected the boy to up and run off the way he had. In his heart, he had expected a minor show of rebellion, then an uneasy peace.

All hope had died on a night when Sam had picked up the telephone and found the police on the other end, asking him to come down to the hospital in Idaho Springs. He'd made that trip down the mountain in record time, refusing to allow Rosa to accompany him, fearful of what he'd find there, a cramping terror in his gut.

What he'd found had been his angry and unrepentant son in the process of being stitched up, his body scraped and bruised from the fight he'd been in with a drug dealer. The jagged knife-cut along his thigh was not life-threatening, but Sam could barely breathe for thinking how a few centimeters one way or the other could have changed that fact.

He was as furious as he was frightened, of course, and even after all these years he knew he had handled the incident badly. Condemnation. Mistrust. The unwillingness to see his son's side of things at all. As a result, Rafe had not come home. Instead, he had disappeared out into the world for twelve long years, and nothing would ever change the loss that defection had brought to their lives.

Sam became aware of movement beside him and discovered his wife slipping onto the arm of the chair, pulling him close so that she could plant a kiss on the top of his head.

"Come back to bed," she said softly. "You can't solve anything tonight."

It was uncanny, how well Rosa knew him after so many years. Still, he had to try to keep her from thinking he had no surprises left to give her. "What makes you think I'm trying to solve anything?" he asked. "I'm just restless."

"Samuel…"

"We need a new mattress. Let's go shopping for one in the morning."

"We don't need a new mattress. Do you want to talk about what we *do* need?"

"No."

"Samuel…"

He knew that tone. He cocked his head at her, settling for a portion of the truth. "He's not going to stay, Rosie."

She didn't need to ask who he meant. She simply shrugged. "He's a grown man. He shouldn't have to stay if he decides he doesn't want to. But if he does, then we'll make a place for him here."

"It won't be easy. The two of us…we don't communicate."

"That's because you are both hardheaded and proud. Too much alike." He heard the smile in her voice. She brought her hand to his chest, rubbing across his heart gently. "But you know something inside you is hungry for reconciliation."

"Perhaps. But on my terms."

"What terms?"

"I don't know the real reason he's come home, but I will not have this family put in harm's way. Not twelve years ago. Not now."

Rosa made a disgusted sound in her throat. "I should have tried harder to make you see reason back then. Rafe would never do that."

"Have you completely forgotten what a rebellious child he was?"

"Children grow up."

"And men grow hard."

She angled her head so that she could catch his eyes. "Sam, I know my children. And in your heart, you do as well. Rafe never did drugs. He would never have brought them into this house. Even that night, the doctors told you there were no drugs in his system."

"Maybe not at that particular moment. But you weren't there, Rosa," Sam said stubbornly, remembering the terrifying spectacle he had witnessed. "You didn't see what I saw. It was a miracle that he wasn't killed."

"You should have brought him home."

He had no reply for that. Since there had been no charges against Rafe, bringing his son home was precisely what Sam had wanted that night, to bring his boy back to the safety and security of the lodge. Instead, he knew he had driven Rafe even farther away.

He couldn't bear to think of all the mistakes he'd made that night, so he said, "Rafe made the decision to walk away from this family. No one else."

"But he's back now. We have been given a second chance." Rosa squeezed his arm. "This is not a bridge to burn, Samuel. It is a bridge to cross."

"You're wasting your time. We might as well be strangers to him."

"I don't believe that."

"Believe what you want. I'm afraid—" He broke off, unsure how to express himself.

His wife slipped off the arm of the chair and knelt beside him. She cupped his hands in hers. "What are you afraid of? That he will stay with us? Or that he won't?"

"We should go back to bed," he said roughly. "Today will be busy with the holiday coming."

She ignored him, instead placing soft kisses along the knobby ridges of his knuckles. When she looked up at him, the sweetest smile was on her lips. "She looks like you, you know?"

"I don't know what you mean," he said, though he knew perfectly well who she referred to.

"Of course you do."

"I find it irritating that you continue to be a woman who enjoys little mysteries."

"There's no mystery, really. Francesca looks like you. I've seen you looking at her. You have noticed the resemblance."

"I'm naturally curious about any child Rafe claims is his."

"And yet you take pains to stay away from her. Why is that?"

"The wheelchair frightens her."

She sighed. "Samuel…"

Annoyed, he lifted his hands out of hers, spreading them in disgust. "Am I not allowed to take my own time? She may be my blood, but that doesn't mean we're automatically *simpatico,* you know?"

"She has your fondness for polka dots." Her hands plucked at the smooth pattern of his pajama sleeve.

One of his favorites—white spots on a royal blue background. "I find that shared quirk rather strange."

"Liking polka dots is not a quirk. And it means nothing."

"She's just a little girl, Sam. No doubt she's frightened by all the sudden changes in her life. I've told Rafe I want her to spend as much time as possible with us. She needs family. More than Rafe, she needs our love and understanding."

"Give me time."

"Your heart understands what your head cannot yet conceive. Trust those feelings."

Sam shook his head. Rosa was too generous, too willing to forget. "He won't stay," he said again, more forcefully this time. "We'll open up our home and our hearts and they'll both be gone by Christmastime. Mark my words."

Her poise could not be shaken by the pessimism of his tone. She simply nodded, as if accepting that possibility. "I have decided that this is a chance worth taking. Meeting your son halfway is no more frightening in the long run than living a life without him."

CHAPTER FOUR

RAFE WAS GLAD TO HAVE EASTER behind him. He wasn't comfortable with family holidays, with their lollipop colors and enforced gaiety. There were too many opportunities for mis-takes.

But Mom's cooking was excellent as usual and the family seemed relaxed and pleased by the lodge guests' eager participation in the planned festivities. Watching the kids collect Easter eggs on the lawn hadn't been too bad, though he'd bet half of them would be sick by dinnertime from eating too many sweets.

His daughter had been on her best behavior. Nick and his wife, Kari, had brought their new son, Ethan, to the festivities, and Frannie always seemed enchanted by the sight of the baby. When she was allowed to hold him, she lit up momentarily and then settled into the responsibility with the most serious look on her face that Rafe had ever seen.

Whatever her reason for good conduct, that, and the fact that Rafe and his father had managed to pass a fairly civil holiday, made him breathe a huge sigh of relief.

The control he exercised around his father could easily fail him. He'd say the wrong thing. Do the wrong thing. And then where would they be? Rafe was trying desperately not to fight in front of Frannie. Hell, when it came to getting along with Pop, he was desperate, period.

On Monday, he drove down the mountain, dropped Frannie back into her kindergarten class, made final arrangements for his daughter to be babysat on occasion by one of the teachers there and then headed downtown. Before going to the newspaper office, he wanted to make a stop at the makeshift construction office he'd put together at the Three Bs. Now that the holiday was over, renovations on the buildings would kick into high gear once again.

He parked on the street and was pleased to see that there were already several trucks and vans there, the workers getting an early start. Standing on the sidewalk, he couldn't help once more admiring the workmanship that had gone into the place.

The inspectors he'd hired to give it the once-over had told him the Three Bs was structurally sound. It would take a good bit of money to make it comfortable and functional, but right now, thanks to years of saving and the money Wendall Crews had left him, money wasn't tight.

Rafe knew he could have found a newer, more affordable, more practical place to call home, but he had a silly attachment to this building. He had an unexpected fondness for Victorian architecture—a sense of history tucked into crazy corners and fancy turrets. Maybe because he'd spent too many years living in nondescript apartments in too many nondescript neighborhoods.

But it was more than that, somehow. Perhaps it was the odd belief that if he could bring the Three Bs back to its former grandeur, he could resurrect his old life here as well.

His father would probably laugh at that idea.

A door slammed behind him, and Rafe turned to find an older man getting out of a battered truck. In the front seat, the biggest German shepherd Rafe had ever seen hung out the window, whining like a puppy when the man joined Rafe on the sidewalk and left him behind.

The guy gave him a short nod, then tossed his chin toward the building. "Gonna be a mess of work to get this place back to what it once was."

"Probably," Rafe agreed. "But it will be worth it."

"Heard you were back in town. You don't remember me, do you?"

Rafe looked at the man more closely, but couldn't place the face. "Afraid not."

"Leo Waxman. Waxman Electric. Good friend of your father's."

Rafe held out his hand. "Of course, I *do* remember. You used to have a lot of shepherd pups in a shed behind your house."

"Still do on occasion," the man said, obviously warming to the subject. Behind him the dog began an earsplitting whine, and Leo turned toward the truck. "Hush up, Brutus." He swung back to Rafe. "I missed the town council meeting the other day. Heard you got elected publicity chairman for the festival."

"Yep. If you're here to tell me you want the job, I won't fight you for it."

"Nah. I've got no interest in the festival, and definitely no interest in trying to get those three committee knuckleheads to agree on a plan." He indicated the building again. "But I also heard you bought this place, among others, and that *does* interest me. You plan on living here, or selling for a profit?"

"I figure four spec condos, plus my own place. Then I want to see about redesigning a few other buildings I've picked up downtown on First Street."

"You gonna need help with the electric? If so, I'm your man."

Leo handed Rafe a business card, and for the next few minutes they talked about what it would take to bring the building up to code, the improvements and modifications Rafe wanted to make to the existing structure. The electrician seemed eager for the work, knowledgeable and forthright. In spite of the differences Rafe had with his father, he knew Sam would never have kept the friendship of someone who couldn't be trusted to do an honest day's work.

Agreeing to get together later in the week, Rafe and Leo shook hands.

Leo grinned. "You know the Three Bs history?"

"That's part of what drew me to it in the first place."

The Three Bs, built in the 1880s, had originally meant beds, baths and breakfast, and had catered to the area's silver miners looking to strike it rich. But widow Ida Mae Culpepper had discovered a more profitable way to make a living, and the social club had become very "social" after a few months in operation. The *B*s soon translated to betting, booze and bad women.

Then during the Korean War, Myrtle Culpepper had taken over, following in her great-grandmother's footsteps to transform the establishment into the perfect place for enlisted men to listen to lively music, drink good liquor and spend a few hours of pleasure in the company of what the newspapers of that time had called "agreeable companions."

Evidently drawing on some memory, Leo laughed. "You know, your father and I spent many a night in this place."

That Rafe *didn't* know, and he was surprised. "Really?"

"Oh, not when it was *that* kind of place. That was before our time. After Vietnam it got turned into just a social club, a place where a bunch of old leathernecks could compare war stories and drink a few beers. I used to play piano back then. Your dad used to pick up extra bucks by playing fiddle with the band." He slid an amused glance at Rafe from under bushy brows. "Bet you didn't know that, did you?"

His father a musician? How could that be? No one, not even their mother, had ever hinted at such a thing. "No," he said, shaking his head. "I sure didn't."

"That's because he was god-awful. Two cats fighting in an alley sounded better, but nobody threw us off the stage. You get a few drinks in a bunch of guys, tell a few war stories, and everyone gets mellow."

"I've never seen him pick up a musical instrument."

"He quit fooling around with it once you kids came along, and things got cranking up there at the lodge. Way too busy to devote the time. Kinda went by the wayside, the way lots of things do once you start a family and you realize what's important."

What's important. For a moment Rafe could envision his father making that conscious decision, putting aside the idle playthings of his younger years and taking on the responsibility of home and family.

Sam had always been able to focus on what needed to get done. He was a practical, goal-oriented man who had never understood the desire to see over to the other side of the mountain when you had what you needed right in your own backyard. It must have been particularly galling to him that his youngest son had refused to toe the line.

"I'll give you a discount, you being Sam's son and all." Leo Waxman cut into Rafe's thoughts.

"Thanks. I'll look forward to working with you."

"You're not afraid of this place?"

"You mean the rumors that it's haunted? No."

In his youth, Rafe had explored the building by popping a broken board off a back window. The place had been deserted for years. He had been fascinated, and the teenage girls he'd brought here had found his arms just the right protection against the whispery night shadows of abandoned rooms. Depending on who you talked to in town, the Three Bs was either haunted or hiding a secret treasure, or both.

"Probably kept the price down," Leo speculated.

That was true. When Rafe had decided to bring Frannie home to the family, he couldn't resist seeing if the old place was still up for sale. He had big plans for it, and he couldn't wait to move himself and Frannie into the place he'd already decided would make a suitable home for them both.

He knew Frannie was benefiting by spending so much time with his family, but he was eager to get out of the lodge, where Frannie must feel confused by all the hustle and bustle that came with running a thriving business. Where the air around his father was thick with tension.

The foreman of the construction site waved at Rafe, and seeing the opportunity to break away from Leo, he shook hands one last time with the man, clapped him on the shoulder and left him at the curb. They were tearing down walls in the club's front room today, and he was eager to see what kind of workmanship lay behind the flocked, garish wallpaper that the Culpeppers had thought so attractive.

Once Rafe was satisfied the work was progressing well, he could move on to his next mission—getting one newspaperwoman to buy into the idea that the second Broken Yoke summer festival wasn't geared strictly to make money for its citizens. Downtown revitalization, worthwhile causes, civic pride rebuilt. Could he persuade her that there was good to be done?

Maybe he was worrying too much. After four years of working for Wendall Crews and his far-flung empire, Rafe had honed the art of gentle, and not-so-gentle, persuasion. He had the talent to spin the festival any way the town wanted it. And just how bright a journalist could this Danielle Bridgeton be if the paper had stuck her out here in no-man's-land?

Besides, big brother Nick had been right. Rafe still had the D'Angelo charm, and though he liked to think he'd changed, that he wasn't prone to the old ways anymore, he hadn't forgotten any of the old tricks.

If all else failed, he'd lay it on thick and deep. He'd make Ms. Bridgeton feel as though she were the center of his universe. He'd have her eating out of his hand.

By the time he was finished with her, she'd give them more newspaper coverage than the winter Olympics.

MAYBE SHE WASN'T the world's best journalist, but Dani thought she could recognize a losing proposition when she saw one. She regarded the three stories spread out on the desk in front of her.

It would be hard to say which would be more exciting. Or which one was more likely to put Gary to sleep when he read it.

She began to feel helplessly angry again at the fates that had dropped her into the dullest news corridor of Colorado. This certainly wasn't the future her mother had scrimped and saved for her daughter to have.

If Wanda Bridgeton could have seen her now, how disappointed would she be?

Not wanting to give in to another fit of useless emotion, Dani decided that maybe a second opinion was called for. After all, she was biased about what interested people in this neck of the woods.

"Cissy," she called out the open office door. "Could you come in here a moment?"

Although she was several years younger, Cissy had become Dani's closest friend here in Broken Yoke. She was a savvy saleswoman when it came to selling advertising for the paper, and she and Dani had discovered a mutual interest in making a name for themselves.

Cissy sauntered in and perched on the side of one of the office chairs expectantly.

Dani picked up the first story. "Tell me which of these pieces would interest you the most if you picked up the Sunday paper." She expelled a resigned breath. "The new forklift that Silver Ridge paid a fortune for this past winter is out of commission because the idiot driving it ran into a ravine."

"Was the idiot killed?"

"No."

"Then who cares?"

Dani picked up the second story. "A guy down at Berthold Pass has grown a squash that has markings like Abraham Lincoln."

"Oh, please," Cissy said, rolling her eyes.

"I've seen the picture the stringer took," Dani said, referring to the photographer she sometimes used. "It really does look like Honest Abe, stovepipe hat and all."

"And that would matter to whom?"

"True." Dani slipped it to the bottom of the stack. She lifted her last and best. "A wolf got into a chicken coop and created havoc for some farmer in Manitou. Killed three of his prize Rhode Island Reds before he chased it off."

"A dozen would be better. More dramatic."

"Just three, I'm afraid. But Farmer Jenkins said his coop is so secure that the wolf had to be the canine equivalent of James Bond to break into it."

Cissy lifted an elegantly shaped brow. "Are you making that up?"

"I swear, that's what he said."

The younger woman pursed her lips, tapping her bottom lip with her finger. "I'd go with that one."

"Why?"

"Death. Destruction. Secret-agent wildlife. Definitely better than an Abe Lincoln rutabaga."

"Squash." Dani placed the story on the top of her pile. "All right. The Double-O-Seven wolf it is. Although Gary is still going to laugh when he reads it."

"I've read your stuff. It'll be great."

"Thanks," Dani told her, but then almost to herself she added, "I've just got to do better than this. There has to be *something* I can sink my teeth into."

Cissy trotted off while Dani sighed again and reflected on how she'd once set aside a space on the top of her fireplace mantle for a Pulitzer. No secret-agent wolf was going to fill that hole on her shelf or in her life.

Damn you, Lorraine Jennings Mandeville. How could one woman mess up her world so completely? Dani wondered.

After she'd been exiled here, she'd briefly considered telling Gary she'd resign before being run out of town, but she wasn't a quitter. Besides, it wasn't forever. She could handle living in Broken Yoke a while longer. She could. It wasn't a horrible place. Kind of postcard-pretty in a lot of ways.

Of course, by the time she finally made it back to Denver and her regular assignments, her career was going to be deader than Farmer Jenkins's poor chickens.

She cupped her head in her hands, massaging a fresh headache with her fingertips. Surely there was some magic she could work with these stories.

She lifted her gaze to discover Cissy had come

back in the doorway of her office. The woman had brightened considerably. Maybe she had come up with something. "Boss, Rafe D'Angelo—"

Dani held up a forestalling hand, too peeved at the moment to bother showing polite interest in a topic of conversation she was thoroughly sick of. "Please. Not one more word about the great Rafe D'Angelo. I don't want to hear about how every woman in town wants him. He's old news, and even if he wasn't, I'm not interested in hearing about a guy who probably has an ego as big as this room. From now on, any discussion about him is off-limits. Is that clear?"

"Yes, ma'am," Cissy said from the doorway, looking uncomfortable. "But I think I should tell you one last thing. Rafe D'Angelo—"

"Is what?" Dani asked, pinning her with a disgusted look. "Is sexy? Is worth his weight in gold? Is the devil incarnate?"

"Is here," Cissy finished for her.

Giving Dani a regretful smile, she stepped aside. In the next moment, the office doorway was filled with the tall, dark, unexpected presence of a complete stranger.

No. Not a stranger. Dani knew him instantly.

"Devil incarnate, huh?" the man remarked with a grin in his voice. "Interested in selling your soul?"

She popped up, feeling flustered at being taken unawares. Her stomach churned. Embarrassing. *Really* embarrassing. He had to know perfectly well that she hadn't intended for him to hear a word she'd said, but it was too late to save face now. Better to brazen it out.

Dani came around the desk, a weak smile on her lips. "I'm so sorry, Mr. D'Angelo," she began.

She got her first good look at his face. Her smile froze on her lips as she took in the sight of dark eyes, dark hair and a slightly crooked nose that kept this man from being classically handsome.

She remembered that nose. Those eyes. She remembered this man. How could this be the infamous local hotshot, Rafe D'Angelo? This was Oz, the casino pit boss she'd worked with briefly six years ago.

A man whom she may or may not have slept with.

The snake in the grass who had disappeared out of her life before she'd ever had the chance to find out.

Oh God. Did he recognize her?

It didn't appear so. His features remained bland and unremarkable as he relaxed into the chair in front of her desk. She didn't know whether she should be glad or unhappy about the fact that she hadn't stirred his memory.

Of course, she'd looked different back then. Dolled up like the rest of the plastic princesses who had worked in Native Sun's casino. The night she'd gone after the story of her life—city government employees who spent a hefty portion of taxpayer money on gambling and hookers—she'd worn enough makeup for the entire chorus.

In spite of years spent trying to put that incident out of her memory, she couldn't help remembering how the tables had gotten turned. How the lowlife she'd gone after had slipped something in her drink. How he and his friend would have raped her if they'd had the chance.

This man—Oz—had evidently stopped that from happening. Her memory was fuzzy, but she definitely recalled waking up naked next to him. He'd seemed somewhat amused by her reaction when she'd rolled over and spotted him, propped up on one elbow beside her. He'd told her that she was safe, that he'd take care of her, and she'd believed him. It hadn't helped that she'd fallen asleep shortly after that. At least, she *thought* she had.

Had they had sex?

She still wasn't one hundred percent positive. When she'd finally come to again, she was still naked, but her head was clearer and Oz was gone. Vanished. From the room. From the casino. From her life.

Oh, it was too humiliating to think about, even now.

Given the way things had turned out, she realized she was perfectly happy *not* to take a trip down memory lane. No, better to stay away from that subject and hope that in addition to being the local ladies' man, Rafe D'Angelo had a memory like a sieve.

She sat down limply behind her desk, suddenly conscious that her hair was a mess and she hadn't bothered with makeup today. "Who— What brings you to my little part of town?" she asked, trying for her most professional tone.

He seemed perfectly willing, thank goodness, to put aside any conversation of a personal nature. "I'm sure you've heard the town has an interest in hosting a summer festival?"

"I've heard there's been some discussion."

She could tell he found that assessment funny. His mouth curved upward—in the kind of quiet, private delight that could make a woman's toes curl. Dani suddenly remembered that several of her fellow show-girls had particularly loved that smile of his.

"Discussion," he said, as though hearing the word for the first time. "That's a polite term for it. A festival committee has been established, but they've yet to agree on a theme. I was elected the publicity chairman."

"Ah."

She understood now. Flacks—which was what the newspaper called PR people who constantly ran around doing their smoke-and-mirrors thing—drove her crazy. They were experts at spinning the truth to fit their own needs, and she had very little use for them. Whatever else Oz—Rafe—might be, it didn't surprise her one bit that he'd been elected to handle the PR slot. Hadn't he always been an expert at subtle persuasion back at Native Sun?

She realized he was frowning at her. "Ah? What does that mean exactly?" he asked.

"Nothing really. Just that I think I see where this is going."

"You do?" He cocked his head. "And where exactly are we going, Mrs. Bridgeton?"

"Miss."

"Ah."

It was her turn to frown. "What does *that* mean?"

"Nothing. Just nice to get all the players straight, I suppose. Especially since I'd like us to spend some time together."

The words came out in such a hot, silky tone that she almost forgot what they were talking about. "I beg your pardon?" she said, trying to dissolve the sudden lump of something strange in her stomach.

"Spend time together. For the sake of publicizing the festival."

Relief stretched through her. "Oh, of course. What did you have in mind, Mr. D'Angelo?"

"Please call me Rafe."

She inclined her head politely in agreement although she had no intention of calling him Rafe. Or Oz. Or anything. In fact, the sooner she could shoo him out of the office, the better she'd like it. Life was getting too darned complicated.

She ran a hand over her hair, glad suddenly that she'd chopped off several inches a year ago so that it fell to just below her shoulders. The shorter, less-dramatic style she currently wore probably set off no memory bells for him. Giving him another professional glance, she said, "I assume you're here looking for coverage."

"I am. In the best interest of the town."

"I plan to cover it, of course. If it's still going to take place on a Saturday, I'll have a piece running the next day in the *Telegraph's* Sunday supplement."

"I was thinking of something a little more extensive than that."

Dani's eyes narrowed. "Such as?"

"Reasonably priced ad space. Perhaps an article or two in the weeks leading up to the festival. We want to attract as many people as possible. It's critical that it be a financial success."

"Mr. D'Angelo, perhaps you don't understand. The paper isn't interested in covering any festival just so that this town can make money."

"I understand that we can't use the paper simply to fill the town's coffers," he said, not at all put off by her attitude. He withdrew a sheet of paper from his jacket pocket. "I've asked the mayor to furnish you with a commitment list of all the projects the town intends to use the proceeds for. As you can see, it's quite extensive."

Dani quickly scanned the list. He was right—it was impressive. The *Telegraph* wouldn't object to being used to further these kinds of causes. She set the paper aside.

"What angle is the festival going to take?" she asked.

"I'm afraid that's still undecided. The committee is leaning toward one of two themes proposed at the last town meeting."

Oh, she'd heard all about that town meeting. Free-for-all was more like it. "Was that the town meeting where one member threatened to deck another with his oxygen tank?"

He laughed lightly, a warm, mellow sound that made a good companion to his smile. "I'm not sure that specific threat was ever made. But I see you're familiar with the people I'm dealing with, Miss Bridgeton." He inclined his head toward the nameplate that sat on her desk. "May I call you Danielle?"

She nodded quickly. Clearly he didn't remember her as DeeDee Whitefeather. "I heard that tempers flared," she said. "If you got strong-armed into this job, then you have my sympathy."

"Thanks. As I was saying, no definite decisions have been made, but if we could, I'd like to schedule some time with you tomorrow."

Her nerve endings began to fire like pistons in a car. "Why?"

Was he surprised by her obvious lack of interest? She didn't imagine that Rafe D'Angelo was used to women being at all reluctant to keep him company. Even when she'd known him as Oz at the casino, he'd been way too sure of himself. He hadn't been nick-named the Wizard of Women for nothing. The pig.

He was silent for a moment, his dark eyes holding her like a hypnotist's though there was nothing in his look that told her what he was thinking.

Then he said, "Two very different events have been proposed. Both parties have prepared presentations. I thought we could check them out. I'd welcome your input."

"What are the two suggested themes?"

"One would celebrate Broken Yoke's pioneer days. Reenactments of the founding of the town. Concessions, games and craft booths built around the town's silver heyday."

"Are you originally from this area, Mr. D'Angelo?"

Did he stiffen in his chair a little before he answered? Hard to say. "I've been away a while, but I was born here."

"Then surely you know that Colorado needs another summer festival like a drowning man needs a brick. And while the state prides itself on celebrating the unusual, more than half the towns choose the same type of event. Founder's Day. Pioneer Days. Rough and Ready Days. You can hardly tell them apart."

"Then it'll be my job to find a way to entice visitors here. I'm certain I can do that."

Oh, this was bad, very bad. She could actually feel herself responding to that overwhelming presence of his. She felt too hot. DeeDee Whitefeather wouldn't have been so affected.

Straightening in her chair with a deliberate sigh of boredom, she asked, "What's the second suggestion?"

"A Christmas in July celebration."

Dani wasn't expecting that and found her interest piqued before she could remember that she wanted nothing to do with this man. "That's a little different."

"It has possibilities. The fellow pitching it feels we can capitalize on the winter activities we have around here. Find ways for people to enjoy the same things, only in the summer. His wife is one of the teachers at our elementary school, and he's enlisted students to help."

"Skiing in July? Sounds problematic."

"True," D'Angelo agreed. "But he's chosen some sample venues. Do you have a photographer available? It might make for fun pictures."

She pursed her lips, intrigued in spite of herself. "I have a freelance stringer I can call on."

"Then do we have a date? I could pick you up at nine in the morning."

"What?"

"We could make a day of it. Perhaps have an early dinner afterward and discuss which idea might do the most good. Whether the paper would have any interest in covering one of them."

She hoped she didn't look as cornered as she felt. "I—I'll need to work out the details with Chester, my photographer."

"Of course."

She really ought to see what the town had in mind for the festival. But there was no way she wanted to spend almost an entire day in this man's company. Even if he didn't remember her. Inspiration came at the last minute. "It would probably be simpler if I met you at these places. Why don't you give my secretary the addresses and we can arrange to link up?"

She stood, determined to take the upper hand and show him that she wasn't going to be maneuvered. This meeting was over.

Dani came around the desk, stretching her hand out once more. Rafe D'Angelo rose quickly, placing his long-fingered hand in hers.

"Thank you for the offer of dinner," she said. "But I'm afraid I have plans tomorrow night."

A curtain lifted in his eyes. They were suddenly alive with interest and amusement. "I'm disappointed," he said. "Are you sure we can't have dinner? Don't you want to catch up on old times, DeeDee?"

CHAPTER FIVE

RAFE WATCHED THE SHOCK take over her features.

Oh, yeah, she remembered who he was, and she obviously didn't like the fact he remembered her, too. By the set of her jaw, he had a feeling she didn't want to discuss the past.

Eager to get *some* kind of reaction, he reached out and pulled her closer. "Now *that's* the DeeDee I remember so well. All haughty superiority. What have you been up to all these years, darlin'?"

She slipped out of his arms, and he let her go. In another moment she was back behind her desk, a safe barrier between them.

"All right," she said at last. "So you know I used to be DeeDee Whitefeather. I remember you as Oz. Six years isn't long enough to erase those memories completely. But so what? We're different people now. I don't see why it should be a problem that we were friends in Vegas."

He did a double take. "Friends? I'd say we got to be a little more than that."

She paled, and he wondered if she remembered just how "friendly" she'd tried to get with him. She turned away in exasperation, pulling a hand through her hair. Six years hadn't changed the bright luster of it, that great complexion, those eyes like storm clouds over the mountains. Had she really expected him to forget those eyes?

She remained silent, thoughtful. It occurred to him suddenly that she was desperately trying to put all the pieces together about their one close encounter, but was coming up empty.

"Come on, DeeDee," he said. "It's not that bad, is it?"

She turned quickly back to face him. "Look, we both know that night in Vegas was... I'm not sure how or why it happened, but it did. I vaguely remember waking up side by side with you on one of the big beds at Native Sun, so I assume somewhere along the way..."

That wasn't exactly how it had stacked up, of course, but he was interested to see just how good her memory was. "I definitely was the one to take your clothes off," he agreed. "In fact, whatever high you were on, you couldn't wait to get out of them."

She cringed and covered her face momentarily with her hands. Finally, she said in a soft, desperate voice, "Whatever we did or didn't do that night, could we just forget it ever happened? I'm not particularly proud of it...."

He realized she didn't have a clue about what had

happened between them, *or* what had transpired after he'd left the room that night. But some time after that, the influence of the drug she'd been under *must* have worn off. Since she'd so cavalierly quit her job the next day and had put his welfare behind her, he wasn't sure she deserved an explanation.

She looked up at him, her teeth drawn between her lips. "Couldn't we just agree not to talk about it? I'm obviously not DeeDee anymore. You're obviously not Oz. No more discussion needs to take place."

He almost told her the whole thing right then. But nothing in her face gave him the impression that she'd believe a word of it. His reputation was clearly there in her memory, and Oz didn't put himself out for any of the girls at Native Sun who happened to get themselves in trouble. The fact that he'd actually taken a beating for her and she hadn't even been grateful enough to stick around to thank him didn't seem to play into it.

So be it. Let the past stay a mystery.

"All right," he conceded. "Tell you what. I agree not to bring up our past…relationship, on one condition."

She gave him an annoyingly suspicious look. "What condition?"

"That you agree to meet me tomorrow and check out the two festival proposals. Whatever happened between us six years ago shouldn't have a bearing on what this town wants to accomplish. Be fair. Give the presentations an unbiased look, then make your decision about coverage. What do you say?"

She chewed her lip a moment in thought. Then she sighed and said, "Agreed."

She even held out her hand and shook on it. Though, he noticed she couldn't seem to release his fingers fast enough.

THE NEXT DAY, IT WAS nearly noon by the time they got to the oxen.

Rafe and the Festival Committee—Mort, Howard and Polly—had already endured two incredibly boring hours. Bill Lawler's reenactment of the planting of Broken Yoke's first aspen tree. A lecture on how to tell the difference between the various minerals found in the area's mines. A demonstration by Bill's wife, Letty, of a typical miner's supper. And, a homemade diorama of the 1846 westward movement of the pioneers from Denver, complete with plastic cowboys and cardboard wagons.

Never a morning person, Rafe tried to pretend an interest he didn't have, but thankfully, they were finally coming to what Bill called the pièce de résistance—the actual founding of Broken Yoke.

Rafe watched as Bill drove two harnessed oxen hitched to a wagon out of his barn. The man maneuvered the lumbering beasts to within a foot of Polly Swinburne's feet, pulled the animals to a halt, then jumped down from the wagon seat.

He grinned at the four of them. "Well, what do you think?" he asked. "Aren't they magnificent?"

No one said a thing.

Letty, standing beside Bill, was nearly as excited as her husband and wasn't a bit bothered by the lack of response. "People love animals," she said.

No, Rafe thought. People loved *wild* animals. Or circus poodles, or really fine horseflesh. There was nothing exciting about these two enormous cows. A whole *herd* of them wasn't going to thrill anyone.

But the Lawlers had put a lot of time and thought into this presentation. Rafe kept quiet, knowing that the committee would have the final say-so. No reason he had to be the one to burst the Lawlers' bubble.

Mort Calloway smiled noncommitally as he reached out to pet one of the oxen. "They're certainly impressive."

"Impressive!" Bill exclaimed. "They're practically direct descendants of the original team. Imagine it. They'd be the last event of the day."

Polly, who never had a problem speaking up, inclined her head sharply. "Last event of the day? You really think we'd get this far? I suspect everyone will have fallen asleep long before you haul these two out of the barn."

"They do reflect how Broken Yoke got its name," Howard Hackett pointed out, playing the peacemaker. Of all of them, he'd seemed the least bored by everything so far.

Letty Lawler couldn't resist trying to make a stronger case. She nudged Rafe to draw his attention.

"Picture it. We have a couple dressed like settlers make their way into the city park. They're tired. Thirsty. Night's coming. Then suddenly, the oxen's yoke breaks."

"Oh, horrors," Polly added.

Ignoring her, Letty motioned excitedly to the beasts hitched to the wagon. "These two come to a halt. The weary settlers climb down from the wagon. What to do, what to do, they wonder...."

Polly Swinburne sniffed in annoyance. "They're not the only ones wondering what to do."

Sensing he was losing his audience, Bill Lawler jumped into role playing with his wife. They clearly envisioned themselves as the poor, distraught settlers. Rafe tried to look suitably impressed. He didn't know what the weary settlers had in mind, but he was pretty clear about what *he'd* like to do right now.

Run.

Finally, the Lawlers stopped spouting hokey lines and stood staring at the committee, waiting expectantly.

Polly looked disgusted. Howard seemed disappointed. Mort, sucking air from his portable oxygen tank, turned to Rafe. "You've been awfully quiet. What do you think?"

Rafe held his hands up. "I don't have a dog in this race," he said quickly. "I'm just here to see what angle the festival is going to take and then figure out how to publicize it."

"So where is this reporter you talked to?" Howard

asked. "I thought you got her to agree to meet with us today."

Rafe glanced at his watch, although he knew perfectly well what time it was. "She should have been here by now," he said. Privately he thought she was the lucky one to have missed this snoozefest.

"Looks like you've been stood up," Polly said. "Some of the D'Angelo charm must have worn off over the years."

The men chuckled, and Rafe laughed along with them. "Just as well. We may have been a bit premature in asking her to come this early in the game."

Bill Lawler, trying to recapture everyone's interest, swatted one of the oxen on the rump. "Let me show you what else these big boys can do," he said.

Inwardly, Rafe groaned.

Twenty minutes later, after promising to give the Lawlers' festival suggestion serious thought, the committee headed to the school to meet up with Phil Pasternak so they could check out his proposal, Christmas in July.

On the way over, Rafe had the chance to replay in his head yesterday's meeting with DeeDee—Danielle—or whatever name she was going by these days.

Admittedly, it had been a shock to walk into that office and discover someone from his past—a very interesting some-one—standing right in front of him again. But he thought he'd recovered quickly enough.

He hadn't been able to resist teasing her a little, but

now that he'd had time to think about it, he probably should have let the past stay buried. Pretended for both their sakes that they were strangers to one another. That year in Vegas—*all* those years of selfish, drifting antipathy until Wendall Crews had hired him—needed to be locked away in some mental file cabinet marked Untouchable.

He'd learned a lot working for Wendall, not just about business, but about being a better person. Things like honor and decency and trust.

And once Frannie had come into his life, hadn't he made a solemn vow to become a new man for her sake? To let go of all the bad habits and old ways so that she could have the kind of home and security she needed and deserved? He could do better. He could *be* better. And he would.

But it was too late now to fix yesterday. And he and Dani had a deal, damn it. So why hadn't she shown up?

Some time between then and now she'd changed her mind, lost her nerve. Or maybe just decided that she didn't owe him or Broken Yoke a thing.

Just like six years ago, she couldn't really be trusted to do what he expected.

THOUGH DANI SUSPECTED Rafe D'Angelo would never have believed her, standing him up for their meeting had not been intentional.

She'd never let him think that he intimidated her in any way, or that being around him for a few hours made her uncomfortable. Their past was officially off-limits. She had his word that they wouldn't discuss it. And though she didn't really trust him for one minute, if he tried to bring it up, she wasn't so meek that she wouldn't be able to shut him down completely.

What she *hadn't* counted on was that her photographer would be late picking her up, then have the unfortunate bad luck to get a flat tire on the deserted road that led out to Bill Lawler's farm on the outskirts of Broken Yoke.

By the time she'd finally arrived at the Lawlers' place, it was clear they'd missed both Rafe and the Festival Committee, as well as the Founder's Day presentation. Racing to the elementary school where the second proposal was to be staged, another half hour passed. It was clear when they got there that everything was well under way.

With Chester in tow, Dani crossed the teachers' parking lot and saw Rafe standing with a group of older people who had to be the committee. They were deep in discussion with another man, a slick-looking business type. Probably Phil Pasternak.

When Rafe looked up and saw her, his reaction didn't surprise her. He looked annoyed.

And then, as she got closer, she realized it wasn't annoyance so much as a look of disappointment, as though he'd been hoping she wouldn't show up.

In another hour, she understood perfectly well what had generated that look.

Phil's presentation, though well-meaning and innovative, was a disaster. Like any salesman, he'd put a lot of energy into the ideas, but not a lot of thought into the execution and logistics.

From the mountain's higher elevations, he'd had snow brought down to create a huge area for kids to indulge in snowball fights. Only problem, the children from his wife's third-grade class, stuffed into their winter snowsuits, had quickly overheated and two had actually come close to fainting.

He'd had wheels put on sleds and marched a few of the kids up the hill behind the school. But once they took off, they bogged down in the wet ground. The kids were forced to walk the sleds the rest of the way, complaining loudly.

In a temporary pen out in the parking lot, Phil had enclosed twenty deer for a makeshift petting farm dubbed Santa's Forest Friends. Unfortunately, none of the animals were tame. They had no interest in the people who kept trying to feed them. One parent got butted from behind, landed in a heap on the asphalt and quickly stormed off in embarrassment with his two kids in tow.

Even considering that any presentation could suffer glitches and little slipups, it was clear that Phil's idea wasn't going to work without some major reconsideration.

Dani knew it. The Festival Committee knew it. And so, quite plainly, did Rafe, who took great pains to keep his features blank.

Polly, Mort and Howard, taking their duties as members of the committee seriously, went off to the teachers' lounge to discuss what they'd seen so far. Chester was busy taking pictures at the disastrous petting farm. Dani stood with Rafe and Phil Pasternak, watching a third child get hauled off by the school nurse to cool down. The kid's face was beet-red.

"Big baby," Phil complained as the kid went wailing past them.

Evidently Rafe couldn't resist commenting any longer. With a sigh, he said, "Phil, if it's too warm even now, don't you think that it might be just a little too hot in July to pull off a winterfest?"

"It will be fine. You'll see."

"I'm not sure how many parents will want to take the chance of having their kids faint during a snowball fight."

"We'll tell them to dress normally then. Let them fight in shirtsleeves."

Dani couldn't resist trying to add weight to Rafe's very valid argument. "They'll get soaked to the bone, Mr. Pasternak. Especially once the snow melts and turns to nothing but slush."

"So? They'll dry off quickly."

Rafe motioned toward the sledding hill and gave Phil a close look. "Suppose one of those sleds turns over and hurts someone? Have you considered what the liability could be for the town?"

Losing patience, Phil threw his hands out in rejection. "For Pete's sake, when I was a kid we used to do the very same thing in the summer with a broken cardboard box for a sled. Sure, we got a few grass burns. That's all. It never stopped us."

Dani watched a muscle in Rafe's jaw twitch in annoyance.

"What do *you* think?" Phil posed the question to Dani. Obviously he thought he had a better chance talking to her, though she was in complete agreement with Rafe's assessment. "You can see the potential, can't you? Great pictures and a fun story."

She tossed a quick glance toward Rafe, who was shaking his head infinitesimally. "I see the potential for a lot of things, Mr. Pasternak. But it's not really up to me. As Mr. D'Angelo says, this is a decision the committee will have to make."

Phil glanced disgustedly toward the building where the committee was still entrenched in the teachers' lounge. "They haven't even looked at everything yet," he muttered. He swung a look back at Rafe and Dani. "Wait until you see the big finish. Santa, pulled on a wheeled sleigh down the center of town. Dexter Robbins makes a great Claus. I haven't got all the bugs worked out, but you'll get the idea."

That was the other thing about salesmen. They seldom took no for an answer.

Evidently unable to endure waiting any longer for the committee to reemerge, Phil made one last push for his idea. He dragged Dani and Rafe off to watch Santa—Dexter—red-faced and broiling in his wool suit, take his place in a large sleigh pulled by six mismatched horses. They looked skittish and uncooperative as Santa picked up the reins.

Rafe frowned at Phil, motioning toward the horses. "Is this a professional team pulling Santa?"

"You mean, like the beer wagons use?" Phil asked.

"Something like that."

"No," the man admitted. "We haven't found the right six horses to work together yet. But we will. How hard can it be? They just have to pull together in the same direction at the same time."

Rafe looked openly skeptical. "I worked on a ranch once. It's not as easy as it sounds to get horses to work side by side. They tend to—"

About that time, the sleigh went flying past them, with Santa pulling madly on the reins, yelling at the top of his lungs. The six horses ran as if demons were after them. They disappeared out of the parking lot, down the drive and rounded the corner out of sight.

"Oh, that Dexter," Phil complained as he watched his big finish disappear. "Forget Ho, ho, ho, you idiot. Try Whoa, whoa, whoa!"

Without further comment, he hurried off after Dexter and the sleigh, along with a few of his helpers.

Rafe looked at Dani. She tried hard to give the impression that she wasn't laughing and cleared her throat. "Well," she said. "Phil was right. That *was* a big finish."

The tight line of Rafe's lips told her he was trying

to avoid expressing a truthful opinion. Obviously he'd hoped for good results from this demonstration, and he certainly couldn't be pleased that she'd witnessed such a fiasco. For the next few moments she distracted herself by glancing around the school grounds, trying to come up with something encouraging to say. It wasn't easy.

"The kids look cute in their elf outfits," she said, pointing out the teenagers Phil had hired.

"And sweltering."

"I like the idea of a Christmas tree–decorating contest."

"Uh-huh."

"Maybe Phil's right. Maybe everything just needs some fine-tuning."

He chewed the inside of his mouth a moment before answering. "Sure. I'll speak to the committee. Give them my take on all of this. It's innovative. Everyone likes Christmas, so it's bound to put people in the mood to buy things from the arts-and-crafts booths." He dropped his head suddenly and placed his hands on his hips as though deep in thought. When he finally lifted his eyes, there was a twinkle of bleak amusement in their dark depths. "Oh, who am I trying to kid? *I* know it's a disaster. *You* know it's a disaster. There's no way this will work. Certainly not with someone like Phil in charge."

Seeing his face so stained with wry discontent, Dani couldn't resist trying to be upbeat a little longer. "It's very…festive looking."

Rafe clearly understood her motives. He smiled at her. One of those slow, intimate looks of his that made her stomach take a helter-skelter dive for just a moment.

"You're being generous, and I know it," he said in a lighter tone. "I also know I shouldn't have hauled you out here yet to see this mess. Phil convinced the committee that he was prepared. They want to make a determination pretty quickly, but having you come out…it was premature, and I apologize."

The apology surprised her. The old Oz would have never shown regret for anything he did or said. She wished suddenly that he wasn't standing so close. "Actually, I don't know what the Lawlers had to offer at their place, but this has been the most exciting thing I've seen since I've been in Broken Yoke."

They laughed together for a moment, a pure, honest sound that carried none of the caution they'd been using with one another from the moment they'd reconnected. It felt surprisingly nice.

Dani had to remind herself what she was doing. She'd only come because he'd practically twisted her arm. She wasn't supposed to enjoy his company. Not at all.

"Dani—" Rafe said.

There was a sudden commotion behind him—the wail of a small child. They both turned to find a young girl coming toward them, her hand clutched firmly by a harried-looking older woman. The two stopped in front of Rafe. The child's free hand pressed a tissue to her lips. The woman seemed annoyed and uncertain.

"Mr. D'Angelo," she said. "I'd like to speak to you. It's about Frannie."

Rafe knelt in front of the child, taking her thin shoulders between his hands. "What about Frannie?" he asked. His voice sounded worried, but matter-of-fact.

"As you can see, we've had a little accident. At the snow-ball fight."

"You didn't have my permission to let her participate, Mrs. Gravis."

"Yes. Well, that didn't stop her from running out to the playground the first chance she got," the woman complained.

Dani suspected she was some sort of teacher—day care, maybe, since she'd noticed that there was one connected to the elementary school. And Mrs. Gravis had that authoritative air about her.

"It's not serious," the woman went on. "Before I could get to her, one of the balls smacked her too hard in the lip. Barely broke the skin, but she won't stop crying."

"Let me see," Rafe said. He tried to pry the tissue out of Frannie's hands.

The child allowed him to look at her lip after a stubborn moment or two. Dani realized quite suddenly that this had to be Rafe's daughter. The resemblance was remarkable. Of all the futures she'd envisioned for Rafe since yesterday—family man wasn't one of them.

He patted Frannie's arm after inspecting her lip, which was puffy, but hardly scratched. "It's all right. You'll be fine."

The girl frowned at him for a full five seconds. Then unexpectedly, she jerked out of his grasp and pressed herself against the teacher's skirt, emitting a fresh wail of fear. "I don't want you," she cried. "I want Aunt Addy."

Rafe stood ramrod straight. "Aunt Addy isn't going to tell you any different."

"I don't want you. I want Aunt Addy!"

"Sorry. You're stuck with me. Aunt Addy's busy."

Mrs. Gravis spoke up. "The last time we called your sister, she was able to get here very quickly."

Rafe frowned at the woman, obviously not pleased by the suggestion that reinforcements should be called in. *Just how often does this happen?* Dani wondered.

"I want her," Frannie wailed again.

"All right," Rafe said with a long sigh. He didn't seem certain of anything, only desperate to prevent a scene. "Let's go make a telephone call."

The teacher turned and began to head toward the school with Frannie. Rafe swung back to Dani, who wasn't sure what to make of what she'd just witnessed. She knew only one thing. Rafe didn't appear very adept at fatherhood, and his daughter seemed absolutely uncomfortable in his presence.

"Sorry," he said to Dani. "I think I have to deal with this."

"You have a daughter." It was a statement of the obvious, but she couldn't keep the surprise out of her voice.

He nodded. "Maybe we could still have dinner later, talk about the festival and what can be done to salvage the idea."

In a way, Dani was glad for the interruption. Before Frannie had burst on the scene, she'd been having too many charitable thoughts about this man. She mustn't be swayed—not even for a second—by that devilish, teasing smile.

She shook her head. "I think you have your hands full trying to salvage your personal life. Don't worry about dinner. I think I've seen more than enough."

CHAPTER SIX

"DEARLY BELOVED, WE'VE COME together today to join this man and this woman in holy matrimony…."

Dani sighed and settled back in her chair, tempted to tune out the rest of the ceremony.

Weddings weren't her favorite kind of story. In fact, if you'd given her a choice between writing a juicy obituary and chronicling the union of two giddy love-birds, she would have taken the dead any day.

But she supposed she didn't really have much choice. The marriage of Matt D'Angelo to Broken Yoke's favorite nurse, Leslie Meadows, was consid-ered big news for this area, and since the wedding was not a ridiculously lavish extravaganza, and the happy couple weren't given to indulging in silly love stuff every chance they got, it wasn't such a chore.

She already knew that Lightning River Lodge was one of the most respected establishments on the Front Range. It was certainly situated in one of the prettiest parts of the state. It wasn't a huge conglomerate. In fact, its small size was probably what accounted for its reputation for down-home hospitality. Guests got treated like members of the family, and personal touches were everywhere you looked. And since the D'Angelos were prominent members of Broken Yoke, it only made logical sense to give the wedding its fair share of newspaper coverage.

Besides, it gave her the perfect opportunity to scope out Rafe D'Angelo's home environment. And that had been the primary drawing card as far as Dani was concerned.

These were Rafe D'Angelo's roots. This was the place he'd grown up. And according to Cissy, who was proving to be a valuable source of information, those formative years had not been without their share of strife.

Evidently there was some bad history between the father and the youngest son that no one seemed willing or able to clarify. The only thing that Cissy knew for sure was that Rafe had left home at eighteen, never to return.

Until a few weeks ago.

So, like most of Broken Yoke, Dani couldn't help being a little bit curious.

The lodge's spacious, friendly lobby had been transformed for the wedding. The focal point of the room, an enormous stone fireplace, was festooned with silk and satin, and the scent of fresh flowers filled the air.

Dani cast a glance around surreptitiously, studying the wedding party, which was small and obviously made up of family members. She recognized Matt

D'Angelo's father and his brother Nick, both of whom she'd met once, as well as several females on the bride's side whom she'd just been introduced to today. The guests numbered less than a hundred, and every one of them looked thrilled to be here.

Up in the front row, she thought she saw Rafe, seated next to the little girl she'd seen last week at the school. Frannie. His daughter.

It was still difficult to imagine the man she knew as Oz as a parent.

Not unexpectedly, the child seemed restless. Dani barely caught sight of the side of Rafe's face when he bent to speak to her, but his clean-cut profile and broad shoulders were unmistakable. No doubt about it. He was one of those men who radiated confidence even without saying a word.

There was a murmur of pleasure from the guests, and Dani realized that Matt D'Angelo and his bride had just turned to be introduced as Mr. and Mrs. Everyone clapped, and in spite of her skepticism about the state of wedded bliss, Dani had to join in because the newlyweds looked so happy.

When Matt D'Angelo planted a kiss on his new wife's lips, the gentle sharing of a perfect moment, Dani's stomach even gave a funny little tingle. What must it be like to stand up in front of everyone with someone you believed to be your one and only soul mate?

She couldn't imagine it. She had no frame of reference. Her own mother, a single parent who had struggled year after year to give her daughter a good home life and the education she herself had never known, hadn't believed much in Happily Ever After. According to Wanda Bridgeton, anything good that happened to you in life came about from hard work and perseverance, accomplished mostly on your own since men were completely untrustworthy. And after Dani's disastrous relationship with Kirk, and a few others she didn't want to think about, she couldn't say she disagreed much with that theory.

After the ceremony, the reception was held in the lodge's dining room. It was very informal, very easygoing, with lots of laughter and flowing wine. Guests were encouraged to make themselves at home, to wander the various downstairs rooms of the lodge and the grounds as though they were visiting with their own family. Dani sipped champagne and took notes and tried to imagine being part of a large Italian family that didn't appear to know a stranger.

It seemed an odd sort of family life for Rafe to have grown up in. Back in Vegas, with the exception of his dating habits, he'd been pretty much a loner.

The reception was in full swing. She'd gone down the receiving line, listened to a couple of effusive toasts to the bride and groom and was now feeling the beginnings of a small headache behind her eyes. She hadn't seen Rafe since the ceremony and couldn't help wondering where he'd taken off to.

After a while, she found the library and was delighted to discover it empty. A high-backed leather chair in one corner offered the perfect place for her to get her thoughts together and see if she had taken enough notes to do the occasion justice in the paper's Sunday issue. She hoped Gary would be pleased. In spite of her lack of interest in stories that clearly would win her little recognition, he seemed to think she had a flare for striking just the right tone.

She was sitting quietly, thinking how to describe the simple but elegant ceremony when she became aware that people had entered the library and she was no longer alone. Two people from the sound of it. And neither of them in a festive, wedding mood.

"You have something you want to say, Pop, then just say it," she heard Rafe say.

"I don't know what you're talking about."

That had to be Sam D'Angelo, Rafe's father. And he didn't sound any more pleased than his son. In fact, both men sounded so alike in temperament that it was amazing.

"I'm tired of hearing about the great accomplishments of Jeremy Waxman," Rafe went on.

"He's my best friend's son. My godson. Now that he's made state prosecutor in record time, don't I have a right to be proud of him? Especially when I remember how much grief Jeremy gave Leo when he was growing up."

"So that's what this is about," Rafe said sharply. "Not how proud you are of Jeremy, but how different he turned out from the way everyone expected. Did it ever occur to you that maybe Mr. Waxman didn't put enough faith in his son? Any more than—"

Rafe broke off, and Dani heard him release a harsh sigh. She couldn't see him, but she would have guessed that the flicker of impatience would be in his eyes. That his jaw would be rock-solid.

"Any more than I did you?" Sam D'Angelo challenged. "Is that what you want to say?"

Dani realized that she was in an incredibly awkward position. Technically, she was eavesdropping. She should have made her presence known immediately. But the conversation had moved so quickly, and something kept her in her chair, quiet, pressed back against the cushion as though she could make herself invisible.

"It doesn't have to be your way or nothing, Pop," Rafe said. "I might not be a doctor, or the new state prosecutor, but I have a certain amount of financial success and stability now. I'm here, trying to make a good home for Frannie and myself. Why isn't that enough for you?"

"Who said it wasn't? Stop behaving like a jealous child."

"Then stop treating me like a failure."

The older D'Angelo clicked his tongue in a sound of disgust. "There is no talking to you."

"Stop talking. Try *listening* for a change. Hear what I'm trying to say to you."

"So say it."

"I want to stay here, but I can't when you continue to give me no reason to. And I *won't* stay if there's no forgiveness for what you see as the sins of my past— real or imagined."

"I didn't need much imagination for what I witnessed that night in the hospital. It was perfectly clear. And what wasn't clear was explained to me thoroughly by the police."

There was a huge, uncomfortable silence. Then Rafe said quietly, in a tone of precise anger, "Maybe it wasn't the police you needed to ask. Maybe it was your own son."

Dani heard the creak of metal and suspected that Rafe's father, moving as well as he could with the help of his crutches, had headed for the door of the library. "I will not have this day spoiled," he told his son. "I have a toast to make for your brother."

There was silence again, uncomfortable and thrumming with tension that hovered in the air even after Sam D'Angelo had vacated the room. She wished she had never heard this conversation. It was too personal. Too filled with hurt. On both sides, from the sounds of it. How long had that anger between the two men been simmering?

She should have known she couldn't escape unnoticed.

Rafe came farther into the library, stared out into the mild sunlight offered by the room's windows for a few moments, then turned to leave. He stopped in his tracks, seeing her sitting there.

Blood surged through her and her whole body tightened. For a split second, he looked at her as if he'd never seen her before. She expected to see cold disapproval in his eyes, but surprisingly there was none.

Dani wanted to do something to ease the discomfort, but she couldn't think of a single thing. She sent him a tentative, uneasy smile. "Sorry," she said. "I'd have let you know I was here, but the two of you seemed…a little distracted."

As though distancing himself physically would help distance him emotionally, Rafe moved away, pressing his back against one of the floor-to-ceiling bookshelves. He folded his arms and stared at her.

Then his gaze softened and the battle-ready tension in his face disappeared, replaced by a mask of indifference. He shook his head, though she suspected the gesture was directed at the situation, not her. "Not the best father-son discussion I've had lately," he remarked.

Relieved at his response, Dani said, "I guess I'm not the only one who's found you to be a hard guy to get along with sometimes."

He huffed out a short laugh. "I inherited it from my dad, who's been a pain in the ass all his life."

In spite of the casual complaint, she felt the emotional power behind those words. It surprised her. Maybe he was more complex than she realized. Who would think he could be?

Her notepad was on her lap, and suddenly desperate to have something to focus on besides his face, she closed it with a snap. "I wish I could say something to help, but parents have been driving their kids crazy for thousands of years. Nothing new in that, I'm afraid."

"Did you get along with your folks?"

"I never knew my father. He was already out of the picture by the time I was born."

"I'm sorry."

"Oh, don't be," Dani said with a shrug. "You don't miss what you've never had. And my mother was my best friend until the day she died. She sacrificed all her life for me."

He cocked his head at her. "So you could be the prettiest showgirl in Las Vegas?"

"Hardly," Dani said. She tilted the notepad on her lap, a reminder to him of why she was here at the wedding. "So I could have the career I wanted. Big-time reporter for a big-time newspaper."

His lips quirked in an amused grin. "Still working on that, I take it."

"Well, sometimes a career takes a few detours."

There was a sudden flurry of movement from the door again, and for a moment, Dani thought Rafe's father had returned. But when she looked in that direction, she discovered Frannie making a beeline for her father. The little girl didn't acknowledge Dani's presence. She looked too mutinous for manners.

"I'm supposed to find you and ask," the child said. "Nonna Rose says so."

Dani watched Rafe draw a deeper breath and straighten. "Ask me what?"

Frannie plucked at the frilled collar of her yellow blouse and tugged at the matching skirt. It was a pretty confection, but by the look on the girl's face, she was finding it not one bit to her liking.

"To see if I can take this off yet," she said.

"Have all the pictures been taken?"

"Nonno Sam says he wants more. Of all of us."

"Then you can't."

"Why not?"

Rafe sighed. "Why do you want to change clothes right now?"

"Because I look stupid."

"No, you don't. You look very pretty."

The child shook her head wildly. "The other kids— I look stupid."

"That's not so."

"It is. I know. I just know."

Dani hid a smile behind her notepad as Rafe rubbed wearily at a spot along his eyebrow. She had no idea what the true family dynamic for these two was, but from Cissy she'd heard that no mother was in the picture. From the looks of it, they could have used one.

"Fine," Rafe said at last. "Take it off."

Frannie looked suddenly uncertain. "Really?"

"Really. What have you got on underneath?"

"Shorts."

"Then let's take off the skirt."

The little girl's face screwed up in consternation. "Won't that make Nonno Sam mad?"

"There's not much in this world that won't make your Nonno Sam mad here lately. Come on. Off with the skirt."

Frannie was too delighted to question her father further. She began tugging at the frilly material.

Over the child's head, Rafe met Dani's eyes. She gave him a rueful look that said he was probably making a big mistake.

"You think I'm making the wrong decision, don't you?" he said.

"What do I know?"

"I've been talking to a child psychologist lately who says that kids need to feel empowered as much as possible."

Dani rose and lifted her hands as though in surrender. "I'm staying out of this. I'd like to stick around to see the fireworks, but I've got work to do."

She gave him a mock salute and made her exit, leaving the two of them to sort out the problem.

Whatever unpleasantness there might be between Rafe and his father, whatever uneasy relationship existed between this child and Rafe, Dani was beginning to suspect one thing about this entire family. When it came to being a D'Angelo, life was never boring.

CHAPTER SEVEN

A FEW DAYS LATER, Dani was sitting behind her desk at the newspaper office when Cissy told her Gary Newsome was on the telephone. She grimaced. Having sent the editor the latest batch of "newsworthy" items from the towns in the area, as well as her report on the D'Angelo nuptials, she wasn't exactly expecting a positive response.

But Gary surprised her sometimes, and as always, he got right to the point.

"I love it!" he said without wasting time with a greeting.

"Love what?" Dani asked, truly confused.

"The report you did on the wedding, of course."

"You're kidding."

"I never kid about the news. You know that."

Dani made a sound of disbelief. "I'd hardly call a report on a wedding ceremony 'news.'"

"Not in the true sense of the word perhaps. But honestly, Dani, it was terrific. Wry without being sarcastic. Touching without getting too sentimental. Even funny, but not silly. I liked it so much that I'm putting it in the full run."

Wow. Not just tucked away in the Neighborhood section for this area, but in *every* paper. That surprised her. A lot. "Oh, good grief. I've finally reached the point where you feel sorry for me."

"I never throw reporters a bone, if that's what you're thinking. This is good work. Take the compliment."

"Thank you."

"That's better," he said, sounding pleased. "I want more."

"More what?"

"More of the same," Gary persisted. "I don't think you realize what I'm telling you. The pieces you're sending out of those small towns are inspired. They're some of your best work, and I want you to keep doing what you're doing."

Dani rested her chin on her hand. As pleased as Gary sounded, it was hard to find the good in what he said. Not for her career, anyway. She frowned into the phone. "Nothing I'm sending you is serious journalism, Gary."

He was silent for a brief moment. Then he said plainly, "Dani, sweetheart. Did it ever occur to you that maybe serious journalism is not the best fit for you?"

Dani went bolt upright in her chair. "What? That's all I know. What I've been trained for."

"So maybe you trained for the wrong thing," Gary suggested. "I'm telling you, the stories you've been sending me lately have the human-interest touch. You *connect* with people out there in those small towns, and it shows. I have high-priced, big-gun columnists who aren't giving me the warm angle you're bringing me. Keep it up."

He sounded so sincere that Dani slumped back in her chair, a little stunned. Was it possible that she did have a feel for the small-town beat? How could that be? She'd always thought of herself as a big-city girl, someone who loved being around the movers and shakers.

"It's not easy," she said. "Not much exciting happens out here."

"It doesn't have to be exciting. It just has to have your special touch. You did an excellent job on that story about the woman trying to raise triplets by herself. And the reunion between the two sisters who'd been separated during the Vietnam War. I showed it to Pauline, and she cried buckets."

"Your wife is a notoriously soft touch."

"Now what about these D'Angelos?"

"What about them?"

"They seem like an interesting family."

"I suppose they are. They're certainly prominent in the area."

"Then they probably know everyone for miles. Milk that connection if you can."

That stopped her. More contact with the D'Angelo family could mean more contact with Rafe. Scrambled images played across her mind. Conversations they'd shared. The way his hair touched the back of his collar when he turned his head. The quick indentation that appeared in one cheek when something amused him. She wasn't sure any closer communication with Rafe D'Angelo was such a good idea.

"I'm not sure milking that connection is possible," she said.

"Why not?"

"Personal reasons."

As she could have predicted, Gary hooted that down with a harsh laugh. "I'm going to pretend you didn't say that."

"I'm serious, Gary."

"Well, then, I'm serious when I say this. Get over it. Put personal reasons aside, and don't miss any opportunities that present themselves."

"But—"

"Trust me on this," Gary said, and a lower, less amused tone suddenly came into his voice. "You want back in the publisher's good graces? This is the way to do it, Dani. We got a lot of great calls and e-mails on that chickens-versus-the-wolf story. The Abraham Lincoln vegetable worked well, too."

"This is impossible," she said, unable to imagine how she could continue to produce anything so unnewsworthy. "Who would want to read this stuff?"

"You'd be amazed."

"I can't build a career based on weird-shaped squash and Italian weddings."

""Of course not. That's just color. But when you dig into those people's lives, find the story that speaks to everyone, then you've got something. And you know how to do that. Work the angles you're given, Dani. Remember, great careers have been built on a lot less."

THIRTY MINUTES LATER, Dani was still seated in her chair, trying to understand that telephone call from Gary, when she heard the front office door open and close. Cissy had gone across the street to get them both something for lunch, leaving the reception area unmanned.

"Hello," Dani called out. "Be right with you."

She started to rise, but in another moment, Rafe D'Angelo was in her office doorway. He looked casually handsome in jeans and a flannel shirt. Barely even thinking about it, Dani sent a nervous tongue over her lips.

He pressed a shoulder against the doorjamb and folded his arms. "You were right," he said.

Dani hated that flicker of excitement that lit her insides whenever she was in the company of this man. "Doesn't anyone say hello anymore?"

"Hello," he replied with a smile. "You were right."

"Good to know. What was I right about?"

"All hell broke loose when I let Frannie take off that skirt."

Remembering their conversation in the lodge's library the day of the wedding, Dani grimaced. "Your father?"

Rafe nodded. "He hardly spoke to me for two days.

Although all things considered, that wasn't such a bad thing. A lot more peaceful."

Dani laughed. "So are you looking for more advice? Better check with your child psychologist, because I'm fresh out."

Rafe moved away from the doorway, coming farther into the room. The tiny office seemed even smaller with him standing directly in front of her desk.

"Actually, I've come to issue an invitation," he said.

Feeling suddenly awkward and uncertain, Dani swept up a handful of papers on her desk and tapped them together. "Someone else getting married?"

"Not yet. I know this area can't be offering you much in the way of news, and you probably need all the stories you can get. So I thought you might like to come over to my place."

That caught her off guard, which was probably what he'd intended. She frowned up at him. "Your place?"

"The Three Bs, actually."

Dani had heard all about the former social club and its renovation. In fact, she'd been kicking around the idea of doing a story about it. Only the fact that Rafe was involved with the place had kept her from walking down the block to check it out.

"I thought it was only a construction site right now," she said.

"Most of it still is," he told her. "The space I've carved out for me and Frannie is pretty much done. We move in tomorrow, which ought to make my father happy. No more trying to make small talk when we run into one another at the lodge."

"If I remember correctly, you weren't much into small talk, yourself."

He acknowledged that comment by dipping his chin and giving her a knowing look. "True. So will you come over?"

"When?"

"In about an hour."

"Uh…" She wasn't sure what to say. This conversation was flowing too fast for her. Why exactly was he inviting her to come over?

"I have a reason," he added.

"Oh. Good. Because I'd need one."

He cocked his head at her. "You know, you're a very suspicious woman."

"I know. Men have made me that way."

"Then you've hung around too many of the wrong kind."

"If there are good ones out there, I certainly haven't run into any lately."

"Maybe you're looking in the wrong places," he said.

The look on his face made her miss a couple of heartbeats. She had to admit, whatever else Rafe D'Angelo was, he could certainly make a woman feel as though she were the center of his universe. Even for a little while. What a good thing she was so immune to him.

She sat up straighter, sensing that she'd better keep

the conversation as impersonal as possible. "So what's this about?" she asked.

"My motives are pure," he told her. "I want you to come strictly for your professional benefit."

She lifted an eyebrow at him, caught in spite of herself. "I'm listening."

"My construction chief was just in my office. His team is getting ready to break through one of the upstairs bedrooms. Solid brick, but it'll come down easily enough once they get started."

Dani gave him a playfully sour look. "This *does* sound exciting."

He held up a forestalling hand. "Patience. I'm getting to the good part. The thing of it is, he thinks there's an actual room behind the wall. One that doesn't show up on the only original floorplans we've been able to get our hands on."

He had her full attention now. "What kind of room?"

"We don't know. That's why I thought of calling you before we tear it down. I thought you might like to be there for its official unveiling."

Dani finally nodded in understanding. "Like Geraldo Rivera exposing Al Capone's vault on national television."

"Something like that. There was always talk about secret rooms in the Three Bs. I never took any of it seriously, but just the fact that there is one ought to be worth a walk over to the place, don't you think?"

She thought about the conversation she'd had with

Gary. Milking the D'Angelo connection had seemed unthinkable to her an hour ago. She'd made up her mind that staying as far away from Rafe was the smartest thing she could ever do. Lots of lectures in the middle of the night about letting the past stay buried popped into her head.

But the truth was, she was sexually attracted to Rafe in spite of the past. Being stuck up here in Broken Yoke was tough and lonely, and she had to fight the need to make a connection with him. Any connection. Especially when she didn't sense it was unreciprocated.

She sighed. "You know, you might be right. I'll come."

He seemed pleased. That devastating dimple appeared in his cheek once more. "Good. One hour." His gaze raked her body, and she felt tingles up her spine. "You might want to change clothes. Even if there's nothing inside, the room's bound to be dirty."

"I'm not afraid of a little dirt. I'll come hoping for secret treasure."

"I can't promise anything."

She nodded. "If I remember correctly from Vegas, you never did."

THE CONSTRUCTION BOSS, Lane Beaudry, picked up the sledgehammer with one beefy hand, then unexpectedly held it out to Rafe. "You want to do the honors, boss? It's your place."

Rafe took the sledgehammer. Its weight felt odd in his hands. It had been years since he'd made a living at manual labor. "I suppose I can still handle one of these."

He moved over to the wall. Behind that worn red brick, who knew what they'd find? Trash? Treasure? Nothing?

Still, Rafe felt his heartbeat trip a little faster. It was exciting to think of exposing a part of the Three Bs that hadn't been seen in years.

He got the feel of the sledgehammer between his hands, then swung it back. He stopped mid-swing as he became aware of movement and a camera flash went off in his face. Dani Bridgeton had moved forward until she was almost beside him. Since her photographer Chester hadn't been able to come at the last minute, she was taking pictures with a simple-looking camera she probably kept in her office just in case. He could tell she was excited by the gleam in her eyes.

He lowered the sledgehammer, having no intention of seeing his face on the pages of her newspaper. "What are you doing?" he asked her, pointing to the camera as she took another few shots of him.

"Taking pictures of the main event."

"I'm not the star. The room is." He came to her, took her by the shoulders and marched her backward until she was pressed nearly against Lane. "Stand here. Don't move until the bricks come down. Understand?"

She frowned at him. "You didn't say there were 'conditions' when you asked me to come over. I want—"

"I don't need a lawsuit from your paper when you get struck on the head by flying debris. Stand there and wait until I tell you it's all right."

She gave him an annoyed look, but nodded. Rafe lifted the sledgehammer and swung it with all his might against the wall. Immediately, bricks caved inward. He swung again, and again and again, until a decent-sized hole opened up, large enough for a man to slip through. He moved forward, sticking his head through the opening first, smelling the scent of stale air and dust. Particles of brick sifted against the collar of his shirt.

"What do you see?" Dani asked behind him, her voice filled with excitement. "Darn it, tell me what you see."

Withdrawing a flashlight from his back pocket, Rafe played the light around the room. It was small, dark and seemed cluttered with shadowy colors—red, yellow and the glint of silver. It was impossible to make out what he was looking at until his eyes adjusted.

"If you don't tell me this instant…" Dani threatened.

"Stuff," he said. "I see stuff."

"What kind of stuff? Gold? Silver?"

"Come look."

Turning sideways to fit through the opening he'd made, Rafe moved into the hidden room. Dani was right behind him, so close he could hear her breathing. An arc of light joined his on the far wall and he realized that she had brought her own flashlight.

The room was eerie, quiet and dead feeling, like a

tomb that had just been exposed after centuries. In a way, it was.

"Lane," Rafe called over his shoulder. "Can you get us a little more light in here?"

"Right away, boss."

The man went off to do as he'd been asked. Rafe moved farther into the room, cautious of where he stepped. His eyes had started to adjust, and now he could make out the shapes of countless objects, a cornucopia of things from another time.

"The room's smaller than I thought it would be," he said.

"Oh, my God," Dani said in an awed voice. "What is all this? Just look at it."

Rafe let his flashlight travel over the right wall. The beam picked up a sea of gold-fringed drapes, a stack of old chairs, a heavy-looking bookcase filled with dusty books. "I *am* looking. It's like being in an episode of *Antiques Roadshow*."

"Think any of it's valuable?" Dani asked in almost a whisper.

"Who knows? Maybe from a historical perspective. The room was obviously used for storage and the club has been closed for decades. But some of this may be from Ida Mae Culpepper's time."

"The original owner?"

"Uh-huh. That means we could be looking at 1880s, 1890s."

Dani had wandered a little away from him. She

poked at an umbrella stand made out of an elephant's leg. It was filled with canes with ornate heads, some of them silver and gold and winking in the beam of the flashlight. "Look at these," she said.

"What the well-dressed john wouldn't be without."

"Does Broken Yoke have a historical society?"

"Yes."

"Who's in charge of it?"

"Burt Beckerman, I think."

"You should call him. He'll have a field day looking at all this stuff."

"Great."

"You sound disappointed."

"Just what I need," Rafe said on a laugh. "Another attic that needs cleaning out."

"Stop complaining. I mean, really." She ran the flashlight along the top of a scratched three-legged bureau where a small collection of scrimshaw tusks lay coated with dust. "Some of this has got to be historically meaningful to the town."

Rafe's attention had been caught by a stack of miscellaneous paper sitting under a pewter pitcher. He lifted the first item gingerly off the stack. It looked to be a receipt for a piano—total cost, twenty-two dollars. "I wouldn't mind a few barrels full of gold and silver," he complained. "Maybe a couple of chests of priceless gems."

Dani laughed, a hollow sound in the darkened room. "We haven't seen everything yet. Be patient."

She moved over to a huge horsehair trunk that sat against the left wall. "Here you go," she said playfully, running the light over the object. "I'll bet this is filled with treasure. Ida Mae's life savings."

The hinge creaked noisily as she lifted the lid, and it took both hands to wedge it up. She played the flashlight's beam over the contents.

"Well?" Rafe asked from across the room. "Am I rich?"

She sighed and looked back over her shoulder at him. "Afraid not. It's an accordion. Do you know 'Lady of Spain'?"

Rafe grimaced. "I know her, and I hate her."

"It's not in bad shape," Dani said. She lifted the edge of it and the instrument exhaled a small, wailing protest. "It needs to be cleaned up, of course, but it looks to be in good—"

She gasped suddenly and jumped back. Rafe came to her side immediately. In the light she looked pale and wide-eyed, and he could see her shaking visibly. "What's the matter?" he demanded.

"Something touched me."

"Sure it did," he said skeptically.

"I'm serious. You look."

A mouse? Cockroaches, maybe? Impossible. The room had been airless, sealed up for too many years for any living creature to survive. He narrowed his eyes at her, wondering if she was joking. "Stop playing games."

She made an annoyed face. "Just look."

He bent over the trunk and cautiously lifted the accordion. It was the old boxy kind that weighed a ton.

Beside him Dani gasped again. She stared down into the contents of the trunk, her mouth parted as though it were difficult to draw breath. "Oh, my God," she said in a whisper. The beam of her flashlight shook. "Oh, my God."

Rafe swung his beam into the trunk. He thought she'd been playing, but with gut-wrenching clarity, he saw suddenly what she'd seen—the skeletal remains of a human being folded into the trunk like a suit of clothes.

He wanted to believe that it was some sort of Halloween joke or one of those skeletons they used to teach med students. This room had obviously been a receptacle for any number of oddities over the years. But as they both stared down in silence at the body, he knew it wasn't any such thing. This was real. This was no joke.

The secret room of the Three Bs didn't hold treasure. It held death.

CHAPTER EIGHT

"WELL, RAFE," SHERIFF BENDIX said. "You do know how to liven up a quiet town. In all the years I've been in Broken Yoke, I've never had to deal with a murder."

Murder.

Dani couldn't help shivering just thinking about it. It seemed impossible. And yet, how could the dead body in the trunk be anything else?

The investigative team that Bendix had called in from Denver had come and gone. They'd spent hours studying the secret room from every angle. The remains of the body had been carefully bagged and removed, along with the accordion and the trunk. It was now past dinnertime and Sheriff Bendix was finally leaving.

Dani had seen very little of Rafe since the discovery. He'd spent most of the afternoon in his office with his construction boss, as though dead bodies were found on his property every day. Now he looked at the sheriff with a raised eyebrow. "Don't you think we should wait for the report to come back before we start making the assumption that it was murder?"

"Oh, it was murder," Dani spoke up.

Rafe turned toward her. She couldn't tell if he was annoyed or disappointed. "How do you know that?"

"Because I've just spent hours pumping the forensic team for details, taking pictures as much as they'll let me, and generally making a nuisance of myself. The back of the Accordion Man's head was bashed in, and he didn't put *himself* in that trunk."

"The Accordion Man?"

"Well, he's got to have a name until I can come up with who he really is and what happened to him."

Sheriff Bendix looked at her, disapproval clearly evident on his features. "Maybe you ought to leave the investigating to the authorities."

Dani knew better than to offend the sheriff, who could be a reporter's most valuable asset when it came down to accessing information no one else could get. "Of course," she said in her most agreeable tone. "But I'd certainly like to do all I can to help. My resources will be at your disposal, Sheriff."

"Not sure what good any of it will do," he said with a short laugh. "If the guy's been in there since the 1800s, you're talking about a pretty old crime. Not many records available and no one left alive to interview."

Dani smiled at the man. "I'm a reporter, remember? It's my job to dig for the truth."

"Good luck on this one," the sheriff said. "Looks like we've got a real bona fide mystery on our hands."

"I can't wait to get started," Dani said with enthusiasm. In that exact moment, her stomach growled noisily, and she pressed her hand over her abdomen. "But first, I have to eat something. I'm starving."

Sheriff Bendix grabbed up his hat, and Rafe pulled his jacket and Dani's off the coat tree that sat in one corner of his office. "Come on," he said. "I'll walk you back to your office. We can stop by the Silver Saddle on the way and I'll buy you a burger."

She was a little surprised by the invitation. He'd ignored her most of the afternoon, and he'd been fairly uncommunicative with the investigative team as well, as though he resented their invasion of his property or was indifferent to the discovery in the secret room. She gave him a regretful smile. "I can't. Now that you're part of the paper's investigation, I'm not allowed to accept a freebie from you."

He scowled. "It's a burger, not a condo on the Riviera."

"Sorry. Company policy."

"Come on," he said, holding out her coat so she could slip her arms into it. "If you're going to be such a rule follower, how about this? I buy dinner tonight. You buy the next time."

The idea that he already envisioned a "next time" for them shocked her even more than the initial invitation. She debated his reasons, but nothing came to her. Finally, she decided not to look gift burgers in the mouth and allowed Rafe to help her on with her coat.

"All right," she told him. "But it really does have to be my treat next time."

He stood behind her, so close she could feel his breath stirring her hair. "It's a date," he said in a low, amused tone, and she had to swallow a sudden thickness in her throat before she could turn her head to look back at him.

With the promise to be in touch with any news, Sheriff Bendix left them outside the Three Bs, and they made their way back down the street. It was a mild night, good for walking, and neither one of them seemed inclined to break the silence.

The Silver Saddle was a warm, cozy place, with only a few patrons seated at the bar and no one at the tables. Rafe led her to a dimly lit corner toward the back, and almost as soon as they were seated across from one another a waitress appeared to hand them menus.

Dani quickly settled on what she wanted, then took a few moments to watch Rafe. The table lamp picked out blue-black highlights in his hair. He needed a haircut, she thought, and then smiled to herself. Rafe had never cared one bit for what fashion dictated and obviously still didn't.

The waitress looked at her expectantly.

"I'll have the biggest burger you've got," Dani told her. "With everything. A large order of fries, a side salad with blue cheese and a chocolate shake. What do you have for dessert?"

"The cherry pie is fresh."

"Save me a piece, then."

The waitress scribbled the order down on her pad, then switched her attention to Rafe. He closed his menu and handed it back to her. "I'll just take whatever you have on tap."

The waitress nodded and left. Dani cocked her head at Rafe. "You're not eating?"

He grinned at her. "I may have to take out a loan to pay for your meal."

"Sorry. I eat when I'm excited."

"And you're excited about a dead guy in a trunk."

"Aren't you?" Dani asked, still mildly surprised that he wouldn't be bursting at the seams to find out more about the discovery they'd made today.

"No."

"For heaven's sake, why not? It's got to be the most interesting thing that's happened in this town in years. Aren't you the least bit curious to know who the Accordion Man is, and who sealed him up in that room?"

Rafe pursed his lips, as though giving the idea some thought. "Not really," he said at last. "Whoever did it is long dead by now."

"Still, it definitely tops anything I've written since I've been up here." Dani played with her napkin a moment. His attitude was so laid back. Too laid back. She pierced him with a close look. "What's bothering you about all this?"

He responded by smiling obliquely and then looking away, seemingly interested in his surroundings for the first time.

At the bar there was a sudden whoop of laughter. Three men were huddled around their drinks. Dani recognized one of them as Gus Jefferson, a construction worker who poured concrete at the new motel going up by the interstate. She didn't like him much. A week ago he'd been in the office, trying to strong-arm Cissy into going out with him. Catching the girl's silent plea for help, Dani had sent him on his way by pretending to need Cissy's assistance.

Rafe caught her attention again when she heard him sigh heavily. "What do you know about my reputation in Broken Yoke?" he asked her.

She thought of all the talk there had been between Cissy and several of the women who often stopped by to share the latest news. While there was a definite fascination with Rafe's comings and goings, a lot of it seemed like outlandish speculation. Admittedly, she hadn't been able to resist listening to every bit of it.

"Very little," Dani said at last, though she doubted if the words sounded sincere.

Evidently not. Rafe made a disbelieving sound. "Be honest," he told her. "You're a reporter with your ear to the ground. And small towns love gossip."

"I'm not interested in rumors. I'm interested in facts."

"Well, some of the facts about my past aren't particularly flattering," Rafe went on, clearly not buying her denial. "I made a lot a mistakes when I lived here before."

"You were young."

He conceded that with a shrug. "Let's just say that, in the old days, I never overlooked an opportunity to shock. There are probably a few people who are sorry that I've come back. Having a murder attached to my name is exactly what I don't want right now."

"What difference does it make? *You* didn't kill the guy."

"I've come back here to live permanently, to raise my daughter in an environment that will be good for her. I don't want her frightened, and I don't need that kind of publicity."

The waitress returned at that moment, bearing Dani's salad and shake, plus Rafe's beer. Her stomach growled in appreciative anticipation. It was nice to have company for a change, and she was glad Rafe had sprung for dinner.

Suddenly she felt uncomfortable. When the waitress had disappeared back to the bar area, Dani leaned across the table. "Is that why you offered to buy me a meal? So you could talk me out of writing the story?"

"No," he said without hesitation.

Was he telling the truth? She decided to believe him and picked up her fork. "Good. Because I have to cover this."

She dug into her salad while he took several swallows of his beer. The lettuce was surprisingly crisp and the shake was the old-fashioned kind, thick and rich. She polished off half the salad, and the silence became long, but not uncomfortable.

Eventually, she found herself saying, "I'll try to keep your name out of it as much as possible."

The slight frown between his brows eased a bit. "I doubt it will help, but I appreciate that."

He sounded so serious. Did he really care so much what people thought? She couldn't connect the Rafe she'd known in Vegas to the man sitting across the table from her.

"All right," she said with a sharp nod of her head. "I'll do my best to keep you out of it, and in return, you allow me access to that room and not hold back anything you know or find out."

"Since I don't know anything, that's not a hard promise to keep. Agreed."

"Good."

When her burger came, she took two bites from it before finally deciding to put words to her confusion. "You know, sometimes when I talk to you, I can't believe you're the same man I used to know."

He looked down, running a fingertip through the water ring left by his beer glass. "I'm not the same man."

There was no mistaking the note of regret. Everything inside her hummed with curiosity. "What happened to you?"

He tilted his head at her. "I thought you didn't want to talk about the past."

"I don't want to talk about *our* past. But I'm naturally curious about what brought you back to Broken Yoke."

"Off the record?"

She hated having to make that concession, but Rafe seemed unlikely to tell her anything unless she agreed to his terms. And frankly, she was suddenly eager to know more. "Off the record."

"I guess I'd have to say that two things changed my life."

Dani took another bite of her hamburger, then wiped the corner of her mouth. "Both of them involving a woman, I'll bet."

His mouth twisted, but he didn't look offended by that remark. "No. The first one was a man, actually. A millionaire by the name of Wendall Crews. I was a river raft guide down in Arizona one summer when he signed up for a week's trip. Three days into it, our boat hit a rough patch. He fell out and completely panicked. Nearly drowned."

"But you saved him?" Dani asked, though she could guess the answer already.

"He seemed to think so. When the week was over, he offered me a job in Los Angeles. I was smart enough to know a good opportunity when I saw one, so I went. He mentored me for four years before he died." Rafe polished off the last of his beer. "Treated me like one of his own sons."

Those words were simple enough, but something about the way he'd added that last bit struck a chord within her. How much better had he gotten along with Wendall Crews than his own father? She couldn't bring herself to ask him. Not yet, anyway.

"Did you inherit his money?" she ventured instead.

He shrugged. "Enough."

Dani mulled that information over for a few moments. Then she looked up at Rafe again. "You said two things changed everything for you. What was the second?"

"My daughter. Frannie came into my life a few months ago—just before Christmas. She's the main reason I've come back to Broken Yoke. I'm a father now, and I'm not going to let her down."

Dani looked down at her plate. She bit her lip. *Whoa,* she thought. Oz, willing to take on the responsibility of raising a child. *You weren't expecting that, were you?* This man was full of surprises. "It won't be easy. She seems like a rambunctious child and it will be hard to get a handle on all that energy without breaking her spirit."

"I'm discovering that."

Snatches of the conversations she'd heard between Cissy and her friends came to her suddenly. The fact that Rafe was seldom seen with his daughter. The incident she herself had witnessed at the school, when the child seemed more eager for her aunt's company than his. Just how often did he make time for Frannie in his life? Maybe she was giving him too much credit.

"What are you thinking?" he asked her.

She cleared her throat. "I was thinking that there's more to being a father than just providing clothes and food and a secure place to live."

He frowned. "What's that supposed to mean?"

She pulled another napkin from the container that sat on one side of the table. *Might as well tell him.* "Do you spend much time with her?" she asked. "Quality time?"

The words came out more harshly than she intended. She felt color steal up her neck. She didn't really want to spoil this time between them.

"Sorry," she said in a milder tone. "I didn't mean that to sound so judgmental. I guess absentee fathering has always been a sore spot for me. My own father couldn't get away fast enough when he found out my mother was pregnant."

"I'm not planning to run away," he said with a shake of his head. "Though I have to admit, she scares the hell out of me."

It was a startling admission for someone like him to make. Dani thought of Rafe as a cocky loner, the kind of man who sailed through life untouched and unfazed. She couldn't imagine a little girl giving him one second of discomfort.

But before she could comment on that, Dani became aware of movement beside their table. Gus Jefferson had left the bar and now stood beside her, his hand resting behind her on the booth.

"Hello, Rafe," he said.

"Gus."

The man tilted his head to look at her. "Miss Bridgeton, isn't it? How ya doin'?"

"Fine."

His gaze swung back to Rafe. "Heard you found a dead body over at the Three Bs."

"News gets around fast," Rafe replied. He sounded disinterested, though Dani thought that the tightness of his jaw indicated he didn't care for Gus any more than she did.

Gus nudged her shoulder and Dani caught the whiff of whiskey on his breath. "You know, me and my buddies made a bet when we heard Rafe here was back in town. I win, I guess, 'cause I said it would be less than two months and he'd have trouble knocking on his door."

Annoyed, she gave Gus a hard look. "Really? Looks like we both win, then, because I bet Cissy that it wouldn't be a month before I saw you drunk on your feet."

Gus's face, already flushed with drink, went tomato-red. He wasn't the kind of man to like mouthy women, and Dani's muscles tensed. Maybe it had been a mistake to antagonize the guy. She kept watching him, hoping her sudden apprehension didn't show. From the corner of her eye, she was immediately aware of Rafe leaning across the table to catch the man's attention.

"You'll hear all the details soon enough," Rafe said. "In the meantime, why don't you and your buddies have a drink on me? Miss Bridgeton and I are in the middle of a private conversation."

Evidently unable to resist the offer of a free drink, Gus's annoyance subsided. He drifted back to the bar, where his friends waited with a fresh beer. Dani watched him go, feeling relieved. When she turned back to her burger, she found Rafe looking at her with a funny half smile on his face.

"What?" she asked.

"You didn't have to chase him off. Gus is basically harmless."

"He's an ass."

She took a bite of her burger, chewed with deliberate care, then sipped long and hard on her milk shake. All the while she was aware that Rafe was still watching her with an indulgently amused demeanor. Finally he shifted back against the booth's seat, all long limbs and lazy grace. He shook his head at her, still smiling.

"What's so funny?" she asked.

"I'm not used to having a woman fight my battles."

"It wasn't like that," she protested. "I just didn't want my burger to get cold while he rambled on."

"I see."

He didn't believe her and he didn't take any pains to make her think he did. His dark eyes were intent on hers, glittering with amusement and something else that made her stomach flutter as though she hadn't eaten a thing. It was the look she'd seen him use on any number of women in Vegas—intoxicating, unhurried appreciation. It was lethal. Small wonder half the girls in Native Sun's chorus line had been head over heels in love.

She had to do something to get him to stop looking at her that way. Anything. *Quickly.*

Something impersonal would be best. She said the first thing that popped into her head. "I wonder why we didn't smell him."

Rafe frowned. "Gus?"

"The Accordion Man," she retorted, glad to get back to their original topic of conversation. "After all, a decomposing body…"

Rafe seemed willing to be sidetracked, thank goodness. He shrugged and took a final swallow of beer. "If he's been in there for over a hundred years, there can't be much smell left. Solid brick walls. An airless room."

"Poor man. If Ida Mae had that wall built, she had to have something to do with his death, don't you think?"

He gave her a knowing look. "I think you won't be happy until you find out."

"You're right."

"Tell me something," he said, his head tilted to one side. "How did you get from a Las Vegas chorus line to working for a big-city newspaper?"

They were back to personal matters. But at least this was a conversation Dani felt she could control. She dabbed her lips with a napkin and pushed the empty plate toward the center of the table.

"When I was at Native Sun, I was actually working for the *Phoenix Star*," she said. "I was investigating city employees who went to Vegas, supposedly on business, but who threw away tons of taxpayer dollars on gambling and women."

"Men like the one I saw you with that night at the craps table?"

She nodded. "Gil Rodgers, the city manager, and the city auditor, Frank Westcott. They were eventually charged with a laundry list of crimes that sent them away for ten years."

"Because of you?"

"I like to think that my investigation helped bring them down."

"So that's why you were so determined that I get lost and leave you alone that night."

She smiled agreement. "That's why."

"I assume you weren't expecting one of them to drug your drink."

Heat suffused her cheeks. Even after all these years, she was still embarrassed to remember how badly she'd miscalculated that night. "No. I have to admit, that came as a complete surprise."

He gave her a close look. "As big a surprise as waking up to find me in bed with you instead of them?"

She frowned, irked with herself for allowing him to steer the conversation to dangerous territory once more. The man was impossible. She gave him a broad, bright smile that said she wasn't going to be maneuvered any further. "I thought we agreed not to talk about that."

He offered a rueful smile. "So we did. But it occurs to me that maybe we should just get everything out into the open."

"I—"

"Ready for your cherry pie?"

It was the waitress, back at their table to complete their order. Dani could have kissed her for showing up.

"I don't think I have room for it after all," Dani told her. "Could we just get our check?"

Nodding, the woman ripped it off her order pad and placed it facedown on the table. Without waiting for further comment from Rafe, Dani slid across the booth and rose. Time to end this strange day. Time to rid herself of whatever madness had made her think more time spent in this man's company was desirable. Or even sensible.

While he paid the bill, she went back out onto the sidewalk. The night breeze ruffled her hair, and she inhaled deeply, hoping to clear her head. She had thought she could remain detached around Rafe, friendly but dispassionate, but somehow it hadn't quite worked out that way. She was quickly discovering that when she was around him, she had about as much control over her senses as a leaf swept up in a hurricane.

He joined her again, and luckily, the newspaper office was less than a block away, so there was no more time for meaningful conversation. She unlocked the door, then turned back to him. He was so close. He smelled nice. Like wood smoke and earth. On him, it was a very appealing combination.

"Thanks for walking me back," she said. "And for dinner."

"My pleasure."

"I'm sorry your secret room didn't hold a fortune in gold."

"Me, too," he said dryly. "But in spite of the way it turned out, I'm glad you came over."

He reached out unexpectedly, tracing a fingertip down the line of her jaw. The pad of his thumb rubbed along her throat. It was too dark to read his expression clearly, but she got the distinct impression that his gaze ran over her. Twice.

She put a hand up against his chest. "Don't…"

"Don't what?" he asked softly. "Don't start, or don't stop?"

"Don't think you can add me to your list."

"What list?"

"The list of women you plan to seduce in this town."

He laughed. "I don't have a list."

"That's not what I hear."

"What do you hear?" he asked with a slight frown.

"I've heard your name linked with everyone from the mayor's teenaged daughter to some gorgeous doctor in Idaho Springs."

Unexpectedly, she caught the flash of his teeth as

he grinned. "I thought that as a reporter you liked to deal in facts, not rumors."

"I'm a woman, too. I suppose, I can't help being curious."

"Curiosity is a very dangerous thing." He moved closer, and Dani didn't pull away when his hand touched her cheek.

She knew he intended to kiss her now. She ought to stop him. She told herself she wanted to. But a part of her wanted to know if the feelings he stirred in her wandering imagination could possibly be real.

The touch of his lips was warm and light on hers, yet oddly devastating. It sent jolts of pleasure through her, and desire came swift and hard. It had been a long time since she'd been kissed by a man, and certainly Kirk had never brought her to such quick excitement. She suddenly understood why all those women in Vegas had looked so dazed around Rafe most of the time.

When he lifted his head, she eased away from him until their bodies were no longer in close contact. Her breathing felt ragged, disorganized, but she looked him in the eyes. "Why did you do that?"

His mouth quirked, and she caught the sparkle in his eyes from the corner streetlight. "I guess if I'm going to be accused of being a serial womanizer, I might as well go after the one woman in Broken Yoke who truly interests me."

"Oh."

"Good night, Dani," he said with another smile.

Then he backed away, too, and headed off down the street, back in the direction of the Three Bs. She watched him go, feeling excited and unnerved and more than a little confused.

One thing she *was* certain of. Whether she wanted to admit it or not, things between them had definitely changed.

CHAPTER NINE

ROSA'S FAVORITE TELEVISION program was on, but when Sam saw his wife trying to stifle a third yawn, he felt compelled to say something. The day had been a long one, with more turnover than usual for this time of year. Good for the lodge's bottom line, but exhausting for everyone.

He struggled up from his chair and into the cuffs of his metal crutches, then made his way to the couch where Rosa sat. She scooted over to make space for him, curling her feet under her like a sixteen-year-old.

He captured her hand and her attention. "Go to bed, Rosie. You look done in."

She smiled. "When Rafe gets home."

Rafe had called earlier, telling them about the discovery in the Three Bs and asking them to babysit Frannie until he returned. Rosa never minded. She said it was nice to have children in the house again, and an hour ago she had put the child to bed in what had once been Rafe's old bedroom.

"Given his history," Sam said, "who knows when he'll show up?"

"Samuel…"

He knew that tone. Rosa hated the fact that Sam and their youngest son were still prickly with one another. But they had been estranged for so long, and there were no easy answers. No point in pretending otherwise.

Rosa hid another yawn behind her hand.

"I'll keep an eye on the girl," Sam told her. "You go to bed."

"I don't know. When I looked in on her a few minutes ago, she seemed restless. She wasn't asleep yet…."

"I haven't forgotten how to handle children, Rosa. Leave her to me."

"I'm not sure…."

She gave him such a hesitant look that he felt suddenly determined to have his way. "I am."

She reached out to place her hand against his cheek. "All right. But try to remember that she's just a frightened little girl. Be gentle. I want her to love her grandparents, and once Rafe moves her into their new home, we won't see her as much. I want her to…*want* to come up here to visit us."

"Dio!" he growled, more than annoyed now. "Do you think I'm some kind of ogre?"

"I don't, but perhaps Francesca does. The kind who eats little children."

He took his wife's hand away from his face and placed a kiss in the center of her palm. "Go to bed, you wretched woman. Before I forget all the reasons I married you in the first place."

With a final kiss good-night, Rosa made her way toward their bedroom. Sam turned off the television and sat in the silence for a while. It wasn't very late, but the lodge was surprisingly quiet.

In spite of the fact that his hip ached from the day's demands, Sam made his way slowly around the ground floor of the lodge. He liked to see for himself that everything was as it should be at the end of the day—the lobby tidied up, the fire dying in the grate, the dining room readied for tomorrow's breakfast guests.

When he was satisfied that the rooms felt warm and full of well-being, he returned to the family's private quarters and decided he'd better check on Frannie.

Rafe's old room, which, at Sam's insistence, had long ago been turned into a spare bedroom, lay in shadows. He stood in the doorway and vividly remembered how it had looked when his youngest son had lived here—a cluttered mess of sports equipment, school projects and discarded clothes.

There was a double bed in the room now, and the tossing lump in it indicated that his granddaughter had not yet settled down to sleep. She looked very small, and Sam had to acknowledge that his wife was probably right. Francesca was just a scared little girl who needed to know her extended family would always love and look after her.

He made his way to the side of the bed. In the

meager glow from the night-light Rosa had left burning, two dark, sparkling eyes met his.

"Why aren't you asleep?" he asked the girl.

"Don't want to," she replied in a soft, hesitant voice.

Sam snorted. "Just like your father. He never liked to sleep, either. He was always afraid he'd miss something."

The child tilted her head at him, a frown marring the silky smooth brow. "Don't you like him even a little?"

"What kind of foolish question is that?" Sam asked in surprise. And then, because he hated the roughness in his voice that made Frannie blink several times, he added with forced calm, "Of course I like him. I *love* him. He's my son."

"Then how come your mouth always goes down when you talk about him?"

There was a moment's silence while Sam acknowledged that observation. He felt a complicated mixture of anger and sadness stir within him. Anger because he knew the child was right—Rafe had turned their relationship into a war zone. And sadness because there wasn't a damned thing either one of them seemed to be able to do about it. He wasn't, however, going to discuss any of that with Rafe's daughter.

"You ask a lot of questions," he told Frannie, hoping his tone would encourage her to snuggle down into the blankets and close her eyes.

It didn't. The child seemed more awake than ever.

"Did my daddy really sleep in this room when he was little?"

"Who told you this was his room?"

"Nonna Rose."

He let his gaze drift around the bedroom, now decked out in soft pastels and lace curtains. How many times had Rosa argued with him over the mess Rafe had made here? Unlike their other children, the boy had never put things back where they belonged.

"Yes," Sam said. "This was his room."

Frannie lifted up on one elbow. "It's awful pretty for a boy."

"That's because we changed everything after he left home."

"It would be nicer with polka dots."

Sam had to laugh. He'd once thought the same thing and had been foolish enough to suggest that to his wife. "I agree. But don't say that to your Nonna Rosa. She just doesn't understand about polka dots."

The girl smiled, a heart-catching stretch of her wide mouth that made Sam's breath stall. Whatever else he thought about the circumstances surrounding her birth, he had to admit that the child was a beauty.

He reached out and pulled the blanket over her shoulders. "You should close your eyes now and try to sleep."

"My mommy always read me a story first."

He gave her a sharp look. "And I know for a fact that your Nonna Rosa read you *three* stories before putting you to bed tonight."

"When Daddy lived here, did he like you to read him stories?"

"No. He was a very foolish boy who thought bedtime stories were for babies."

"See?" Frannie said, pointing a finger. "Your mouth goes down when you talk about him."

"You're an observant little monkey, aren't you?" Sam said without rancor.

"What's that mean?"

"It means you are too smart for your own good." He tucked the covers and bent to place his hand against the child's forehead. "Now go to sleep, *mia bella*."

"Tell me a story first. Tell me one about Daddy when he was little."

"You need to—"

"Please."

It wasn't a trick of the light. Frannie's eyes were filled with an earnest longing that was heartbreaking. How little she must know about her father. But Sam was hardly the one to share fond memories with. Where Rafe was concerned, the most vivid tales always involved disobedience and arguments and suspended allowances.

But Frannie looked so pathetically eager....

"All right, all right," he said with a sigh. "Stop bouncing about like a crazed poodle and scoot over."

Quickly, the child wiggled away from the edge of the bed, and Sam lowered himself with the help of his crutches. He rubbed his chin, trying to think.

"Tell me a *funny* story," the girl demanded.

That was a tall order. But there had to be some. If he just stretched his mind back far enough…

"Let's see…" he said thoughtfully. "Once, when your father was about your age, we were all out on the lake fishing…."

AFTER LEAVING DANI at the newspaper office, Rafe had returned to the Three Bs to finish up some paperwork and leave instructions for the construction crew tomorrow. Though most of the workers had pretended to ignore the excitement, the discovery in the hidden room had brought progress almost to a standstill.

Sheriff Bendix was right. It wasn't every day a mysterious death happened in Broken Yoke. By now, everyone in town must be speculating about the Accordion Man.

Personally, Rafe wasn't interested in who the guy had been or how he had ended up in that trunk. If he'd been in there since Ida Mae Culpepper's time—which seemed likely given the time period of all the items found in the room—there probably weren't many clues left. Certainly no murderer remained alive to prosecute. The Accordion Man deserved a decent belated burial, and then he needed to become nothing more than a footnote in Broken Yoke's history.

Rafe hated the idea of publicity and his name attached to it. He was trying hard to fit in here. To be a decent father to Frannie, even though most of the time he had no clue what he was doing. He didn't want her frightened. He didn't need people turning his new home into a sideshow.

He wondered if he stood a chance in hell of getting Dani to downplay the incident any more than she'd already agreed to do. Not likely. The sparkle in her eyes when she'd talked about investigating the mystery had made his nerve endings sing.

Of course, that wasn't the only reason his senses were thrumming. There had been a lot to like about her today, and all the way up the mountain road to the lodge he had to resist the urge to turn around to find out if Dani was still at her office. To find out if there was any chance of finishing what they'd started.

He hadn't planned that kiss, not really, although somewhere in the back of his brain he could admit he wasn't a bit sorry it had happened. Almost from the day he'd reconnected with Danielle Bridgeton, he'd been feeling a raw, primitive craving whenever he was around her, and he'd been dying to find out what it was all about.

Now he knew.

Pure, uncontrolled desire.

He'd given the matter a great deal of consideration and had come to a pretty basic conclusion. He wanted Dani, and he knew he could probably get her by falling back into his old habits, by doing what he'd always done in the past when he wanted a woman. He'd been blessed with a talent in that department—the ability to become the kind of man a woman needed but had never had.

It would be easy.

But what if it didn't work? She didn't entirely trust him. She was the kind of woman who asked questions and expected answers. She might see through any slick act of his in a minute and laugh in his face.

The idea of Dani laughing at him made his gut ache. That was the last thing he wanted from her. For reasons he still didn't have straight in his head, he wanted her to see him as a man she could respect. Not as the glib, late-night ladies' man from the Vegas strip, but Rafe D'Angelo.

A part of him knew, too, that he ought to forget her. Let her drift out of his life the way she had once drifted in. He was in the middle of creating a new life for himself, and a lot of that revolved around making Frannie feel safe and loved. He didn't need to confuse her any more by bringing a woman into the picture. At least, not until things settled down a little.

Lord, he missed the good old days when life had been simple and he hadn't given a damn what anyone thought.

He parked in Lightning River's parking lot, got out and had to stretch a moment to work the kinks out of his spine. He was more tired and hungry than he expected. The day had been long and strange. After making sure Frannie was safely tucked in bed, he planned to raid his mother's fridge and then call it a night.

He hit the wide front doors with a yawn, waved to

a sleepy-looking clerk at the front desk, then let himself into the family quarters. What luck! The lights were turned down low, the television was off, and there wasn't a soul around to keep him from hitting the hay. Best of all, no pesky questions about the mysterious dead man found in a hundred-year-old trunk.

It would feel good when he could get moved into the renovated portion of the Three Bs, but in the meantime, it was nice to know that the family had accepted his daughter so eagerly. Well, everyone but Pop—although even he seemed to be coming around slowly. Just yesterday Rafe had found Frannie sitting quietly beside his father on the couch while the two of them paged through one of the family photo albums, and Pop told her all about their Italian roots.

His old bedroom was where Frannie had been sleeping, and he headed down the hallway in that direction. The door was half-open, the interior of the room nearly dark. But when he stopped outside to listen, he heard the sound of low laughter coming from within. Obviously, Frannie wasn't asleep.

He pushed the door open. He'd expected to find his mother with the girl, and it surprised him to see his father instead, seated on the side of the bed next to her. They both looked up at him. Smiling. Considering that neither of them did much of that, Rafe was even more shocked.

"What's going on in here?" he asked in a soft voice. He moved to the other side of the bed. He frowned down at Frannie, who lay with her arms folded neatly over her chest. "I thought I'd find you asleep."

"Nonno Sam's telling me stories about you. Funny ones."

Could this day get any weirder? He could easily see his father telling stories about him, but not *funny* ones. Although he spoke to Frannie, Rafe glanced across the bed to Sam, lifting one brow in question. "Is he?"

His father seemed to understand Rafe's astonishment. As though needing to offer an excuse, he explained, "I'm trying to get her to settle down."

"It doesn't appear to be working."

Frannie squinted up at him. "When Aunt Addy was a baby, did you really try to sell her to the garbage man?"

"Afraid so. Babies are no fun to play with."

"And did you really dig up Nonna Rose's garden so you could bury pirate treasure under her flowers?"

"Where else would you bury treasure?"

"Nonno Sam said that when he spanked you for it, you told him you wanted to go to the orphans' home. So nice people would adopt you."

Rafe grimaced and glanced at his father once more. "I don't remember saying that."

"He said it," Sam said to Frannie with a low chuckle. "Little brat spent a week pretending I'd paddled him so hard he couldn't sit down."

Recalling how expertly he'd played the wounded victim, Rafe couldn't help laughing, too. "I suppose it wasn't as bad as I made it seem."

"Ask your mother. It was two well-deserved taps on your rump."

"I guess I deserved that. And more."

Sam shook his head. The smile stretched across his lips was a clear indication he could recount every detail from the past. "You kept me and your mother on our toes, that's for sure."

Frannie yawned. "Nonno Sam says you were always ram...bunkus."

"*Rambunctious*," Rafe corrected automatically, but he couldn't help throwing his father a curious look. *Rambunctious* wasn't the word Sam usually picked to describe him. Of course, the other ways Sam liked to describe his youngest son weren't the things a little girl should hear.

When Frannie yawned a second time, Rafe bent and caught her chin between two fingers. "It's time you went to sleep."

"I don't want to."

"Sorry. You need your rest. We're going to be very busy starting tomorrow."

The child's dark eyes lit excitedly. "Moving into our house."

"Yep. You have to help me figure out how to fix it up. Make it pretty."

With a huge sigh, Frannie nodded. "Okay."

Sam rose slowly. He reached out to ruffle Frannie's hair. "Good night, *bambina*. *Sogni d'oro*. Sweet dreams."

Frannie muttered a response, sounding disappointed, but already she was giving in, relaxing into the gauzy pull of sleep. Her eyes closed dutifully.

Sam was nearly out the door when Rafe called out to him. "Pop, wait up."

His father stopped in the hallway, and quickly Rafe joined him there. He pulled the bedroom door almost closed behind him so as not to disturb Frannie. "Thanks for looking after her," he said softly. "Things got a little crazy down at the Three Bs. I didn't want to have Frannie frightened by all the fuss."

Sam nodded. "She's easy to amuse, and I haven't lost my touch."

"Or your ability to tell a story, it seems."

"She enjoyed hearing about her father. And there were plenty of tales to tell."

"Rambunctious, huh?" He gave his father a slight smile. "Coming from you, that's a pretty mild description. I would have expected you to trot out some of my more…inflammatory incidents."

The words brought an awkward little moment instantly, and just as quickly Rafe regretted them. The hard edge returned to his father's jaw as the smile dropped from his lips. His dark eyes were serious and stern as the years of disagreements they'd shared arched up between them once more.

"She's only five," Sam said. "There's time enough for her to learn all the ways a child can break a parent's heart."

He continued down the hall. Rafe watched him go, knowing that the temporary bridge of easy understanding they'd crossed in Frannie's room had disappeared like smoke.

Disappointed, but not really surprised, Rafe went back into the bedroom. Quietly, he retrieved the chair from in front of the writing desk and pulled it up beside his daughter's bed. Frannie was still, her eyes closed, her hand tucked under her chin as she lay on her side. For a few long minutes he stared down at her.

He'd spent so many years alone. It felt strange to have this small being, helpless and trusting, so dependent on him. He was discovering that fatherhood was complex, mysterious, but he had to admit, watching a child sleep, *his* child, made something tight within him unspool and relax.

Frannie sighed heavily in her sleep. Her eyelids fluttered and she saw him sitting by the bed in spite of the near darkness.

"Mommy?"

"It's Daddy, honey," Rafe said softly. "Go back to sleep."

"I miss Mommy…."

"I know you do. But just rest. I'll be right here."

Her fingers walked along the sheet, searching, and Rafe reached out to take her hand. Her mouth worked for a moment or two; he couldn't tell if she was disappointed or relieved. Then she seemed to fall asleep once more.

How could Ellen have walked away from this child? Could the new man in her life really be such a catch? Granted, Frannie was a spirited kid, a handful, but it didn't seem possible that any woman would give up all her rights as Ellen had agreed to do. But then, he hadn't been drawn to her because of her maternal instincts.

Rafe yawned and squinted down at his watch. It wasn't late, but it sure felt that way. His back ached. His eyes felt like grains of sand had been thrown into them. But as restless as Frannie was, it might be a long time before he was able to slip off to his own bed.

Well, he thought, feeling her fingers tucked warmly against his palm, what would be wrong with that?

CHAPTER TEN

THE DAY AFTER THE BIG discovery at the Three Bs, Dani rose and was at the newspaper office by 6:00 a.m. She might as well have stayed there all night since she'd been unable to sleep. Her mind was filled with possible ways she could find out who the Accordion Man was and how he'd ended up in that trunk.

She spent the morning searching through federal, state and county data banks for information about the Three Bs Social Club and its chain of possession. The earliest records were pretty skimpy. It had stayed in the Culpepper family until Ida Mae's great-granddaughter Myrtle had died in the 1950s in a car accident. After that, the property had been sold to various companies over the years. None of them had done much with the place, and none of them looked as though they might have something to hide. No bankruptcies, court judgments or criminal activity. Not a whiff of scandal involving any of the previous owners.

Satisfied about the history of ownership, Dani

moved on to specifics. She searched the paper's archives for mention of the Three Bs, Ida Mae and Myrtle Culpepper, Broken Yoke and even accordion players. She got a lot of random debris, one or two historical tidbits about the place, but nothing significant. For an establishment that had spent a lot of its existence as a "social club," it appeared to have been surprisingly law-abiding.

Around ten, Dani heard the front door open. A few moments later, Cissy appeared in the doorway of her office, coffee cup in one hand and a take-out bag from the local diner in the other. "I knew I'd find you here early," the young woman said.

Dani barely looked up from her computer screen. "Why is that?"

"I stopped for coffee at the Sun Dial this morning. Everyone was talking about what happened at the Three Bs yesterday. Did the dead guy really fall on top of you?"

"No," Dani said with a frown. She motioned toward the bag in Cissy's hand. "Is that for me?"

Cissy nodded and handed her the bag. It held a steaming cup of the Sun Dial's best coffee. Dani kicked back in her chair and sipped in delight. Broken Yoke might be out in the sticks, but they sure knew how to do a great cup of coffee.

"I assume you're digging for clues," Cissy said. "Any luck?"

"Not yet."

"Anything I can do to help?"

Dani plucked her camera off her desk and tossed it to Cissy. "Can you get prints made?"

"Sure." Cissy held the camera between two fingers as thought it were radioactive. "Are these pictures of the Accordion Man?"

"I hope so. They're all I could take before the forensic team got there and closed off the place."

"Wish I'd been there to watch. I'll bet it was just like television."

Dani was barely listening. Feeling frustrated by the paltry information she'd been able to glean, she shut down her computer. The Internet usually saved hours of research time, but in this case, it hadn't given her very much.

Cissy was making her way back to her reception desk. "I can't ever remember a murder in Broken Yoke. We just don't get stuff like that happening here."

Chin in hand, Dani glanced out the small office window and had to admit that she shared Cissy's dismay.

From this angle you could see a corner of the city park and beyond that, the gingerbread trim of Holly's Fudge Kitchen, all pink and cream. Next to it, window boxes of bright red tulips invited passersby to stop in the hobby shop that catered to recreating Victorian homes as dollhouses.

Sometimes, when she looked a little closer, as she got to know more and more of the townspeople, Dani stopped thinking of Broken Yoke as Hicksville. It really had a certain charm all its own. A certain energetic vitality.

And she definitely couldn't imagine a murder happening here.

A sudden thought occurred to Dani, and she sat up straighter. "How long have you lived here, Cissy?"

Cissy turned. "All my life, I'm afraid."

"Do you recall if the town ever had its own paper? Not just a local section in the Denver Sunday edition?"

"Sure. But it stopped running a while back. No one read it much."

"Who published it?"

"Herb McKay."

"Does he still live in town?"

"He died a few years ago. But his wife Geneva is still around."

Dani grabbed her purse and jacket, and scooped up the notes she'd made. "Can you get in touch with her? I'd like to talk about back issues. Today, if possible. Call me on my cell."

"Okay." As Dani swept past her, heading out the door, Cissy called out, "Where are you going?"

"Sheriff Bendix's office. I want to find out what he's thinking, and if he's heard anything yet from Denver."

AN HOUR LATER, DANI LEFT the sheriff's office and headed for Geneva McKay's home on the outskirts of Broken Yoke. Cissy had set up a meeting for noon.

Dani was still feeling thwarted. Sheriff Bendix had

been less than helpful. It wasn't that he didn't want to share information, it was simply that he saw no reason to throw himself into a full investigation. In his mind, it was a crime too old to worry about. He was perfectly willing to wait until the forensic team in Denver came back with their findings. Until then, he had other things to do.

What those things might be, Dani couldn't imagine, but she kept her annoyance in check and got as much out of him as she could. He was a long-time resident of Broken Yoke and had furnished Dani with several names of people who might have more information on the Three Bs—old-timers like Burt Beckerman of the historical society; Mayor Wickham, who came from a long line of town politicians; Shirley Cauthen, the postmistress. Even Rafe's parents were on her list, their family having established overnight cabins back when Broken Yoke had first tried to become a tourist destination.

Some of these people must be very familiar with the Three Bs, she reasoned. If nothing else, it was a start.

When she arrived at Geneva McKay's house, she discovered that the woman was thin, about seventy. She had spark-ling blue eyes, hair done up in a messy topknot and a warm smile. She ushered Dani into her home as though she'd been waiting for her all her life.

"You're just in time to join me for lunch, dear. Nothing fancy, I'm afraid, but it fills a body up."

Hesitating in the foyer, Dani said, "Perhaps I should come back later. I don't want to inconvenience you."

"The more the merrier," a male voice replied from somewhere nearby, and Dani turned to find Rafe's father making his way slowly toward her. He smiled at Geneva. "Right, Ginny?"

"That's right," the older woman agreed. To Dani she said, "I believe you know Sam D'Angelo."

Dani hadn't seen him since his son's wedding, and it surprised her a little to find him here. She held out her hand. "Of course. Nice to see you again, Mr. D'Angelo. How are the newlyweds?"

"Still flittin' around the country on their honeymoon. Doing what lovebirds do."

Dani smiled.

"I hope you two like tuna salad," Geneva said. "Shall we eat?"

She led the way through the living room. Her home was neat, cozy and filled with evidence of her interests. With a reporter's natural curiosity, Dani took the time to study her surroundings. Her gaze was particularly drawn to side-by-side portraits that hung on one wall. A man and a teenage boy, beautifully executed with bold, precise strokes.

"Those portraits are lovely," Dani said as she came into the small dining room and took the seat Geneva indicated. "Extraordinary, really. Are they family?"

Geneva nodded. "My husband Herb. And my grandson David, when he was eighteen. He lives in Los Angeles now."

"They're very handsome, both of them."

The comment seemed to please her. The lines in her face shifted and resettled as she smiled. "I'm afraid the artist wasn't very objective. She was quite in love with her subjects."

Sam D'Angelo had set his crutches aside and taken the place opposite Dani. "Ginny painted them," he told her.

Something clicked inside Dani. She looked at the old woman in surprise. "Are you Geneva St. John?"

The artist's work hung in some of the finest galleries in the country. But she'd seemed to drop out of existence years ago, and nothing new from her had ever surfaced.

"I used to be," her hostess said, blushing slightly. "Now I'm just plain Geneva McKay."

"You're still the best," Sam said in a no-nonsense tone. "That's why I want you to paint Rosa's portrait." He glanced across the table to Dani. "My wife's birthday, but don't tell her. It's a surprise."

"What a lovely idea."

"Anything for my Rosa." Then Rafe's father winked at her and grinned. "Besides, women are like cars. Take good care of them and you won't have to have a new one every few years."

They all laughed at that, then Dani dug into the mound of tuna salad on her plate. She listened quietly as the two older people chatted a few minutes about the portrait Sam wanted to commission. She made a mental note to speak to Geneva about her past at some later date. There could be a good human-interest story here if the woman was willing to share it.

Finally, Geneva lifted her hand to halt Sam's effusive compliments. "Enough business for now, Sam." She looked at Dani. "Your receptionist told me you were interested in the paper Herbert used to print. I'm afraid it died with him. I wouldn't have been very good at it, and to be honest, it would have been too painful to continue."

"I certainly understand," Dani said. "But do you recall how far back it went?"

"No, I'm sorry, I don't," Geneva said with a regretful frown. "Herbert was a CPA, but he always dreamed of being in the newspaper business. After he retired he was quite excited about taking it over from the fellow who sold it to him." The woman brightened suddenly. "But I do remember him saying that it had been around nearly as long as the town."

Dani felt her heart take a leap. "Would you happen to have any of the oldest issues archived? I was hoping to get a look at them."

"You searching for information on the Accordion Man?" Sam spoke up.

Dani looked at him in surprise. "Rafe told you about yesterday?"

"Ha!" The older man jabbed his fork in her direction. "As if my son would volunteer anything but the basics. I got a call this morning from a friend who filled in the details. News has a way of getting around pretty fast." He shook his head. "But it was a shocker, all right."

"I'd like to gather as much information as I can about the Three Bs," she told the two of them. "Perhaps it will help me find out who the Accordion Man was."

One of Sam's salt-and-pepper brows rose. "Does Rafe know that?"

"We spoke about it over dinner last night. He understands—"

Sam leaned forward suddenly, skewering Dani with a close look. "You two had dinner?"

"Well actually, I ate, he watched. But he understands that I'd like to help identify the poor man who ended up in that trunk."

"Yeah, poor man," he said quickly. "You two dating?"

"I beg your pardon?"

"You know…a couple."

"Sam!" Geneva cut in. "What a question. You're embarrassing her."

"Why?" Sam asked with a frown. "What's to be embarrassed about?"

Dani cleared her throat and swiped her tongue over her lips. She wasn't sure just why she found his questions so unnerving, but she did. Thinking about the Accordion Man hadn't been the only reason she hadn't been able to sleep much last night. Memories of Rafe's kiss kept curling through her, alive in each exquisite detail.

The problem was, she shouldn't have found any of

that to her liking. While she no longer actively hated Rafe for what he'd done in Vegas, she was supposed to be feeling completely indifferent toward him.

So how could she have spent half the night wishing he had never kissed her, and the other half wishing he had never stopped? Oh, anything involving Rafe had always been such tricky business, hadn't it?

"Shouldn't be such a hard question to answer," Sam said with a short laugh. "You two seeing each other, or not?"

"No, Mr. D'Angelo," she said in the most neutral tone she could manage. "We're not dating."

"Call me Sam."

He was still eyeing her with the kind of close scrutiny that made Dani feel as though she were a butterfly on a pin. She couldn't tell if he thought her an acceptable specimen or whether she'd been found wanting. Maybe she could steer the topic of conversation to safer waters.

She turned a blinding smile on Geneva. "Mrs. McKay, about the back issues…"

"I'm afraid I gave them to Burt Beckerman for the historical society. But he's very organized. I'm sure he'll be able to help you."

Sam made a disparaging sound as he set his iced-tea glass back on the lace-covered table. "Help from Burt Beckerman? That's as rare as finding a lawyer in heaven."

"Sam!" Geneva admonished.

"What Connie ever saw in him, I'll never figure out."

Geneva turned to Dani. "Connie was Burt's wife. She died a few years ago," she explained, then stared pointedly at Sam, "and since then the poor man's been very lonely."

"Hmmph!" Sam complained. "Is that what they're calling rudeness these days?"

Geneva gave him a censuring look. "He just needs another good woman in his life. I'm thinking of setting him up with Polly Swinburne."

"Paranoid Polly! I'd rather hook up with a sick grizzly."

"Well, we're not talking about you."

"Burt can't get remarried anyway. He's too old. The rice would knock him over."

Geneva pressed her lips together in disapproval, and before the older people could go off on any further tangent, Dani spoke up. "Could you tell me where he lives?"

Geneva nodded sharply. "I'll do better than that. I'll call him for you. Connie and I were very close. If I pave the way, perhaps it will help him to be a little less…"

"Nuts?" Sam posed.

"Reserved," Geneva corrected sternly.

"I would appreciate anything you could do, Mrs. McKay."

"Ginny, dear. More iced tea?"

Sam gave Dani a speculative look. "You know, if it's the lowdown on the Three Bs you're after, I can tell you about the place. Used to play in a band there several nights a week. That was before we found out we had more enthusiasm than talent."

"I'd be interested in hearing anything you remember. I have to start somewhere."

"Well, then…" Sam said, looking enthusiastic. "Ginny, we're going to need some more tea."

Over peach cobbler, Sam launched into one story after another about the Three Bs, with Ginny adding an occasional anecdote of her own. The place had apparently been a popular spot for dancing and having a few drinks with friends during the Vietnam War. Ginny, older than Sam by a few years, even remembered when veterans from Korea had found the Three Bs the best place to swap war stories. But although their memories were good, their minds sharp, neither of them could recall much about the place before that.

The years between Ida Mae's ownership in the late 1800s and Myrtle's possession sometime in the 1950s was one huge blank. And neither of them could ever recall an accordion player working there.

Eventually they ran out of stories, and Dani had filled half her notebook. It was mid-afternoon. Eager to pay a visit to Burt Beckerman, she rose and said her goodbyes.

"Thank you both for your time," she said at the door. "And for lunch, Ginny."

Geneva clutched both of Dani's hands in her own. "Come by anytime, dear."

"I'll walk you out to your car," Sam said, an offer

that surprised Dani since the man must have difficulty managing his crutches on the steep front steps.

They made their way slowly to her car, and when she had opened the door, she turned to Sam once more.

"Thank you again, Sam. You've been very helpful."

"I hope you won't be sorry you asked all those questions."

"What do you mean?"

"Since my son owns the Three Bs now, I expect he isn't going to like all this poking around in the past."

Dani frowned. "Why? It's a very old crime, but someone's going to want to solve it. If it can be solved." She gave Sam a closer look. "I know he'll hate the attention this will bring, but did he tell you specifically that he didn't want me to investigate?"

"Didn't have to. Rafe and I don't talk much, and we spent an awful lot of years apart. But I know he's always been the private sort."

"He certainly has," Dani said without thinking. "Oz never did like the man behind the curtain to be seen, did he?"

Sam's head lifted, as though he were a wolf on the scent of prey. "Oz?"

She realized her mistake immediately. "Oh, that's ancient history. I'd better let him tell you about that. I didn't realize that you didn't know."

Sam leaned back in his crutches, his dark eyes glinting. "I'm afraid there are a lot of things about my son that I don't know," he said, his voice sinking back as if it had begun to tire. "And I probably never will."

THAT EVENING, RAFE HAD one heck of a headache.

It had all started the moment he'd heard that an emergency town meeting had been called by the Festival Committee, and it didn't look like it was going to end anytime soon. The back room of the Silver Saddle was filled with Broken Yoke citizens, all of them in various stages of excitement, most of them talking over one another as they argued their point. So far, nothing had been agreed upon, but one thing was certain.

It was going to be a very long evening.

Rafe had arrived with his father. He wished Nick had come with them, but his brother had taken his wife to dinner in Vail. Lucky guy. Much better to spend the evening in the company of a beautiful woman like Kari than to have to deal with the local head cases here tonight.

He tried to pay attention to the old codger who had the floor at the moment. Burt Beckerman was weighing in with his thoughts on the matter. Although usually quiet and almost shy, Burt had quite a head of steam up right now.

Rafe happened to agree with him. The Accordion Man would *not* make the perfect focus for the upcoming town festival.

"This is a ridiculous idea," Burt sputtered, his thin

face nearly as red as his sweater. "You don't build an entire festival around a dead man!"

"Why not?" Mort Calloway asked. "This state has a reputation for quirky celebrations. This *town* was once the wild frontier. It could put us on the festival map."

"It's in bad taste," Burt said.

Harvey Delacroix stood up from the back of the room. Harvey ran the local used-car dealership. "You people don't know the first damned thing about salesmanship! This is a natural. This dead body is a gift from God."

Burt swung around quickly to face Harvey. It wasn't easy since Burt was asthmatic and looked as fragile as a shell. "It's obscene. We're talking about someone who was probably murdered."

"A hundred years ago, Burt. It's not obscene. It's like finding a mummy. It's…it's history!"

Shirley Cauthen, the postmistress, clearly still uncertain about the idea, spoke up. "I don't know…. A festival to celebrate someone who died horribly just doesn't seem very respectful."

"Tell that to Crested Mesa," Sheriff Bendix said with a laugh. "Don't they celebrate the anniversary of the Donner party freezing their keisters off every year?"

Ralph Harris, a jock with a Southern frat-boy manner, waved his hand to catch everyone's attention. "And what about Longview? They have Roaring Twenties Days in honor of that guy. That dead guy…"

"The Great Gatsby," someone supplied.

"Yeah, him."

Shirley shook her head in disgust. "That doesn't count."

"Why not?"

"Because Jay Gatsby wasn't real."

"He wasn't?" Rafe heard Ralph say. "I never knew that."

Oh, brother. These people were never going to arrive at a consensus.

"We could go back to my suggestion to have a Christmas in July celebration," Phil Pasternak spoke up. In spite of the fiasco at the school, he had never given up on his idea.

Several people laughed outright.

"I thought that plan died when your Santa Claus said he was going to sue you for reckless endangerment."

"It doesn't have to be Dexter. I could get someone else to play Santa."

"Not anyone with half a brain," Howard Hackett said.

Shirley spoke up again, looking a little more persuaded. "A festival built around the discovery of the Accordion Man would certainly be unique."

"And unlike *some* ideas we've had, definitely not boring," Polly muttered.

The tension in the room seemed to lessen a little as more and more people began to see the possibilities. Rafe bent his head to hide his dismay and annoyance. These people couldn't be serious. Could they?

"We could do musical competitions for the best band to make use of an accordion."

"How about a bordello theme in honor of the early days of the Three Bs?"

"That ought to bring in the whole family," Rafe said under his breath. He'd been hoping he wouldn't have to add his two cents to this bizarre discussion, but it looked as if sooner or later he'd have to speak up.

"Nothing too risqué, of course," Polly went on. "Maybe we could have awards for the prettiest or funniest costume."

Mayor Wickham raised his hand for attention, then looked across the room at Rafe. "Would you be willing to let us run tours through that secret room of yours?"

It seemed as though every head in the room swung in his direction.

"No."

"We could charge a fee."

"*No.*"

"People will be curious."

"People will have to stay curious."

"They'll want to see the room. I heard it was filled with treasure, not just the dead guy."

"You heard wrong."

The mayor was tenacious, if nothing else. He looked past Rafe for support. "What about you, Miss Bridgeton? You represent the press, and you know this area. Do you think we could draw a crowd?"

Rafe turned and spied Dani at the back of the room. She must have come in late because he hadn't noticed her before. He willed her to back him up, but she never once looked in his direction. Instead, she nodded at the mayor.

"Yes, I do," she said.

People began to talk among themselves, nodding and smiling as though they'd just latched on to the secrets of the universe. Only Burt Beckerman still looked grumpy. Feeling as though he were the last sane person on the planet, Rafe cleared his throat to get everyone's attention.

"In a few weeks' time, all this excitement will die down," he said loudly. "People will be interested in something else. They won't even remember who the Accordion Man was."

Beside him, his father moved forward on his crutches, equally intent on capturing the floor. "Then we need to have the festival sooner than July. To capitalize on it while it's hot." He turned to look at Rafe. "What's your real problem with planning a festival around the Accordion Man and the Three Bs?"

"I don't want the publicity. People will be hauling off souvenirs, peeking in the windows—"

"Once word gets around about the Accordion Man," Dani said, "some of that is inevitable. Whether this town has a festival or not, you can't keep it from happening. And I'm certain I can get my editor to run a short piece about the mystery before the festival. That should drum up even more interest."

If she'd been closer, Rafe could have cheerfully strangled her. Instead, he dragged a hand through his hair and faced the room again. "Look," he said in his most reasonable tone. "Maybe you could get people to come up here strictly out of curiosity, but once the renovations are finished, I want to market those units as condominiums. No one is going to want to buy a place where a man was murdered."

"People do it all the time," Mort Calloway said. "And as I understand it, that room will be part of your home, not a unit you plan to sell. Isn't that true?"

"Yes, but—"

Sam spoke up. "Seems to me you'll get a better response from buyers if you're honest and open with them about what happened there. Show them it's no big deal, that there's nothing to hide. They might even think it's pretty nifty. It could enhance the value. But cover it up, try to downplay it, and people get suspicious."

His father's opinion didn't surprise him. Sam never took Rafe's side. In anything. He gave himself a few moments to find his patience. "Being open and honest about it is not the same as having a festival in celebration of a dead musician."

Burt Beckerman made a grumbling sound low in his throat. "This is unthinkable. How can we even consider—"

Polly nudged him. "Oh, stop being such a fuss-budget, Burt. I say we take a vote."

Mayor Wickham moved quickly to second the idea, and in no time the motion carried with only two negative votes—Rafe's and Burt Beckerman's. Even Shirley Cauthen deserted them.

Another few minutes were spent to determine the right time to have the festival and to set up subcommittees. Everyone was so enthusiastic about the idea that few people declined to offer help.

Annoyed, Rafe left the building. His father was still talking to several people, and although Rafe had already decided not to be a poor loser about the whole thing, he saw no reason to stand around and pretend he was thrilled.

He leaned against the front of the building and waited, hands in his pockets, head down. Thinking. People streamed out of the building for a while, then dribbled out as the place emptied. His father was taking his own sweet time. No surprise there, either. He probably knew Rafe would be unhappy with him, and the drive back up to the lodge would be a silent, tense one.

When the front door opened and Dani emerged, Rafe reached out and tugged on her coat sleeve. He pulled her against the building with him, then brought one arm up to trap her there.

"Don't run off," he told her. "I want to talk to you."

Surprisingly, she went stiff in his arms. He saw right away that she was in no mood to be friendly. "Well, I don't want to talk to *you*."

"What's the matter?"

"You lied to me. You broke your promise."

He frowned. "What promise?"

"The one where you promised you wouldn't stand in the way of my investigation."

"And I haven't."

The look in her eyes said she didn't believe him. "I talked to your construction foreman today. Lane. At least I tried to. He said you told him not to talk about the Three Bs or the Accordion Man. Is that true?"

"In a way."

"What way? He stonewalled every question I asked, and when I tried to take another look at the room, he wouldn't let me."

"Lane took me too literally," Rafe said with a small smile. "I told him I didn't want a bunch of nosy busybodies hanging around trying to get all the gory details from him and the crew. Not while I'm footing the bill. And I certainly don't need any lawsuits from nitwits who fall down trying to get a closer look. But that didn't include you. I'll tell him first thing in the morning that you have carte blanche."

"Good," she said simply, though he noticed that she still looked a little skeptical.

"You don't trust me very much, do you?"

"You haven't given me a lot of reasons to," she replied.

A few more people came out of the Silver Saddle, and they were both sidetracked with saying good-night to them. When they were alone once more, Rafe decided they needed to forget about questions of trust for the moment.

"So you got invited to this insanity?" he asked her.

"No. Any time I see a bunch of townies collecting in one place, my antennae start quivering. So I crashed."

"Where's the camera?" he asked.

"What camera?"

"The one that tells me all this was some sort of TV prank."

Her eyes crinkled with amusement. He'd forgotten how penetrating-gray they were. "Sorry, I think it's real."

She gave him a tentative smile, all unpleasantness tucked behind them for the moment, and the world seemed to narrow to just the two of them. He thought he could actually feel the warmth of her presence so close to him.

"Are you angry with me for influencing them to vote yes?" she asked.

"No. Anyone who didn't vote yes was in danger of being lynched." He shook his head. "Idiots."

"Does that include your father? He voted against you."

"My father would swear I was wrong if I said the sun rises in the east every day."

Dani gave him a sharpened look. "What is it with you two?"

Rafe shrugged. "Too long and too stupid to talk about."

He didn't want to discuss his father. Dani's mouth was the most beautiful he'd ever seen, and he was having to fight the urge to lean down and capture it. What would she do if he did? She hadn't tried to stop him the last time. Would she tonight?

"If you don't talk about it, it will never get fixed," she told him.

"Who says it has to get fixed? Some things are better left alone."

"True," she acknowledged. "But it seems to me that a man trying to raise a little girl in a town this small might want to have the support of his family. *All* his family."

His brow lifted. "Suddenly you're as wise as Dear Abby?"

"Suddenly you're as clueless as the village idiot?"

He leaned closer, giving her a playfully severe look. "I don't discuss my relationship with my father."

She waved that statement away with one hand. "So don't discuss it with me. But you might want to try discussing it with him."

He watched her throat work as she swallowed and realized that she wasn't immune to his presence at all. The knowledge pleased him greatly.

Never taking his eyes from her, he reached out and repositioned a stray tendril of dark hair in front of her shoulder. He could see that she held her breath. "Why do you care so much?" he asked.

"I hate to see grown men act like children."

Her words irritated him, but they did battle with the sheer pleasure he took in having her so near. "It's too late for us," he said softly.

"It's never too late." As though coming out of a deep trance, she straightened suddenly and shot him a disapproving glance. "I spoke with your father quite a bit today. I didn't get the impression that your relationship was such a closed door."

"Where did you run into my father?"

"At Geneva McKay's place. He was checking on some painting he's commissioned from her for your mother's birthday. We had lunch, as a matter of fact. Unlike Lane, Geneva was very helpful with my Accordion Man investigation. So was your father. I found him to be charming and funny and very smart. A man like that can't be completely unreachable."

"He's also stubborn, temperamental and unforgiving."

"That's funny."

"What?"

"I'll bet if you asked him, he'd describe you the same way."

Before Rafe could stop her, Dani slipped under his arm and headed down the sidewalk.

CHAPTER ELEVEN

LITTLE MORE THAN A WEEK LATER, the town sponsored a Prepare-the-Square weekend.

The festival had been set for late May to capitalize on Memorial Day, and the rush was on. The center of Broken Yoke, the town square, would host craft and game booths, food vendors and a huge stage for performers. The word went out that help was needed to turn the park into a proper setting. Armed with paint, tools, lumber and greenery, nearly every-one in town showed up to make the transformation happen.

The day was bright, clear, the kind of weather that could make you forget how miserably cold winter could be. In every direction the mountains rose sharp and visible. The atmosphere was playful, but determined. People seemed united in their resolve to make the festival a success.

Since she'd come to Broken Yoke, Dani had never seen so many of the townspeople in one place. Laughing, chatting, they seemed united in a commu-

Play The Lucky Hearts Game

and get...
FREE BOOKS & a FREE GIFT...
YOURS to KEEP!

Yes! I have scratched off the silver card. Please send me my **FREE BOOKS** and **FREE MYSTERY GIFT**. I understand that I am under no obligation to purchase any books as explained on the back of this card. I am over 18 years of age.

Scratch Here!
then look below to see
what you can claim...

U8II8

Mrs/Miss/Ms/Mr _____ Initials _____

BLOCK CAPITALS PLEASE

Surname _____

Address _____

_____

Postcode _____

Twenty-one gets you
2 FREE BOOKS and a
MYSTERY GIFT!

Twenty gets you
1 FREE BOOK and a
MYSTERY GIFT!

Nineteen gets you
1 FREE BOOK!

TRY AGAIN!

DETACH AND POST CARD TODAY!

The Mills & Boon® Book Club™ — Here's how it works:

Accepting your free books places you under no obligation to buy anything. You may keep the books and gift and return the despatch note marked "cancel." If we do not hear from you, about a month later we'll send you 4 brand new books and invoice you just £3.69* each. That's the complete price — there is no extra charge for postage and packing. You may cancel at any time, otherwise every month we'll send you 4 more books, which you may either purchase or return to us — the choice is yours.

*Terms and prices subject to change without notice.

THE MILLS & BOON® BOOK CLUB™
FREE BOOK OFFER
FREEPOST CN81
CROYDON
CR9 3WZ

NO STAMP
NECESSARY
IF POSTED IN
THE U.K. OR N.I.

If offer card is missing write to: The Mills & Boon Book Club , PO Box 236, Croydon, CR9 3RU

nity effort that she seldom saw in her neighborhood back in Denver. Watching them, she couldn't help but hope they were doing the right thing, that their efforts to plant and paint and pressure wash would not be wasted.

Determined to do her part, she spent the morning on the square, working up a festival story. Something fun and interesting. She interviewed young and old alike, and had Chester, her photographer, snap so many shots that he complained about being overworked.

By mid-afternoon, she was tired and almost hoarse, but she felt surprisingly energized. Everyone was so enthusiastic, and she realized that she was, too. Her conversations with several people had netted her the possibilities of at least half a dozen human-interest stories that begged to be written. She couldn't wait to share them with Gary.

Accomplishing something specific was certainly a welcome change from the way the rest of the week had gone.

Her visit to Burt Beckerman had been a bust. It was clear he regarded her request to view back issues of the local paper as a bother and a waste of time. He wasn't far wrong about that. Very little was computerized, and her search for information brought nothing particularly noteworthy.

There was still no word on the Accordion Man from the medical examiner's office in Denver. Sheriff Bendix claimed they were short-staffed and bogged down right now with current cases. It might be months before they had news.

For reasons that she preferred not to consider, she was disappointed that the week passed without a single sign of Rafe. She knew he was busy getting settled into his place at the Three Bs, but Cissy reported that he'd been seen a couple of times with a good-looking woman from Idaho Springs named Heather. Dani tried to pretend that it didn't matter to her one way or the other what Rafe D'Angelo was up to.

There was a sudden flurry of activity around the gazebo at one end of the square. New shrubbery and flowers were being planted, and a group of women and children were busy applying a fresh coat of white paint. Dani decided to check it out.

She spotted Rafe's sister Addy among the lineup of workers, as well as Frannie, who was painting with such serious intent that she didn't even glance up when Dani came to stand beside them.

"Hi there, worker bees," Dani said. "Need some help?"

Addy turned, looking delighted to see her. "Reinforcements! Hurray! Grab a brush." She gave Dani some supplies, then motioned toward the gazebo. Under her breath she said, "This thing's got to have *three* coats according to our fearless leader and resident slave driver, Stacey Merrick."

She inclined her head meaningfully a few feet down the line of workers. A statuesque blonde in designer jeans and a blouse cut too low for common sense was issuing orders to a couple of other women. She didn't have a spot of paint on her.

Dani had only met Stacey once, briefly, but she knew her type well enough. Spoiled, arrogant and artificially beautiful. The kind of woman who enjoyed giving orders and cracking whips. Dani tossed Addy a sympathetic look of understanding.

Rafe's sister smiled. "Matt says I'm just jealous, but I swear, she's the perfect example of how some people let power go to their heads."

"Matt and Leslie are back from their honeymoon?" Dani asked.

Addy nodded. "Leslie's up at the lodge. With the exception of me, the women are holding down the fort today while the menfolk do the hard labor." She pointed toward the back of a large nursery truck on the street, where dozens of plants were being unloaded. "Matt and Nick are helping out over there. Pop's watering in the new tulips they planted around the drinking fountains."

And Rafe? Dani realized she was longing to ask. *Where is he?*

As though she'd heard the unspoken question, Addy motioned toward the entrance of the square where a new, larger entrance sign was being placed. "There's Rafe."

Dani had no trouble distinguishing him from the other two men digging post holes. She thought she would have recognized that tall, solid frame of his anywhere, the way every move seemed like effortless grace, and yet overwhelmingly masculine. What stunned her more was the shiver of pure, sensual awareness that ran through her. It was the absolute antithesis of the woman she thought herself to be.

She was almost relieved when Frannie drew her attention away by sidling up to Addy. "I need more paint," the child said, pointing to her empty bucket.

Addy lifted her own gallon and poured the majority of it into Frannie's container. "Here you go. Have a ball."

The girl returned to her spot and began carefully laying on paint once more. There were a few other children helping out, but Dani noticed they were having more fun than actually accomplishing anything. Their clothes and hands were a mess. Frannie's outfit was spotless, her face intent. Was this kid always so serious? Dani wondered.

The sudden lack of productivity on Addy's part had caught Stacey Merrick's attention. She approached them with hands on hips, a frown marring her smooth brow. "Adriana, if you're not going to work, do us a favor and get sodas and snacks for everyone."

Without waiting to see if Addy was willing, Stacey turned to one of the other women, pointing out a spot that needed another coat.

Addy made a face at Stacey behind her back, then saluted. "Aye, aye, Captain." Under her breath she whispered to Dani, "See what I mean? Slave driver."

She went down the row of workers, taking orders. Dani took up where she'd left off, slapping paint across the boards. When Addy returned to Dani's side, she said, "Will you keep an eye on Frannie while I go over to the Sun Dial? I shouldn't be too long."

For just a moment, Dani considered saying no. She didn't think she had any special affinity for children. She'd been an only child and had seldom even babysat. Kids were a real mystery to her. But with Frannie within earshot, what could she say?

She nodded, and Addy called to the girl, "Frannie, I'll be back in a few minutes. Do whatever Dani tells you to. All right?"

"Okay," the kid agreed.

This might not be too bad. The child seemed to be on her best behavior today. Calm. Malleable.

"How are you, Frannie?" Dani asked as she dipped her brush.

"Okay," Frannie said again without glancing up. "Painting wood isn't fun like painting pictures in school."

"Well, you're doing a great job."

"Daddy said that, too." She stopped painting and gave Dani a knowing look. "Grown-ups like to say things like that just to make you feel good."

Not knowing how to respond, Dani decided to concentrate on her work. A few minutes passed in pleasant silence. The task was boring, and Dani couldn't help that her eyes strayed every so often to see how progress was going with the new sign. The men were still hard at work. No one glanced in her direction. Least of all, Rafe.

On the other side of Frannie, a woman in a T-shirt and cutoff jeans plopped her paintbrush into her can. She stretched and sighed heavily. "That's it for me. I'm beat."

Stacey was at her side instantly. No slacking for recruits. "Not too much longer, Nina," she encouraged. "Then we can all take a break."

Nina wasn't buying that promise. She shook her head, then pulled a ragged towel from around her neck. She stared off into the distance. Her face was alarmingly flushed.

"Do you need to sit down a while?" Dani asked quickly. "Are you overheated?"

"No," the woman said. "In fact, I wish it would get hotter."

Stacey looked at her in surprise. "For heaven's sake, why? That would just make everyone miserable."

"Maybe," Nina said. "But I wouldn't mind if the heat made a few people take off their shirts." She jerked her chin toward the front of the square, where Nick and Matt D'Angelo were wrestling shrubs into holes that had been dug along the sidewalk. "I *do* so appreciate the sight of a well-sculpted male back. And you can't beat those D'Angelo brothers for good looks."

Stacey laughed. "Forget it. They're married."

Nina lifted one brow and let her glance shift to Rafe, still hunched over the new sign. "Not all of them."

Stacey frowned. "I wouldn't waste my energy thinking about Rafe D'Angelo."

"Why not? He's still the same hottie he was in high school."

"And he's probably still got the same alley-cat morals he had back then. Or don't you remember how half the cheerleading squad wanted to sleep with him and the other half wanted him dead for breaking their hearts?"

Nina gave Stacey a wicked grin. "But I'd be *sooo* good to him, he just might mend his sinful ways."

Stacey laughed. "A lot of good it would do you. Rafe isn't the kind of man to stick around. He's never liked responsibility. Not then. Not now. Mark my words, he'll be gone before the end of summer, off searching for the next adventure."

Dani took a step forward, intent on reminding them that Rafe's daughter was nearby. The little girl didn't need to hear what these two witches thought of her father, and Dani had no idea how much nastier they'd get.

But before she could say a word, Frannie was at her side. The child looked up at her, those eyes as clear and bright as the alpine sky overhead. "I need more paint," she said.

Dani frowned down at Frannie's half-full bucket. "You have enough to finish up," she told her. "Once you use that up, how about we go across the street and get ice cream?"

"Okay," Frannie said.

Relieved that the child evidently hadn't heard the two women's conversation, Dani patted her on the head. Frannie headed off again, paint bucket in hand. She walked no more than half a dozen steps when she passed Stacey Merrick—and unceremoniously dumped her can of paint over the woman's feet.

Stacey squealed like a boiled cat. There were gasps from several bystanders, including Dani. Those shoes may have been open-toed, but they had looked darned expensive. Frannie just stared at Stacey's feet.

Before Dani could stop her, Stacey bent and grabbed the girl by the arm, shaking her. "Why don't you pay attention to what you're doing?" she snapped.

But that's *exactly* what she had done, Dani thought. Frannie *had* paid attention. *Close* attention to Stacey and Nina's conversation. And she hadn't liked it one bit.

Oh, the kid was devious. A girl after her own heart.

Dani rushed forward, removing Stacey's hand. "It was an accident," she said. "She tripped."

Stacey started to make another comment, her mouth twisted with nasty intent. Then she must have realized that several people were staring, waiting to see what her next move would be. Verbally flaying a child would not go over well. With one waspish, muttered curse, she swung on her heels—at least as much as her glop-covered white feet would allow her—and stalked toward the public restrooms across the square.

Everyone nearby watched her go, and Dani couldn't help sensing that some of them weren't nearly as horrified as they'd seemed. "Poor Stacey," Nina said, but the look on her face didn't exactly convey distress. A moment later, she headed off in the direction of the cars parked along the street.

Dani didn't give the woman a second thought. She stared down at Frannie, wondering what was going through the child's mind. She looked completely unrepentant, sticking stubbornly to indifference. No tears, no nervous smile asking for understanding and forgiveness. The kid was one tough little cookie.

"Frannie, why did you…?" Dani began, then let her lips close on the rest of her words. She knew why the girl had done it. Heck, given another few moments, Dani might have been tempted to do it herself.

The child drew herself upward in tight control, prepared for the worst.

Dani crouched in front of her. "Never mind," she said. "I'm going to see if I can salvage this situation somehow."

"What does *salvage* mean?"

"It means I'm going to try to make things right and keep you out of the doghouse. Now stand right here until your Aunt Addy gets back. Don't move. Don't breathe. And for goodness' sake, don't touch the paint. Got it?"

"Okay," the girl replied in a maddeningly mild way.

It didn't take Dani long to reach the restrooms. When she entered, she saw Stacey Merrick sitting on the vanity, scrubbing her feet with paper towels. She looked very undignified with them propped up in one of the sinks.

"I came to see if you needed help," Dani said.

Stacey glanced up. Her face was pinched, sour, and she threw a soggy paper towel into the nearby trash. "I don't need any help. Unless you'd like to give that little monster the whipping she deserves." She motioned toward the floor, where two white globs that used to be fancy footwear lay in a sad heap. "Look at my shoes. Do you know how expensive they were?"

"No, but—"

"More than most people make in a week."

"I'm sure Rafe will replace them."

Her eyes narrowed, and as she tossed her head, the flagrant false brilliance of her blond hair caught the light. "You speak for Rafe D'Angelo these days?"

"No, of course not."

"They're ruined," she said in exasperation. Her lips disappeared as she bit them. "And I looked like such a…"

For just a moment, Dani almost felt sorry for her. Women like Stacey Merrick didn't like to look foolish. "I'm very sorry," Dani heard herself say, struggling her way toward peace. "I should have kept a closer eye on Frannie. But it was just a horrible accident. You know how clumsy kids are."

"No, I *don't* know. But I'll tell you this, I'm not sure that it was an accident at all. I don't know what that miserable kid has against me, but if I had my way, she wouldn't stop crying for a week."

The woman's hateful tone sent a fierce sense of

anger right through Dani. Stacey Merrick wasn't entitled to sympathy. Her ego, so dependent on such nasty behavior for its nourishment, was not worth feeding any longer. She was a gossipy witch who had gotten what she'd deserved.

Dani gave her a level look. "Maybe she just didn't like the idea of her father being called an alley cat."

"Oh, I get it," Stacey said in the same, deadly calm tone. "You haven't come here to help me. You've come to give me a lecture. Well, don't bother, because I'm not interested."

"That hadn't been my intention, but… Look," Dani said with an air of great reasonableness. "You're a grown woman. You should have known better. Frannie might be little, but she can hear perfectly well. And what you said was very hurtful."

"There's no excuse for bad behavior."

"Exactly."

The change in Stacey's expression was as sharp as a slap. A thin current of antagonism seemed to eddy between them. "Ah. I see what this is all about," she said in a tone of pure venom. "You think you can get in Rafe's bed by playing protector to his kid? I'll tell you the same thing I told Nina. He's not here for the long haul, and you'd be just another notch on his bedpost by summer."

"I'm not trying to be anything to Rafe—"

"Of course you are. You wouldn't be a woman if you didn't think he was worth going after. He's one hell of an attractive man."

Communication was dead between them. No point in pretending otherwise. "Yes, he is," Dani acknowledged. "But I'm not concerned about him. I'm concerned about his daughter. Frannie didn't need to hear your opinion of her father's morals. If you have any human decency at all, from now on you'll watch what you say around that little girl."

Stacey's face flushed vividly. Their gazes locked like crossed sabers. "Are you threatening me?"

"Of course not. I'm only promising you—if you hurt Frannie's feelings again, it won't be paint you'll have to deal with. It'll be me."

She didn't wait to see Stacey's reaction. She didn't have to. She knew the woman would be furious, and she didn't care a bit. Swinging around, Dani stalked out of the restroom, riding a rush of emotion she couldn't define.

The moment she stepped outside, she nearly collided with Rafe.

He stood leaning against the outside wall, arms crossed, his features unreadable.

"Oh," Dani said, stopping short. "Hi."

"Hi. Everything all right in there?"

She couldn't imagine how much he'd heard, if anything. The walls of the restroom were thick. But then, how loud had their voices been? She realized she was frowning, and she stopped. "Sure," she said. "Frannie spilled some paint. You might want to buy Stacey Merrick a new pair of shoes."

"Think she'll accept them from an alley cat like me?" he asked.

So much for wondering how much of that argument he'd heard. God, this was embarrassing.

"I was just—" She broke off, feeling ill at ease and oddly vulnerable. Her anger had dissipated like summer storm clouds, and yet she felt ensnared by Rafe's gaze; she couldn't look away. "I guess you heard everything in there."

"Just about."

"I know it's none of my business really…."

"That didn't seem to stop you."

"I wasn't trying to defend you or run interference. I just really hate it when…"

Uncertain what there was to defend herself about, she looked away. Back at the gazebo, Addy was passing out sodas to the others with Frannie's help. The little girl looked so small and defenseless. How could Stacey and Nina have been so thoughtless?

"Dani." She turned back to face Rafe and felt his hand on her hair. Unhurriedly he tucked a stray lock behind her ear. The fact that the contact was feather-light did not stop it from sending a shiver through her. "Haven't you learned yet how extraordinarily cruel people can be?"

"That doesn't mean you have to accept it."

"No, but sometimes the best way to fight it is to show them that nothing they say or do bothers you in the least."

"Are you going to tell me I was wrong to say anything?"

"No," he said in a perfectly serious tone. "Not this time. In fact, I'm going to tell you that if anyone tries to hurt my daughter, you have my permission to take them apart with your bare hands. Just do me one favor."

"What's that?"

"Next time, come and get me. I'll help you."

SINCE THE THREE Bs WAS only two blocks off Broken Yoke's town square, Rafe and Frannie walked home. The day had been long and tiring, but productive. He still didn't see the sense in making the focus of the festival the Accordion Man, but why continue to fight the whole town? Especially when he wanted to call this place home.

And maybe, just maybe, they were right. Maybe it *could* be shaped into a profitable venture. Everyone certainly seemed determined to give it their best shot. Well, everyone except Stacey Merrick, who'd stormed out of the park barefoot, swearing that she wouldn't have anything further to do with any of it.

Rafe didn't think anyone particularly mourned the loss.

He glanced down at Frannie, who was dragging her feet beside him as though she had a date with an executioner. He'd just explained to her what kind of punishment she could expect for that little prank with the paint.

"So you understand that you have to pay for Mrs. Merrick's new shoes?" Rafe confirmed once more.

"I guess," the child said with a lackluster shrug. "How much?"

Rafe pretended to give that some thought. "Five dollars ought to cover it."

Frannie jerked to a halt and scowled up at him. "Five dollars! That's almost all I have in my piggy bank!"

"Sorry. That's the deal."

Rafe watched his daughter's jaw work as she chewed the inside of her cheek. Her hand in his was warm and so small. It moved fretfully, like a captured butterfly. "Okay," she said at last.

They started down the sidewalk again. He had to admit to feeling somewhat relieved she'd conceded with no more argument. Frankly, he was flying blind here.

But what was so strange about that? When he back-tracked in his mind over the past few weeks—anytime he'd been in Dani Bridgeton's company—he'd been in the same fix, hadn't he? Flying blind.

Whatever was developing between them had him firmly by the throat. He couldn't explain it. He wasn't sure he even understood it. He just knew it was more than desire. He was drawn to her in ways that had nothing to do with how much he longed to take her to bed. Drawn to her stubborn determination. Drawn to her quick mind and honest courage. Drawn to the passionate empathy she could show toward one confused little girl.

"Why did you buy those stupid trees?" Frannie asked, cutting into Rafe's thoughts.

Before leaving this afternoon, he had spoken to the guy in charge of the new, improved landscaping at the park. Two small cottonwood trees, balled and burlapped, were all that had remained in the back of the nursery truck. Rafe had purchased them rather than see them returned to the store. He didn't have much of a green thumb, but Frannie would need *someplace* agreeable to play. A place with grass and shade and soft breezes.

"Because they'll look nice planted in the backyard," he told the girl.

Frannie scrunched up her nose. "They didn't look so good. They might die."

"They might. But we'll give them lots of water and plant food, so they might take root instead."

"They're awful small."

"They are right now. But just think how strong they'll be when they get as high as the roof. And in the fall they'll turn yellow like lemon drops. That will be pretty, don't you think?"

Frannie stopped and stared up at him. She looked very skeptical. "That will take a long time."

Damn it! What was wrong with her? Frannie had the most pessimistic, gloom-and-doom attitude of anyone he'd ever met. Even his father seemed like a cockeyed optimist compared to this kid.

He thought about this afternoon's incident between

Stacey and Frannie. He'd heard enough outside the restroom to put the pieces together, and suddenly he knew what had gotten his daughter so riled up.

Fear. Pure and simple.

Whether her father was considered an "alley cat" or not probably hadn't made one bit of difference to her. Maybe she didn't even know what that term meant. But she knew what it felt like to be abandoned by a parent. Left with strangers. And listening to that big-mouthed bitch Stacey Merrick talk about his habit of never staying in one place too long had probably scared the hell out of her.

He knelt in front of Frannie and brought his hands to either side of her head so she couldn't look away from him. Her eyes were huge, but she didn't blink. "You're right," he said. "It will take a long time for those trees to grow. But we have the time, Frannie. You and I are going to live here. Together. The two of us can keep track of how big they grow."

A trailing uneasiness crossed her features, then dissolved. There was something hopeful in her eyes. The mere hint of it was enough to make Rafe believe he was reaching her.

He brushed her dark bangs out of her face. "I mean it, Frannie. You're stuck with me. We're going to be together for a long, long time. Do you understand?"

He could see her thinking it over, trying on the idea. After a long moment, she gave him a thoughtful nod. "Maybe we can take pictures of them sometimes."

"That's a great idea!" Rafe said, pleased that she seemed willing to be swayed. "We'll take pictures as they grow. You and me, standing in front of them every year. Maybe in the fall, when they turn yellow."

They headed down the sidewalk once more.

Rafe couldn't honestly say that he breathed a sigh of relief. Who knew how long it would take to give this child a sense of security again? But maybe, like the cottonwood trees, the idea had been planted. You dropped seeds into the soil and took a chance that they would take root. It had to be something like that with kids, didn't it?

All he could do was hope.

CHAPTER TWELVE

"IT'S A CRUMMY ASSIGNMENT," Dani said as she closed Gary's office door behind her.

Gary turned from the sixteenth-floor window that overlooked Denver's Cherry Creek Park. He dropped into the chair behind his desk and motioned for Dani to take the one in front of it. "Of course it is," her boss admitted. "But it got you back here, didn't it? I know it's only three days, but—"

"Covering the school-board meetings is a rookie's beat."

"Wait a minute!" His head gave that cockatoo tilt he liked to use to show confusion. "I thought you'd kiss my feet for this assignment, even if it's only temporary. Don't tell me you've grown fond of covering the boondocks?"

"No." Of course that wasn't it, Dani thought with an inward scowl. She'd come back to Denver the day before yesterday at Gary's request, and she couldn't have been happier to leave Broken Yoke behind. "I'm delighted to be back. But sitting in on school-board meetings, trying to find my lead in that boring mess of red tape they call conducting business…" She grimaced. "Do you know I almost fell asleep in yesterday's session?"

"You prefer the company of those yahoos in Broken Yoke?"

"Don't call them that," she said with a frown. "There are a few eccentrics, a few bad eggs, but mostly they're nice people. And they're more interesting. At least when you go to a town meeting up there, you can pretty much count on somebody getting ticked off and threatening to punch someone's lights out."

Gary looked so shocked that his mouth dropped open. "Oh, my God. This is like *Invasion of the Body Snatchers*. You're one of them now!"

Dani crossed her arms and gave him a hard look. "No, I'm not *one* of them. I'm just doing the job you forced on me. I can't do decent human-interest stories if I don't get to know those people."

"Why do you sound so defensive?"

"I'm not defensive."

"Well, we needed to meet anyway," Gary said, evidently deciding to move on. "Let's talk about this Accordion Man of yours. Unless the dead guy turns out to be Jimmy Hoffa, tell me why a reader should care about him? What's our angle for advance coverage of this festival?"

They spent the next ten minutes discussing the possibilities, though many of the angles Dani came up with still relied heavily on finding out just who the Accordion Man was. It seemed to her that even Gary didn't show the appropriate amount of interest in finding out. Old news, he said. When she complained that it was still news, he got up, hitched his pants higher and claimed he had a meeting to go to.

As he removed his coat from behind his chair, Dani stood staring out the interior glass wall of his office. Most of the newsroom was visible from here. For such a long time, it had been the central drama of her life, a second home. A place where her days had often ended in capitulation to a plate of cheap nachos and a Diet Coke.

She could see Kirk, her old boyfriend, bent over his computer. She was unmoved by the sight of him. Could there really have been a time when she'd thought she'd won the boyfriend lottery?

In the far corner she spotted her desk. At least, it *used* to be her desk. Now her friend and fellow reporter Nancy Collier sat there, a pen twirling in her hand as she listened on the telephone.

As though she realized that she was being watched, Nancy turned and waved at Dani, who smiled and waved back. Gary came up beside her. "I had to find a place for Nance once she got back from maternity leave," he said, as though he owed her some explanation.

He didn't. Reporters never got the luxury of carving out a place of their own at the paper for long. Still, she'd thought it would be hard to see someone else sitting at her old desk. Surprisingly, it wasn't. "That's fine, Gary," she said, and meant it.

"Do you still miss it so much?" he asked kindly. "Being here?"

"I thought this is where I belonged." She shook her head. "This *is* where I belong."

"Is it?" When she gave him a confused look, he added, "When you come back, I want you to seriously consider changing the focus of your career."

"Why? Are you going to fire me?"

"No, of course not. You're a good investigative journalist. But you don't have as much of a killer instinct as you'd like to think you have. What you have is heart, and it shows in the stuff you've been sending me lately. You care about people and their lives. The unwed mother. The football coach who's kicked a drug addiction. Their stories matter to you. Can't you feel it inside?"

"I suppose I've come to find those stories more interesting than I ever thought I would," she acknowledged. "Even the strange ones."

"It's a gift, not a curse. Consider nurturing it." As though he'd said too much, Gary cleared his throat and suddenly looked all business. "Can I drop you off someplace?"

"No, I'll walk, thanks," Dani replied. "I want to stop by the medical examiner's office."

"To see where they are with your Accordion Man?"

"And maybe get them to bump the investigation up to a higher priority."

"Talk to Templeton. He owes me a favor."

They got on the elevator, and when the doors opened, they walked together through the lobby and out onto the street. The traffic was noisy, the sidewalk of downtown Denver crowded with people who seemed to be in too big a hurry. Compared to the scent of sweet pine and new earth she was used to in Broken Yoke, the air here felt heavy and thick with the infamous "brown cloud" of smog that sometimes settled over the city.

Gary gave her a peck on the cheek and then a quick hug. "Be a good girl, and don't get into any trouble." He started off down the street, but got no more than a few feet before he turned around.

"I nearly forgot," he called out to her. "Do you want to have dinner with me and Pauline tomorrow night?"

"I can't. I'll finish up with the school board tomorrow morning. As soon as Russ approves the story, I want to start for home."

"Home?" Gary said with a lopsided grin. "Since when did you start thinking of Broken Yoke that way?"

It was a question she had no answer for, even though she thought about it all the way back up the mountain the next day.

Rafe thought that if he heard another accordion wail out "Lady of Spain," there would be more than one dead man found in the Three Bs secret room.

The First Annual Accordion Man Festival arrived

on a Saturday that was blessedly sunny and warm. It was the kind of perfect spring day that Coloradoans loved, and they turned out in droves. He had to give Dani some of the credit for that. She'd done a bang-up job on the article about the Accordion Man. With very few hard facts on which to base it, her article had been intriguing, witty and chilling. Whether they were just curious, desperate for entertainment or genuinely interested, Rafe couldn't tell. But he had to concede one fact—everyone seemed in good spirits.

Mayor Wickham was beaming. The Festival Committee seemed giddy with excitement, which was not a particularly good look on its elderly members. Shirley Cauthen, in charge of festival finances, predicted a huge profit.

Somehow, in just two weeks' time, the town had pulled it all together. A small carnival-ride company had been hired. Area artists and craft vendors—most of them booked every weekend in summer—had successfully been encouraged to get a head start on the season. Favors were called in for tents, generators and printing. Rafe had even managed to wrangle a radio ad out of one of the local country stations. Downtown Broken Yoke sparkled like some sort of Disney movie set.

Silver balloons and red streamers were everywhere—the official colors of the festival. The air was redolent with the irresistible odor of sugared cinnamon and hot French fries from the food stands. The staccato slap of tap shoes, the tuning of various instruments and wind chimes from one of the craft booths created an interesting mix of sound.

And of course, you couldn't get away from the wheeze of the accordion. It was everywhere.

Since breakfast, Addy, Frannie and some little friend of hers from day care named Rhonda had been enthusiastically tracking down green rubber bands, pink paper plates and old gym socks for the scavenger hunt.

Rafe stayed at the Three Bs, giving tours of the secret room and fielding questions he had no real desire to answer. He tried to make sure things ran smoothly and that no tourists wandered into his private quarters.

Surprisingly, no one complained that the Accordion Man wasn't making a personal appearance. The dimly lit rooms of the Three Bs, the twists and turns of cobwebbed hallways, and a faint accompaniment of spooky music seemed to do the trick. Rafe thought rummaging through someone's attic would have provided more of a thrill, but people seemed intrigued by the sight of the Accordion Man's final resting place and a glimpse of the past, a peek into an actual 1880s bordello. How many people ever got the chance to do that? Mayor Wickham had argued. And think what the money was going to mean for Broken Yoke.

So Rafe shut up, kept the lines moving and tried not to grit his teeth every time someone asked if they could take his picture.

He certainly hadn't been in any hurry to get to the festival. He'd heard Addy promise to take the girls to the face-painting booth after the hunt, and he'd be damned if he was going to let anyone paint an accordion on his cheek.

Around noon, Rafe left Mayor Wickham to play tour guide and headed over to the food stands. He heard familiar laughter, turned the corner near the funnel-cake booth, and spotted Lightning River's contribution to this crazy celebration.

He knew that his mother and Aunt Sofia had set up a stand to sell lemon ricotta cake, jam tarts and Rose's specialty, choux pastries. He'd expected it to do a decent business—the smell alone would entice a person to check it out. But he was surprised to see so many people gathered around, especially teenage boys.

And then he saw why.

His two sisters-in-law, Kari and Leslie, were behind the counter as well. Selling kisses.

Rafe waited in line, and when he got to the counter, his mother clapped her hands together and greeted him as though she hadn't just seen him yesterday. *"Bella!* I have your favorite just waiting for you." She pointed toward a tray of fresh choux pastries. "What would you like? Chocolate or vanilla?"

"Chocolate."

"How many?"

"That depends. Do I have to pay for it?"

"Today, yes."

"Then I'll take one."

Rose scowled at him. "Don't be stingy. Buy several."

"Why? I'm planning to talk you out of the leftovers when all this is over."

She leaned across the counter and winked at him. "Under some of the choux we have placed a fake silver coin. If you find one, you can trade it in for a kiss."

Rafe raised one brow. "I'm not sure Nick or Matt would appreciate me lining up to get kisses from their wives."

"You've got that right," a voice said beside him, and Rafe turned to find his brother Matt grinning at him.

Rose shook her finger at Matt. "Stop behaving like a jealous baboon," she told him. She swung her attention back to Rafe. "And you, either buy more choux or get out of the way. We have work to do."

Both men chuckled and moved off, taking refuge under a shady cottonwood not far from the stand. Rafe dug into the pastry eagerly, savoring the rich custard filling and the sweet taste of powdered sugar on his tongue.

He realized Matt was watching him. "I'd offer to share this…" he told his brother as he licked crumbs off his finger. "…but I don't want to."

Matt laughed. "I completely understand."

Rafe swallowed another bite. "Thought you were working at the lodge today?"

"Pop's got the helm. He was having a fit about not being here until Mom promised that she wouldn't sell any pastries to Mayor Wickham."

"Why?"

"He's jealous. He's convinced the guy is trying to replace him."

Rafe polished off his pastry. It looked like he was out of luck. There was no silver coin at the bottom of his bowl.

Nick walked up to join them. He wore his bomber jacket, and Rafe knew that he was giving short rides in Lightning River's helicopters for anyone who had twenty dollars to spare. Not only would it raise money, but it was good advertising for the lodge.

"How's it going?" Nick asked, inclining his head toward Rose and Sofia's stand.

"Judge for yourself," Matt said, then grimaced as he motioned toward one side of the booth where Kari and Leslie were busy swapping coins for kisses. "I know the money's going for a good cause, but do they have to look like they *enjoy* it so much?"

"Spoken like a true newlywed," Nick said.

Matt made a low, displeased sound. "Can't help it. That's the fourth time that curly-headed kid has turned in a coin to Les. If he gets one more, I'm going to pay him to go find something else to do."

Rafe laughed as he tossed his empty bowl into a nearby trash can. Over the sweetly scented air, the sound of "Moon River" being murdered on an accordion wafted toward them. "Lord, I can't wait for all this to be over."

They watched Kari D'Angelo give a kiss to a young man with long hair and a banjo slung over his back.

Then she waved at Nick, pointed toward her watch and held up two fingers.

"Finally," Nick said. There was no mistaking the strained patience of his tone. "Lunch break. She's all mine for one hour."

Rafe gave Matt a sympathetic look. "Looks like Leslie's going to be the prime attraction. You gonna make it, big brother?"

Matt gave a philosophical shrug. "At least she's got reinforcements coming," he said, then pointed toward the opposite side of the booth.

Rafe glanced back at the stand. Dani Bridgeton was just picking up an apron.

For the space of a heartbeat he felt as though he couldn't breathe. He hadn't seen her in some time. He'd been busy with the Three Bs and getting Frannie settled into their new home, and then publicizing the festival had eaten up a lot of his free time. He'd heard that Dani had been out of town for days on end, working, but that hadn't kept him from thinking about her.

He remembered the way her smile brought dimples to each corner of her mouth.

He dreamed about the way her hair could sift over her shoulder like silk when she turned her head.

He thought of how she had been with Frannie that day in the park, the ferocious fire in her voice as he'd listened to her lecture Stacey Merrick. It was a strange feeling, strange but nice, to have someone defend his kid like that.

Oh, yeah, he thought about her. More than he liked to admit.

The truth was, he liked the way he felt when he was around her. Sure, there was a good amount of hormonal lust involved. But it was more than that. When he was with Dani he felt…relaxed. At ease. Totally himself. With her, he never felt the need to pretend to be someone other than he was.

He watched her reach behind her back to tie her apron. The movement sent her breasts upward, exposing the softly rounded swells over the edge of her blouse. This time when his mouth watered, it had nothing to do with the aroma of a dozen different fair foods.

He found himself reaching in his back pocket for his wallet. If anyone was going to kiss Dani, it was going to be him.

Beside him, Matt laughed and nudged Nick. "I told you. Pay up."

Nick sighed and handed Matt a twenty-dollar bill.

Rafe frowned, aware that some agreement had taken place between his brothers. "What's going on?"

Matt slipped the money into his pocket. "I bet Nick that you'd be over there buying kisses within ten minutes of seeing Dani Bridgeton behind the booth."

"I said twenty minutes," Nick complained. "You couldn't have hung on just a little bit longer, little brother?"

"He's gotten so predictable," Matt said. "He's like a lab rat, making all the right moves in the maze."

Rafe slipped his wallet back into place. Not for one minute did he intend to miss out on kissing Dani, but he'd be damned if he'd do it in front of these two idiots. They thought they had him all figured out. Well, maybe they did, but it rankled him to see them so smug about it.

He grimaced at his brothers. "I would think you two have better things to do than give me grief."

"Can't think of anything," Nick replied.

Shaking his head at them both, Rafe walked off. There was plenty of time. And neither Nick nor Matt could hang around his mother's food booth forever.

BY THE AFTERNOON, Dani was convinced that flipping burgers during college had been a cinch compared to working Rose D'Angelo's booth at the Accordion Man Festival. Kari's idea of trading coins for kisses had been in the hopes of boosting sales, but the extra incentive was hardly needed. The mouthwatering smells of Rose's desserts were enough to create a lineup of eager customers.

Now Dani, who had agreed to work at the booth when Kari had called last night, was officially done.

She was kissed out.

"I'm exhausted," she told Kari as she ran a finger lightly over her lips. They felt tender. "I never would have guessed Broken Yoke had so many horny teenaged boys."

"We're almost finished," Kari replied as she slipped

a piece of lemon ricotta cake onto a plate. "Why don't you go home?"

She wished she could. But she'd seldom left the booth the entire day, and if she intended to do a piece for the paper, she needed to see more of the festival than just the inside of a food stand.

Knowing that she couldn't give in to tired feet and an aching back, Dani tugged her apron over her head. She said goodbye to the D'Angelo women, then headed off.

As she wove her way through the crowd, it seemed to her that the day was going well. People looked happy. Near one end of the park, there were squeals of delight from children on the carnival rides. A juggler entertaining a small crowd at the gazebo was getting lots of laughs. And near the bandstand, a young woman who had won the costume contest had just received a standing ovation.

She wondered if Rafe had gone back to the Three Bs. She hadn't seen much of him today. She had seen him buy pastries earlier, but never from her, and as busy as the booth had been, she probably wouldn't have had much time to talk, anyway.

After returning from Denver, she'd made the rounds of the I-70 corridor, stopping by all the small towns in the area that her bureau covered. According to Cissy, Rafe hadn't come by the office while she'd been gone and there had been no messages left for her. It surprised her how disappointed she was by his lack of interest, but she told herself that it wasn't that. He had things to do to publicize the festival, of course.

And then, as though she had willed him into existence, she saw him. He was seated at one of the picnic tables in the park. And he wasn't alone.

Rumor had it that he was still seeing Heather Somebody. Dani had not had the courage to ask his family if that gossip was true. But it must be, because here they were, in close conversation. Rafe's dark head and her blond one made a strong contrast as they bent to hear each other's words over the nearly deafening squall of dueling accordions.

He laughed at something the woman said, and Dani couldn't help the little catch in her breast. She hadn't forgotten what he looked like, but she'd forgotten the effect he could have on her senses.

She couldn't help watching, either. They seemed so right for one another. Two attractive people—strong, confident, poised. Together as though they'd been friends for years.

Rafe had a perfect right to chase after anyone he wanted, of course. But Dani felt annoyed all the same. Where was Frannie while he was making the moves on Blondie? The festival was crowded with families enjoying the day—fathers treating their children to games of chance and sticky clouds of cotton candy and giggling runs through the makeshift fun house. Didn't Rafe's daughter deserve to have fun, too?

Oh, why should it surprise her, really? Wasn't that

just like the man she'd known so long ago in Vegas? Only interested in what *he* wanted.

Determined to shelve any more speculation, Dani spent the next hour interviewing festival-goers, musicians—anyone who looked interesting. It was time well spent. There was nothing big enough to get in tomorrow's Sunday edition, but stories began to take shape in her mind for next week's Features section, mental toys to play with once this crazy weekend was over.

She was about to pack it in and walk back to her car when someone tapped her on the shoulder. It was Addy D'Angelo.

"Doing anything?" the young woman asked.

"Just about to head home."

"I was on my way to get Mom, but you'll do."

"For what?"

"Reinforcements," Addy said mysteriously. She ruffled her fingers. "Come with me." She turned and began walking away.

"Where are we going?"

"Help me convince Rafe to cooperate."

Dani almost came to a dead halt. She didn't particularly want to see Rafe again today. Especially if she discovered him arm in arm with his friend. But Addy was making a beeline toward the bandstand, weaving in and out of the crowd, and Dani couldn't get her to stop.

Rafe's sister finally came to a halt near one side of the raised platforms where half a dozen different events had taken place throughout the day. As Dani approached, she saw Frannie and another little girl with flame-red hair that no ponytail could control. Rafe stood beside his daughter, looking stubbornly determined. Blondie was nowhere in sight.

Uncertain just what family discussion she'd been dropped into the middle of, Dani smiled, then let her eyebrows soar in polite confusion. "What's going on?"

"*Please,* Daddy," Frannie begged, glaring up at her father with a desperate look.

Rafe shook his head. "Frannie, I hate whipped cream. I could never eat enough to win."

Catching Dani's uncertain glance, Addy pointed in the direction of the stage, where chairs were being drawn up behind a long table. "Frannie wants her father to enter the pie-eating contest," she explained. "I think it's a great idea."

Quickly Dani looked back at Rafe, who returned a narrow smile that clearly indicated she'd better side with him in this argument.

"What's the winner get?" Dani asked.

"A brand-new accordion."

Frannie danced about enthusiastically. "I could take lessons if you win."

Rafe frowned. "Then I definitely don't want to enter. There's absolutely no difference between an accordion and the way a cat sounds when you squeeze it."

"But I don't have a cat to squeeze."

Dani hid a smile at the child's logic. She couldn't say she blamed Rafe for wanting to beg off. Was there anything more embarrassing than going face first into a pie plate full of whipped cream? But for some reason, Frannie seemed very determined.

"It doesn't seem like such an outrageous request to me," Dani found herself saying.

"That's because you won't be the one up there," Rafe replied.

"*Pleassse,*" Frannie said again. "Just try."

They watched a few moments as numerous pies consisting of no more than whipped cream in a tin plate were set in front of all the chairs. The announcer was encouraging the crowd to come closer, get involved. Already a few men were heading up the wooden stairs, laughing as their families called encouragement.

The redheaded girl beside Frannie waved to one of the men, who grinned and gave her a thumbs-up sign. Then she turned back to Frannie. "It doesn't matter if your daddy tries or not," she crowed triumphantly. "My daddy's going to win."

Frannie's features darkened. "No, he's not, Rhonda Moseley. Don't you say that. Tell her, Daddy. You can eat all the pies in this whole stupid contest."

"No. I can't, Frannie."

"Yes, you can."

Dani cleared her throat to get their attention. "Even if you didn't win, I'll bet you could give most of them a good run for their money," she said.

Addy nodded encouragement. "What have you got to lose, Rafe?"

"My lunch," he replied grimly.

Frannie threw herself against her father's legs. "I know you can do it. Please, please, please. Show everybody, so they'll see."

"See what?" Rafe asked. "Frannie…"

With a heavy sigh, he lifted his head and locked eyes with Dani. The bewilderment was stamped on his face, and he clearly wanted rescuing.

Dani lifted her brows as if to say, *Sorry, you're on your own.* Really, what harm would it do to look a little foolish if it made Frannie happy?

But she suspected Rafe wasn't the kind of man to let himself be caught at a disadvantage. Not for anyone. Not even a five-year-old child who just happened to be his daughter.

And then, the frown lines across his forehead disappeared. He nodded slowly, even as he muttered a curse under his breath. "All right," he told them. "Let's do it. Let's get this over with."

There were cheers from Addy and Frannie, along with Dani's own startled gasp. Rafe yanked off his jacket and handed it to his sister. His mouth was no more than a thin, pale line of doubt.

"Go, Daddy!" Frannie squealed. She bounced in place as if she had springs on the bottom of her sneakers.

"Good luck," Dani called as he turned on his heel. Over his shoulder he gave them a look of such seriousness that he might have been a soldier going off to war. "If I end up puking my guts out, don't say I didn't warn you."

Then he disappeared into the crowd.

Dani stared after him in disbelief. She thought it was quite possible someone could have knocked her over with a feather.

Maybe Rafe wasn't completely hopeless as a father. Maybe he was learning after all.

CHAPTER THIRTEEN

ALL THE SOUNDS AND COLORS of the bright day were disappearing as the first official Accordion Man Festival drew to a close. Through sun-dappled shadows, the tired but seemingly happy crowd shuffled their way back to cars parked along Broken Yoke's streets. Overhead, the mountains raised sharp, purple peaks against a sunset that would soon turn scarlet.

Rafe had helped his family pack up the supplies from their mother's dessert booth. He'd pulled up stray signs, rounded up money from the vendors and loaded sound equipment into vans that would make the trip back to Denver. He was tired, ready to sit back and relax.

And he never wanted to hear the sound of an accordion ever again.

Seated behind the wheel of his truck, Rafe glared at the big, shiny box taking up most of his passenger seat. Inside was the flashiest, reddest accordion he had ever seen. A monster, heavy and ridiculous.

Flipping the latches, he lifted the lid and studied the instrument with narrowed eyes. Why couldn't first prize have been a piccolo? At least that wouldn't give him a hernia.

Of course, Frannie had been thrilled. He still wasn't sure why winning the pie-eating contest had been so important to her. But once Rafe had devoured enough plates full of whipped cream to choke a horse and been declared the winner, she'd run around them all like an insane chicken.

The accordion glowed brightly in the fading sunlight. Rafe reached out to press one of the keys along the keyboard.

"Don't think you're living with me for long, honey," he said. "You and I have a date with eBay."

He shook his head as he stroked his hand along the smooth, bloodred case. It would be a challenge to talk Frannie into giving up the damned thing, but no way was he going to live in the same house with an accordion. *No way.*

"Awww, a guy and his accordion," a nearby voice said. "What a touching sight."

Turning his head, Rafe discovered Dani at the driver's window. She was smiling at him, her arms folded over one another as she leaned against the door. Just that quick, he was keenly aware of her closeness.

"I suppose you think all this is very funny," he said.

She pretended to be momentarily contrite, then couldn't seem to help herself. Her mouth shaped into a broader smile, the one he'd developed a fondness for. "Actually…I do."

Rafe blew out a disgusted sigh. "I still can't believe I won. I wasn't even trying that hard."

"Oh, come on. It's not so bad."

He couldn't help showing his skepticism. "Do you know what they say when a ship full of accordions sinks to the bottom of the ocean?"

"What?"

"Well, it's a start."

She laughed. It was such a warm, natural sound that the impulse to reach out and capture the back of her head, to bring her lips to his, was like an ache inside him.

"You did the right thing," she said. "With Frannie, I mean."

"That's something I don't hear very often. I'll remind you of that when you get invited to Frannie's first recital."

Dani cast a quick glance around. "Where is she, by the way?"

"I've been ditched for a sleepover."

He realized that he sounded a little resentful, and truthfully, he was. He'd imagined that the two of them could go home and spend the evening together. But after his unexpected success at pie-eating, Frannie had soon been sidetracked by the invitation to spend the night with Rhonda. He was glad she'd started to make friends here at last, but oddly disappointed to discover he could be replaced so easily.

"She left her new accordion behind?" Dani asked, her tone incredulous.

"Out of consideration for Rhonda's family, I insisted on taking it home with me."

Vehicles were slowly making their way down the street to the interstate. Over the muted sounds of the day closing down, the hateful sound of car horns suddenly corrupted the air.

"I suppose I'd better get out of the way and leave the two of you alone," Dani said, straightening.

"Where's your car?" Rafe asked quickly.

"Down by your place."

"Then get in. I'll give you a ride."

For a moment, she looked as though she might refuse. As she studied him, trying to glean his intentions, he could almost hear her drawing all the wrong conclusions. He didn't have any ulterior motives, really. He just wanted to be with her for a little while.

When she finally nodded and moved around the front of the vehicle, Rafe wrestled the accordion into the backseat of the truck's cab. Dani slid in beside him.

Immediately, silence fell between them. Somehow the close confines brought their easy conversational mood to an awkward halt. Dani stared out the windshield, seemingly fascinated by a family of four weaving their way across the street.

Rafe found an opening in the tangle of traffic. By the time he parked behind Dani's vehicle, several minutes had passed and they'd hardly spoken at all. This wasn't the way he'd envisioned their time together.

"Thanks for the ride," she said as he killed the truck's engine.

Her hand was on the door handle. Rafe realized he'd have to stop her now or lose his opportunity. He reached out and caught her arm. "Hold on a moment," he said. "Don't run off."

She looked at him, off guard, as though he'd startled her. Then her expression gradually became more curious than wary. She settled back in her seat.

He tried the effect of a smile to go with the spur-of-the-moment request that she stay a while. "I haven't seen much of you lately."

"I guess we've both been busy."

Her voice sounded a little stiff, but not unfriendly. He knew one topic that would draw her interest and didn't hesitate to use it. "How's your investigation going?" he asked. "Figured out how the Accordion Man got into that trunk yet?"

"No. But I have ten million pieces of useless information I can draw on if I ever want to write a book about Broken Yoke."

"Such as?"

"The Accordion Man Festival isn't the first time this town has sponsored a bizarre celebration," she told him. She seemed to relax a little. "Did you know it once held a bullfight to raise money?"

"No. When I lived here as a kid, I wasn't exactly interested in Broken Yoke history."

"Well, they had one. Just once. The two bulls were

so terrified that one of them plowed through a fence, ran off into the mountains and was never seen again. The other one refused to move and had to be pulled out of the arena."

Rafe laughed. "Not a financial success, I take it?"

Dani shook her head. "Just for the pickpockets and prostitutes."

Her eyes sparkled. Something inside Rafe was hungry for this, this holding of a chunk of time between them that was totally his own. He wanted more. He wanted all of it.

He let one hand dangle over the steering wheel, as if he were in no hurry. As if there were no place he wanted to go or needed to be. "What about his identity? Any news on that?"

"Not yet. I'm hitting nothing but dead ends. Still waiting to hear something from the ME, but I don't have much hope."

Rafe stroked his hand across his chest absently. His heart was racing, as if he'd been running. He took a deep breath, grimacing. "Don't worry," he told her. "After all that whipped cream I ate, you might have another dead body to write about soon. I'll probably have a heart attack right here in the truck."

She laughed. "Well, at least this time we won't have any trouble identifying the body. We can tell it's you by the whipped cream behind your ear. Hold still."

She reached out and flicked her finger against the back of his earlobe. When she withdrew her hand, a tiny dab of whipped cream sat on the tip of one finger. "Got it," she said triumphantly as she showed it to him.

Before she could draw her hand away, he caught her fingers in a light grip, brought the one with whipped cream up and slipped it into his mouth. "Mmmm… Delicious."

She gazed at him, her lips slightly parted in surprise, as full and lush as roses. "I…I thought you hated whipped cream."

"I think I've acquired a taste for it."

For just one moment, the meeting of their eyes was as close as a kiss. It took very little effort to coax her closer. A small tug, a light urging, and she was so near that he could feel her breath fan his cheeks. His gaze never left her face, and though her brows had gone as high as they could go, he saw no rejection of his touch in her features.

"You smell like cinnamon and chocolate," he said, brushing his hand against the side of her neck.

"Your mother's pastries. Good thing I didn't work the fish-and-chips stand, or I'd have every cat in town following me."

She tilted her head a little, allowing him greater access. When she swallowed hard, he felt the movement of her throat under his fingers.

"It was nice of you to help Mom out." He was blathering, they both knew that. But somehow, prolonging the moment when he would really take her mouth with his—a moment he sensed they both wanted—was an exquisite delay.

Dani sighed. "Don't tell her, but after today I may never be able to eat Italian pastries again."

"Me, either."

She frowned. "I didn't see you buying all that many."

He bent his head and allowed his breath to feather her skin, let his mouth plant kisses along the curving, sculptured contours of her throat, her collarbone. She jerked once, then any thought of rebellion died. "I had to be sneaky. In case my brothers were watching."

"What?"

"Never mind. Besides, you were busy kissing pimply-faced teenagers," he said against her flesh. "Why do you think I didn't want to enter that pie-eating contest? I'm still full of choux pastries. Fifteen, to be exact."

"Fifteen!" Dani said, straightening to catch his eyes. "Why would you eat so many?"

He grinned at her. "Why do you think? I wanted one of those coins."

"Oh." The look in her eyes told him that she knew what he was getting at. "And…did you succeed?"

"Not a one, damn it. All I have to show for it is one heck of a sugar high."

Her smile widened, like a bud opening to sun and rain. She slipped her hand into the front pocket of her blouse, and when she withdrew it, a shining, silver coin lay caught between two fingers. "My, my," she said with a teasing lilt to her voice. "Looks like this is your lucky day."

For a moment he was mesmerized with delight. "So it seems," he said at last.

Rafe gathered her close again. When he lowered his head to find her mouth, she turned her face slightly. "Careful. My lips are still tender from all that kissing."

"I'll be very gentle."

When he reached out to take the coin from her, she pulled her hand back and shook her head. "Remember. *One* coin only gets you *one* kiss."

"If I do it right, one is all I should need," he promised.

Stretched beyond the limits of his endurance, he placed his mouth against hers lightly, then ran his tongue across her bottom lip. When she opened for him, he made a rough sound of pleasure. A craving for more of her, all of her, roared into his head, blocking out everything else.

And then, something unbearably sharp sliced through his brain. It was a car horn. Someone honking. Someone close by, damn it.

Dani pulled away from him quickly and Rafe could do nothing but follow her lead. He turned his head to discover that Sheriff Bendix had pulled up in his patrol car and was motioning for Rafe to roll down his window. Rafe could have cheerfully killed the guy.

The sheriff had bent low across his seat so he could make eye contact. Pretending that they hadn't just been caught like two high-school kids necking on

Lightning Lake, Rafe put down his window to acknowledge Bendix with a short nod.

"Hey, you two," the sheriff called. "Did you enjoy the festival?"

Oh God, Rafe thought. *I really am going to kill him.* Beside him, he could sense Dani straightening her blouse, swiping hair away from her face.

"It was…interesting," Rafe said in the best imitation of friendly chitchat he could manage at the moment. "How about you, Sheriff?"

"Just great. Pretty successful, I'd say. Of course, it might end up being our one and only Accordion Man Festival."

"Why is that?"

"I got the ME's report back from Denver."

Dani slipped closer to Rafe and ducked low so she could see the sheriff. "What did it say?" she asked, and Rafe could hear the excited anticipation in her voice.

Bendix looked eager to deliver his news, like a kid on Christmas morning. "He got his skull crushed in by that accordion, all right. But here's the kicker. The things in that room might be antiques from the 1880s, but not our dead guy. He was put there back in *Myrtle* Culpepper's time, not Ida Mae's."

"So he was put in that trunk…in the 1950s?" Dani asked.

"Yep. Looks like it. Know what else that means?"

She nodded. "Whoever killed him could possibly still be alive."

DANI STOOD IN THE MIDDLE of the Three Bs' secret room and shook her head for the third time. "I still can't believe the body is from the fifties," she told Rafe. "This changes everything."

"Not really." From across the room, where he was giving a silver-headed walking stick a closer look, Rafe shrugged. She'd asked to see the Accordion Man's final resting place once more, and he'd complied, but he didn't seem nearly as stunned by the sheriff's news as she was. "So the murder happened around fifty years ago instead of over a hundred. It's still a pretty old crime. The person who did it could be long dead by now."

"Yes, but what if they aren't?" Dani asked, her mind churning with possibilities. "There could be a murderer roaming the streets of Broken Yoke right now."

"There isn't."

"How do you know?"

"Because after today, every single person in this town is too tired to be out roaming anywhere." He replaced the walking stick in the elephant-leg stand with the others and gave her an amused look. "Except maybe Stacey Merrick."

"Will you please take this seriously?"

"Look, as far as I know, there haven't been a bunch of murders in Broken Yoke over the years," he replied. His light, affable tone sounded completely impervious to hostility. "We're probably not dealing with a serial killer."

"Okay, so he's not roaming the streets. He could

have moved away. Or be in jail already, for some other crime."

"Possibly."

Folding her arms, Dani skewered him with a sharp look. "Don't you want to see the Accordion Man get justice?"

"Not tonight, I don't." He gave her an effortless, winning smile. "Tonight, I just want to relax."

"I want to solve this mystery."

He sighed heavily, then motioned toward the door. "Then come on, Inspector Clouseau. Let's talk it out over a glass of wine."

He led the way back through the somber, gaping hole he'd originally made into the brick room. She expected him to suggest they go to the Silver Saddle for a drink. But instead of leading her down the set of steep stairs where today's visitors had entered, he took her in the opposite direction, down a long, gloomy corridor lined with doors. Dani noticed that there were small rectangles cut into the wood about head-high. Each rectangle had a knob, so that it could be opened.

"Are those peepholes?" Dani asked.

"Yep," Rafe said without glancing back at her. "All good bordellos need peepholes into the bedrooms. That way the madam can make sure no one is mistreating her girls or running out without paying."

She wondered how it was that he knew so much about bordellos, but decided not to ask. Before long, they had reached a door at the other end of the corridor, and Rafe inserted a key.

"My place," he said as he swung the door wide.

In another moment, he flipped on a lamp and the room glowed with mellow light.

Dani blinked a couple of times and looked around. So this was Rafe's home, the renovated west side of the Three Bs. She knew he'd moved in recently, but he wasn't exactly the kind of guy to throw a house-warming party.

She was delighted to see that much of the Victorian architecture had been retained. There was a lovely cherrywood staircase off to one side. It led up to a landing where a stained glass interpretation of the Colorado mountains probably provided a rainbow of color during the daytime. Although the paint looked new, the original ornamental wood paneling beneath the chair rails had been kept throughout. In what was designated as the living room, a massive marble-and-English-tile fireplace had been made a focal point.

The place was beautiful. It was also nearly empty.

It was more sparse than any bachelor pad Dani had ever seen. Two love seats sat facing one another, and a thick area rug between them covered the original oak flooring. A television, a stereo and a bookcase completed the living space.

"Make yourself comfortable," Rafe said. "Would you like white or red?"

"White is fine."

While Rafe went off to the kitchen, she wandered a bit. She noticed that his tastes in music ran toward Nat King Cole and Sinatra, that he liked mysteries and autobiographies, and that he didn't have a single picture of his family sitting out anywhere. Not even Frannie.

In one corner sat five or six cardboard boxes, arranged as some sort of make-believe playhouse. They had colored drawings all over them, mostly polka dots. Inside there were blankets and a child's tea service set out as though all the guests had just left. Frannie's domain, no doubt.

She heard Rafe come back into the room and turned. "I like what you've done with the place," she teased as he handed her a wineglass. "I should have known you'd be a minimalist."

"Very funny." He glanced around as though seeing the room for the first time. "Doesn't look like much, does it? I moved us in pretty quickly because I thought Frannie needed a place to call her own as soon as possible. No sense imposing on my family any more than I have to."

"Because of your unpleasant relationship with your father?"

"No, not at all," he replied with a frown. "I *want* Frannie to know both her grandparents as much as possible. And whatever differences Pop and I have, we know better than to air them in front of a child who's already struggling with adapting to changes in her life."

"You sound very sensible. Very...responsible."

He grinned. "Very un-Oz-like, you mean?"

"Yes," she admitted.

"I've had lots of good advice lately."

She wasn't sure what he meant by that. Advice from whom? His family?

Dani took a sip of her wine and inclined her chin toward the cardboard house. "Does she sleep in there?"

"Upstairs, down the hall from me. I let her pick out her own furniture, so I assure you, her room looks like any little girl's."

Settling on one of the sofas, Dani watched as he pushed aside what looked like a mass of bright red yarn, then sank into the couch opposite her. He set the wine bottle at his feet, and for a little while they drank in silence. She wasn't much of a wine connoisseur, but the drink was cool and fruity and pleasant on the tongue.

"So what's your next step, Inspector?" Rafe asked as he swirled the wine in his glass.

Dani shrugged. "I suppose I'll have to go over my notes again. Only this time I'll focus on the right time period. I should talk to anyone who lived here during the fifties." She gave Rafe a speculative glance. "How many old-timers do you think are left in town from those days?"

"I haven't been back long enough to know."

"I'm sure Sheriff Bendix is going to want to question them as well. But I'd like to get a head start if I can."

For the next half hour, the two of them compiled a list of all the citizens in Broken Yoke who might have some knowledge of the Three Bs during the 1950s. Rafe's father made the list since he'd once played with the band there.

By the time Dani put her notebook back in her purse, a second bottle of wine had been opened and drained. She felt mellow enough to take the conversation in a whole different direction, to try to find out answers to questions that had been plaguing her for weeks.

"Mind if I ask you how you ended up being a daddy? Back in Vegas I got the distinct impression that kids would never be in your game plan."

He didn't seem offended by the inquiry. He stared into the golden liquid in his glass, as though it held some secret knowledge he wanted to decipher. "They weren't. But sometimes you're overtaken by events."

"I suppose that happens to all of us once in a while."

His eyes met hers. "Not to me. At least, it never used to. I've often made foolish choices, but I'd never been careless."

He spent a few minutes telling her about the circumstances that had led to him meeting Ellen Stanton again last December, and how one night of moonlight and passion had created that beautiful child.

What kind of woman was Frannie's mother? Probably a beauty. But had the attraction simply been physical? She had to know, and there was enough wine floating in her system to make it possible for her to ask.

"What attracted you to Frannie's mother?" The

words popped out of Dani's mouth. "Besides the physical, I mean?"

He didn't hesitate or seemed surprised by the question. "Ellen was a lot like me. At least, the *old* me. A wanderer. Always wanting to know what was over the next hill. Slightly dangerous and wild. To tell the truth, I was amazed she raised Frannie as long as she did. I think she tried to be a good mother, but ultimately she wanted excitement and adventure more. And she found a rich man who could give it to her. With conditions."

"No children."

"Exactly."

"Poor Frannie," Dani said almost absently.

"I'll make it up to her," Rafe said in a quiet voice. After a long moment, his mouth drew up in a lopsided smile and he sighed. "Not a very interesting or unique story, I suppose. But now you know."

"So you weren't in love with Ellen."

"Honestly? It was years ago. When Ellen called me, it took me a minute to remember what she looked like."

Dani got up. She settled next to him, one leg tucked under her as she faced him sideways, one arm along the back of the couch. "You could have denied your responsibility to Frannie. But you didn't."

He conceded that with a grimace. "Maybe not. But, I have to admit, being a father is a lot harder than I ever expected."

"So you make a few wrong turns. Remember what they used to say in Vegas? You can't expect to win a jackpot unless you're willing to put a few quarters in the machine."

"That's easy for you to say. You haven't been treated to crying jags and temper tantrums and the silent treatment. If I was half as big a handful as Frannie, I must have given my father many a sleepless night." He laughed suddenly. "What am I saying? I *know* I was a royal pain in the butt."

She wondered how the relationship between Rafe and his father had spun so far out of control. From what she'd been able to read between the lines, both men had grudges to bear. She touched Rafe's forearm. "You and Frannie will find your rhythm eventually, and you and your father should learn the art of compromise. I think he loves you far more than you're willing to give him credit for."

As though that comment made him uncomfortable, Rafe shifted. "He has an odd way of showing it." He bent forward and lifted the empty wine bottle. "Shall I open another one?"

She shook her head. Any more and no telling what she'd say or do. "So what do you intend to do now? Once you get settled in here?"

"The rest of the building will go on the market as condos. After that, I intend to redevelop some of the downtown business district. Broken Yoke has potential, but the city planners have no vision. No motivation. It's been allowed to run amok. When I worked for Wendall Crews, I learned how to revitalize communities so that everybody wins. This town can come back. It can prosper instead of falling by the way-side."

"Can I ask a question?"

He grinned at her. "I don't think you've stopped asking questions since we came in here."

"Sorry. It's the journalist in me. But just one more."

"Shoot."

She scooped up the red yarn that sat on one end of the couch and held it up to him. "What *is* this? I've been looking at it for forty-five minutes now, trying to figure it out. Don't tell me you knit. It will blow all my illusions about you."

"You mean you still have some?" he asked with a raised brow. He took the yarn from her hand. "I borrowed this from Mom. It's supposed to be a Fiona wig. If you use your imagination."

"*Whose* wig?"

"Princess Fiona. Didn't you see *Shrek?*"

"The kid's movie about the green ogre? I missed that one."

"It's Frannie's favorite." He motioned over his shoulder toward the pile of cardboard boxes. "So last week we built his house, and she gets to play the kick-butt princess."

"And who do you play? Shrek?"

"No. The sidekick jackass."

"I shall refrain from making the obvious comment."

He tossed the nest of red yarn back on the couch. "Smart lady."

"I don't know much about kids, but trying to find a way to connect with Frannie on her level seems like a good idea to me. And here I thought you spent all your nights out, dating every woman in town."

"I see my reputation is intact. But there's really no point in having children, is there, if you're not going to be home long enough to be a father to them?" Rafe stood and stretched suddenly. "I think I've been humiliated enough for one day. If you're so interested in how I spend my free time, come with me. I have something to show you."

She couldn't help staring at him before he turned away. Who was this man? The play of light left his face partly in shadows, but what she could see was pure masculine strength. Broad shoulders. Granite jawline. A tough guy.

But he also seemed to be a man who had a softer side, a willingness to learn and grow. A person who took his responsibilities seriously. Both men—the man she'd known years ago, and the man she knew today—had one thing in common.

They confused her.

CHAPTER FOURTEEN

RAFE TOOK HER BACK to the side of the Three Bs still
under renovation. With the help of a single flashlight,
he led her down a twisting staircase, through a maze
of so many turns that Dani began to feel disoriented.
The aged house had an eerie way of swallowing sound
and the air seemed cooler. They had to be below street
level now.

Dani realized that goose bumps had risen along her
arms. "Where are we going?" she asked in a low voice.

Rafe looked back over his shoulder, a puzzled
frown marring his brow. "Why are you whispering?"

Feeling silly, she laughed. "I'm glad you're too
young to have killed the Accordion Man."

"What?"

"I'm beginning to feel like a murder victim being
led to her doom."

She saw the flash of his teeth as he smiled. "Patience," he told her.

Finally he came to a halt before a heavy wooden
door. With his hand on the ancient iron latch, he

turned toward her. "There's no electricity down here, so don't move around until I get the lanterns lit."

She nodded, not sure what to expect. She could feel her heart pounding in slow surges. Her eyes struggled to adjust to the gloom. She heard the rasp of a match as Rafe lit a kerosene lantern, then a second. The shadows bounced and leaped fitfully for a moment. Then the room began to take shape and substance.

"Forget what's in the secret room upstairs," Rafe said. "This is the Three Bs' real treasure."

She blinked a couple of times, and at first she could see nothing remarkable. It was a fair-sized room, cut into solid rock, completely devoid of decoration. The most remarkable thing about it was the air around her—moist and warm, slightly steamy.

And then she saw the reason for it.

A few steps away, a bubbling sunken pool of water sent mist into the air like ghostly streamers, a giant witch's cauldron that moved with mystery and light in the lantern's yellow glow. It was big enough to hold about six people sitting down.

Dani gasped in delight. "A hot spring!"

"You've seen one before?"

"The paper did an article last year on the geothermal caves at Idaho Springs."

She approached the lip of the spring, where stone steps had been chipped out of the rock. Slipping out of her sandals, she dipped her toes into the water. It was hot and soothing, and as much as she'd been on her feet all day, Dani couldn't resist a sigh of absolute pleasure.

"One hundred and six degrees," Rafe stated. "I've had the water tested. It's pure mineral."

"It's pure heaven," Dani corrected.

"I imagine the Arapahos in the area thought so, too, when they discovered it. Once Ida Mae Culpepper bought the land and built the Three Bs over it, you can bet she made a fortune off the miners."

"How did you come across it?"

"As a teenager, the place fascinated me. It was boarded up, but I broke in to explore and have somewhere private I could sneak off to. Eventually I found the spring."

She turned back to look at him. "What are you going to do about it now? Keep it for yourself? Or make it part of your condo complex?"

"I haven't decided yet."

Carefully Dani stepped around the edge of the pool. The stone was worn smooth from time, and she could imagine how many people in the past had stood in this very spot, breathing in the spring's healing vapors before they plunged into the water. She gazed into the swirling, dark surface, wondering if it was true what the Native Americans said about places like this—that they were magic, a refuge for gods and spirits.

"Go ahead," Rafe said, and she realized he had come up behind her. "You know you want to."

She didn't need more coaxing than that. She had

worn shorts today, but they weren't her best pair, and besides, what harm could the water do them? Carefully Dani lowered herself to one of the wet stone copings, letting her bare legs slip over the side into the pool.

"Can you touch bottom?" she asked.

"There's a rocky ledge about a foot below the surface, then you hit a gravel bed. The water comes up to about your shoulders. As a natural hot tub, it's just about perfect."

She nodded agreement. The hot water, its content probably filled with iron, magnesium, calcium and half a dozen more different minerals that were good for you, beat against her legs with massaging strength. Oh, it was wonderful!

"Do you know how many resorts in these mountains would kill to have a geothermal hot spring on their property?" she asked. She closed her eyes in contentment. "Skiers go nuts trying to soak away the soreness after a day on the slopes."

"I'm tempted to keep it all to myself," Rafe said. When Dani opened her eyes, she discovered that he was seated beside her, his pant legs rolled up to his knees, his legs dangling over the side next to hers. "For purely selfish reasons."

He was so near she could see the gleam of lantern light in his dark eyes. In the shadows, his cheekbones stood out like arrows, his jaw like an ancient, rugged carving. The air felt close and damp and intimate. She had the sudden, intense sensation that Rafe was about to touch her. For just a moment, Dani thought she should move away, stand up, but something like mutiny was brewing within her, and she remained as she was.

"Why keep it to yourself?" she asked, and some insane urge made her add, "so you can bring women down here for a little…fun?"

He wasn't put off. His mouth twisted into a teasing curve. "You told me you didn't listen to rumors."

"Some of them are too good to ignore."

Dani closed her eyes again and rolled her head. She wished the hot, bubbling water that felt so soothing on her legs could work its magic on her shoulders. They ached from today's workout.

And then, as though he'd read her mind, she felt Rafe's hands descend on them. Something inside her turned over at his touch, but she kept still. She heard herself make a soft, lost sound low in her throat because his massaging fingers felt so good. So good.

"Did you really bring girls down here in the old days?" she asked.

"I'm afraid I took full advantage of the circumstances. Back then, the Three Bs was supposed to be haunted, too. My dates were shivering with excitement."

"So you got to play the big, brave protector." She heard him murmur agreement. Opening her eyes, Dani turned her head to look at him. "And do you bring women down here now?"

"Danielle." He gave her a sexy, sweet half smile. "You ask too many questions."

"That's just the sort of thing I'd expect you to say."

"Then I haven't disappointed you." He stopped kneading her shoulders, and for just a few moments, they simply stared at one another. Then Rafe asked gently, "Do you want to go back upstairs now?"

She felt passion rising powerfully from deep within her, and there was something hot bubbling in his gaze, too. "No," she replied, a mere whisper.

He stroked her hair, a reassuring gesture, as though he knew her thoughts. "Then what *do* you want, Dani?"

"This is so…" She struggled with her voice, pretended to find interest in the cave-like walls around her, then turned back to him. "I think—"

He brushed his hand against her lips. "Stop thinking. Just tell me."

"I'm not sure I can."

"Then let me see if I can guess."

Slowly he turned her toward him. He slid the fingers of one hand into her hair at a spot where it cascaded behind her ear. Tilting forward, he fitted his mouth against hers in a sweet, easy kiss that made her sigh. Then fresh excitement wove through her as he touched the tip of his tongue to hers, and she reciprocated.

He kissed her until she was beyond reason—playful, sultry, gentle kisses—layering sensation upon sensation so quickly that Dani couldn't analyze or isolate what was making her feel so good. She only knew that she wanted this. She wanted it now. And she wanted it never to end.

He brought his hands to her shoulders once more, then pulled her T-shirt over her head and tossed it aside. She looked back at him steadily as he fingered the lacy edge of her bra, her chin angled almost fearlessly upward. Lazily, he hooked his fingers under the front clasp. In another moment, the bra had joined her T-shirt on the stone floor. Everywhere flesh met flesh, Dani tingled.

He let his gaze wander over her bared breasts, lingering, arousing moments that made a great undissolvable lump wedge in her diaphragm. Cupping one hand, he bent forward and scooped water from the spring. He tipped it against her breast, so that it trickled down to the hem of her shorts in hot, tickling rivers.

As sensually exciting as that was, it was nothing compared to the feel of Rafe's mouth as he bent to drink the water from her flesh. With a sure, tender touch he poured water on one breast, then the other. The lovely, wet glide of his tongue across her nipples made her gasp and arch forward; the sudden ache in her lower body demanded appeasement. It was more than she could bear. Inside, her bones were melting.

"Dani," Rafe spoke in a gruff whisper. "Do you know how beautiful you are?"

She couldn't respond. She was trembling, pressed against him with champagne bubbles of anticipation chasing through her veins. Every touch from Rafe brought the promise of gifts to come, and she welcomed them. She wanted to be closer. She wanted to feel more. Life was full of one-time offers, like great sex. It had to be seized on the spot, didn't it?

Through the pleasure spiraling through her, she sensed his growing urgency. He breathed a heavy sigh of satisfaction against her ear. "You don't know…" he said in a soft whisper of sound. "You don't know how many times I've dreamed of this."

She frowned, hearing those words reverberate inside her.

I've dreamed of this…. I've dreamed of this…. I've dreamed of this….

She tried to corner a wisp of memory. She'd heard those words before, hadn't she? But where? The knowledge veered away, turned back, then swooped in to take permanent hold. That terrible night at Native Sun, when he had saved her from disaster. Or had he?

A gust of memory blew cold against her fevered blood, and she stiffened. Passion faded like a dream in the morning. "Rafe, stop."

She pushed against him, and he lifted his head, frowning slightly. "What?"

"Let me go. I want to go back upstairs."

"No, you don't."

She willed iron into her soul. "I do," she said, lifting her chin. "I want to go home."

"Dani…" He shook his head. His voice was husky, uneven. "You don't have to be afraid."

"I'm not afraid. I just want you to let me go."

"What is it?" he asked gently, touching the side of

her face. "Tell me why we shouldn't do this when it's what you want? What we *both* want."

She turned her head away. Inside she felt filled with helpless misery because he was right. She *did* want this. She did. All these weeks she'd only been fooling herself....

No! It was impossible. The moment he had reentered her life, she had vowed to be strong. She had vowed to resist him. How could she be in danger of losing her heart to this man? No matter who he was trying so hard to be these days, he was still Oz. And what he'd done to her all those years ago was unforgivable.

She felt strangled. Weighed down. She pushed against Rafe, and thankfully he sank back away from her. "This *isn't* what I want," she told him in a voice she hardly recognized as her own. "Not now. And not six years ago."

"What are you talking about?"

She reached for her T-shirt and slipped it over her head, then wadded her bra in her hand. "I remember, Rafe. Not very much, but enough. I remember waking up naked with you in the bed. I remember you grinning down at me and saying the same thing you said just now. How you've dreamed of this. Don't you remember saying it?"

He blinked hard. "That was a long time ago. I don't remember what I said to you that night."

"No, I guess you wouldn't want to remember it, would you?" she said wearily. "It can't be very complimentary to your ego. Of all the women you'd slept with back then, I was the only one who had to be drugged out of her head before she'd have sex."

He stared at her a long moment, as if stunned. She wondered how angry her words had made him and found her answer in the line of his clenched jaw. "I didn't drug you," he snapped out. "I *saved* your butt from two lowlifes who wanted to pass you around like a ten-dollar whore."

"And I would have thanked you for that if you'd stuck around long enough. But you didn't." She wouldn't let him paint his own pretty picture of what had happened. "You didn't because you knew that in the end you were no better than they were. You saw your opportunity, and you took it. Because I let you." She bit her lip, trying to calm her breathing. "Maybe you regret it now. I'd like to believe you do. But that doesn't change the fact that you took advantage of the situation. Of me."

He moved so quickly that Dani flinched. One moment, he was seated beside her. The next, he was standing over her, water running down his legs to pool at his feet. He scowled so darkly that a shiver went up her spine. "Hold on, princess," he said. His voice was raw. "I don't know where you got this idea—"

Unwilling to feel at a disadvantage, Dani stood as well. "When I woke up the next morning, you were gone. I had bruises on my upper arms. As though I'd been held down against my will. Did you do that?"

"Yes, but—"

"You did. I know I must have brought some of it on myself, that I must have encouraged you because of the drugs in my system. But you had to know what was wrong with me. That didn't give you the right to—"

She couldn't complete the accusation. From the anger that flared in his eyes, she knew she didn't have to.

Silently, she studied the flame from one of the lanterns, seeking some small focus. The warm, damp air felt thick with tension. Finally, she raised her eyes to his again. "I know you're trying to change, Rafe. You're different than you were back then. And I'll admit, I'm…very attracted to that person. But I'm not sure I'll ever be able to forget who you were. Somewhere deep inside, you're still Oz. And that's not someone I can ever trust." She straightened. "So I want to go home now."

She felt numb. Ragged. Exhausted. A feeling of loss engulfed her because whatever foolish dreams she'd envisioned for the two of them had disappeared into empty air.

As for Rafe, his expression was carefully washed of emotion. Finally, he shook his head and gave a short, humorless laugh. "As an investigative reporter, I would think you'd make sure of your facts before you make an accusation. That isn't exactly the way it went down, and I think it's time we hashed this out once and for all."

"There's nothing more to say."

"The hell there isn't. Let's go upstairs. We can talk this out."

She scooped up her shoes and headed for the door as though in agreement. Dani wanted to go upstairs all right, but she had no intention of letting him persuade her over another bottle of wine and the brand of sweet talk he'd always been so well known for.

Rafe fell in behind her. At the top of the twisting flight of stairs, Dani was saved from having to say anything when she heard his cell phone chirp. She stopped on the dark landing while Rafe answered.

"Is there a problem with Frannie?" Rafe asked quickly, and Dani realized that it was Rhonda Moseley's mother on the other end. A few moments later, he added, "No, you're not disturbing me. Put her on."

Dani listened to Rafe talk to his daughter. His voice had changed. No longer hard and angry, but typically paternal.

"So why can't you sleep, sweetheart?" A pause as Frannie evidently answered. "Which one's Petey? Oh, yeah, the polka-dotted elephant. I should have remembered. Yes, I can bring it over. Hold on a second," Rafe said, then placed his hand over the phone. "Dani, wait…."

She shook her head. "I can find my own way out," she told him. And kept going without looking back.

THE NEXT EVENING, Dani closed up the office and headed for the Sun Dial where she could grab a late dinner. Like her mother, she wasn't much of a cook, and she enjoyed the food at the café.

Truthfully, she also liked the way Jeannine, the head waitress, had begun to recognize her preferences, the waves and smiles of the regular crowd that often greeted her when she showed up. Without a doubt, the more she came to know the people in this town, the sadder she would be when it came time to leave it.

The Sun Dial was busy tonight, and Jeannine motioned Dani toward her favorite table near the center of the room. After she ordered the special—meat loaf and homemade mashed potatoes—she took out her notepad and began doodling aimlessly. Reporters were consummate eavesdroppers, but the trick was not to look like you were blatantly listening.

Most of the conversations around her seemed to focus on the success of the festival. Mayor Wickham was holding court in one corner, loud and jovial, pompously claiming credit for having thought of the idea of a celebration centered around a dead man. Two men at the table next to her were quietly speculating who the Accordion Man might be, but overall, they seemed more interested in finding a way to capitalize on all the tourist contacts they'd made the day of the festival.

Jeannine brought her dinner. Dani ate slowly and tried to drum up some enthusiasm for reviewing the notes she'd made, but she couldn't seem to find much. Gradually the café thinned out, until Dani was the only customer left. The kitchen closed at ten-thirty and, fifteen minutes after that, Jeannine was counting the money in the register.

Realizing she was just wasting time and starting to feel sorry for herself, Dani took that as her cue to leave. She scooped up her bill and purse, and headed toward the front of the restaurant.

"Busy tonight," Jeannine said with a smile as she took Dani's money. "I'm sorry we didn't get a chance to talk."

"That's okay," Dani said. "We'll get the chance another time."

On a couple of occasions, Dani had struck up a conversation with the waitress because she seemed friendly and in-the-know about the town, but Dani had gradually learned that Jeannine had an interesting tale of her own to tell. She'd been a model in New York in her youth, but an accident had left her badly scarred and out of work. Dani had found the woman's history fascinating, and as she'd learned bit by bit, the makings of a great story had begun to take shape in her mind.

But would she get to explore it fully? Sooner or later, she'd be heading back to Denver, of course. And really, what was there to keep her in this town? Clean mountain air? Nice, interesting people? A man? That particular incentive seemed highly unlikely now.

Dani's car was still parked in front of the newspaper office. She walked along the deserted sidewalk, past darkened storefronts whose windows no longer beckoned visitors to come in and see what they had to offer. The streetlights were on, creating warm pools of comfort, but more than a few seemed to be out. Maybe some of that money the festival had brought it should be used to keep downtown lit properly, Dani thought, as she picked her way carefully down the uneven sidewalk.

Dani was almost to her car when she remembered she'd left the phone number of one of the musicians she'd met at the festival on her desk in the office. He'd told her that his grandfather had once played piano at the Three Bs, and had even dated Myrtle Culpepper. He could set up a meeting if she liked.

It was a slim lead, but Dani couldn't afford not to follow up on it. And though it was too late to call him now, she might be able to reach him first thing in the morning before she drove down to Denver to talk to the M.E.'s office.

She went up the four front steps of the office carefully since the light was so poor. Inserting the key into the lock, she twisted the bolt, then frowned. It took her less than a moment to realize that the door was *already* unlocked. Which should have been impossible, since she distinctly remembered locking it earlier.

Her hand was still on the knob, but she couldn't make herself push the door open. Cissy might have returned to the office for some reason, but why wouldn't Dani have seen the lights on from outside?

About the time she decided to retreat and find Sheriff Bendix, the door swung wide suddenly and someone grabbed her wrist. Stunned, she stumbled over the threshold as she was yanked into the dark reception area and then flung aside. She slammed against the front of Cissy's desk and landed on her knees, with one of the visitor chairs upended on top of her.

By the time she scrambled for her purse in the dark and found the can of mace she'd never once used, she realized that she was alone in the darkness. The door to the newspaper office was closed, and she hadn't seen who had grabbed her, had no sense of whether the intruder had been male or female, young or old. Nothing. Some reporter *she* was.

Dani's reaction was emotional and intense. Though the breath shuddered from her lungs and a chill raced up her spine, she was furious.

She stared down the sidewalk, her eyes trying to separate the shadows. At the corner, the trees leaned slightly sideways, like drunks sharing secrets, but nothing else moved. Nothing.

She heard a scraping sound—a shoe against cement?—and turned her head quickly in the direction of the narrow alley that ran between the newspaper office and the electronics store next door. She hurried to its entrance.

"Come out, you coward!"

Still nothing.

She took a step into the alley, then stopped. This was no big-city cave of unknown horrors. She'd taken the office trash out into this alley, sorted through deliveries here. But still…it was dark and looked a lot less friendly right now than it did in daylight.

Quickly Dani returned to her car. She got in, locked the doors and clutched the steering wheel. She was amazed to find that she was breathing heavily, as though she'd just run a marathon, and that her stomach felt tightened in knots. Really, she was more shaken than she'd thought.

Her anger grew with the thought that someone had broken into her office. Who, she couldn't guess. Why, she didn't know. Those were questions better left for another time, when she was feeling less undone.

She wished she could go to Rafe. He'd help her sort things out. But that was impossible now, things being the way they were between them.

There was only one thing to do. Dani started the car while simultaneously dialing Sheriff Bendix's office on her cell phone.

RAFE HAD PROMISED his brothers that he'd help them build a private deck off the back of the lodge, a retreat away from Lightning River's guests, so he and Frannie had come up for the day. He'd spent most of the afternoon pounding nails and cutting wood with Nick and Matt and even his father, who seemed determined to prove to them all that he could hold up his end of the job.

As for Frannie, she was in the kitchen with his mother and aunts. She was supposedly getting the D'Angelo initiation into cooking, but even from out here they'd all heard the tortured-cat squeals from the accordion she'd insisted on bringing.

Three days had passed since he'd been with Dani at the hot spring, and he was still so mad when he thought about it, he could hardly see straight.

You took advantage of the situation. Of me.

Hell, why hadn't Dani just spit it out? *You raped me* was what she'd wanted to say.

Damn her. He should have made her stay somehow. Made her sit down and listen to *him* for a change. Listen to the truth about what had happened.

Granted, since he'd left home at eighteen, he'd done a lot of terrible things. Things he wasn't very proud of, especially in those early years when he'd been so wild with anger against the world that people had melted out of his path after just one glance his way.

But he'd never taken a woman against her will. *Ever.*

He'd been so stunned by Dani's accusation, and then so furious, he could hardly speak. After Dani had left and he'd made the short trip to deliver Frannie's stuffed elephant, when he'd uncorked another bottle of wine and polished it off, he'd finally come to one decision. Let Danielle Bridgeton think what she liked. He would go about his business; she could go about hers. He no longer felt a thing for her, he told himself. They were *refinito,* as Pop would say.

He felt better already. Yes. As long as he didn't allow himself to think of that woman at all, he felt better.

There were plenty of other women out there, and

some of them had made it downright obvious they wouldn't mind reconnecting with him. It was true he had no gift for celibacy, but it didn't have to be Dani in his bed. So what if they didn't have that odd, sexy little swing to their voice that Dani had? Or a scent that was elusively floral, but all woman. Or hair that swept back from their temples like satin—

Damn it, stop!

Rafe frowned down at the nail he'd crookedly hammered into the railing. Her fault. All her fault. He was just physically exhausted from the mental attempt to shut himself out of his own mind.

He tapped the bent nail into a straighter position, then banged it down again. It sheared off and went flying into the grass. He cursed, dug out the shaft and looked around for a box of nails.

Matt was suddenly in front of him, holding out his own supply. "What's eating you today?" he asked. "Or should I say *who?*"

"Nothing's wrong with me today," Rafe replied. The words came out more defensively than he liked. He repositioned a nail into the wood and slammed it home.

"Really? Because you're attacking that board as if you expect it to try to get away from you. You hardly touched Mom's lasagna at lunch. The way you're going through nails, I figure something has you pissed off."

Matt had always played the psychologist in the family, trying to find answers for everything. It was annoying as hell. Rafe opened his mouth wide, pretending to yawn. "Keep talking. I always yawn when I'm interested."

"Yep. I'm betting it's a woman and I can guess which one. Wanna talk about it?"

"Go pedal your theories someplace else, Dr. Phil. I have work to do."

While Rafe ignored his brother and turned his attention back to the railing, Matt levered himself into one of the deck chairs they'd brought out earlier. "Hey, Nick! Pop!" he called. "Little brother here has woman problems."

Rafe's head jerked up and he tossed his hammer down. "What the hell, Matt? Mind your own business." He saw that Nick had stopped working now as well, and that his father was wiping sweat from his brow as he stared at him. "All of you," Rafe added. "Butt out."

Matt grimaced. "Sorry, but the family *is* our business. And whether you like it or not, that includes you."

"Is it Danielle Bridgeton?" Nick asked as he approached.

"It's no one," Rafe snapped. He dug through the nails, pretending that he couldn't find the one he needed. He looked back up at his oldest brother. "What makes you ask if it's her?"

"Because you used to have a great poker face. Never a clue what you were thinking. Now, every time you're watching her, you look like you're either going to start spouting poetry or lop somebody's head off."

"Besides," Matt said with a grin, "Mom ratted you out to us. We know about all the pastries you ate trying to win a coin instead of just buying a few kisses. I'll bet she wouldn't have said no."

"I am *not* interested in Danielle Bridgeton."

Sam had made his way slowly across the new deck. "Why not? She's pretty. She's educated. What's the matter? Is she too smart for you? I'll bet she's got you all figured out, and you don't like it."

Rafe expected his father to say something like that. But he wasn't going to rise to the taunt. "We are not having this conversation."

"See?" Nick said with a laugh, using his hammer to point at Rafe. "There's that look. Mention the Bridgeton woman and he wants to lop someone's head off."

"You're partly right. I *do* want to lop off someone's head. Several someones, in fact. "

Their mother appeared on the deck just then, carrying a tray with a pitcher and glasses on it. Frannie walked carefully beside her, a plate perched between her small hands like an offering to the gods.

"Ready for a break, *famiglia?*" Rose asked. "Francesca and I have brought tea and biscotti."

The men made appropriate sounds of appreciation, and Rafe, eager to put an end to this ridiculous discussion, was quick to make his way to his mother. Drinks were passed around. Chocolate biscotti were doled out carefully by Frannie, who took great care in picking out one for each of them. Rafe noticed that she gave him the biggest. It was the first time he'd felt like smiling in days.

Sam bit into his. He chewed a few moments, then his brow creased in puzzlement. "This is—"

"Francesca helped me make them," Rose cut in meaningfully.

"—wonderful!" the old man finished. "Good job, Francesca."

Frannie frowned at him. "I don't think they're so good. But that's okay. Nonna Rose says I have to practice, and one day I'll be able to cook like her. Someday when I'm really, really old. Like twenty, or something."

They all laughed at that.

Frannie went over to the railing to finger the tools along the ledge. "Can I hammer, too?"

"We're almost done here, sweetheart," Rafe told the girl.

Rose turned toward her granddaughter. "Francesca, will you bring us more napkins from the kitchen, please?"

Frannie skipped away to do as she was asked. She'd been very complacent the past few days. Maybe she sensed that Rafe wasn't in the mood to cut chewing gum out of her hair or fuss with her about taking a bath.

As soon as the child disappeared back into the lodge, his mother tapped Sam's arm. "Sheriff Bendix is on his way up from town. He wants to talk to you."

"About what?"

"About the Accordion Man."

"Why?" Sam asked with a twinkle in his eye. "Am I a suspect?"

"Don't be ridiculous. He didn't say, of course. Just that he wanted to ask a few questions since you used to go to the Three Bs."

"Well, good for him. Since most of the time that man would be out of his depth in a puddle, I'd like to think our tax dollars aren't *completely* wasted." He set down his glass and plate, and fitted his arms back into the cuffs of his crutches. "Better change out of this shirt. If I'm going to be arrested, I don't want to go looking like a hobo."

Rafe caught Nick's eye, then Matt's. He knew what his brothers were thinking. Sheriff Bendix's intentions were probably harmless, but there was no way a protective guy like Nick was going to let his father go through it alone. Matt, too, would be right there by Sam's side.

Just before he hit the back door, his father looked over his shoulder. "You boys can finish up without me, can't you?"

"Sure, Pop. No sweat," Rafe replied for them all.

He knew that in a few minutes both his brothers would find an excuse to go inside as well. They'd do whatever it took to make sure the old man didn't get hassled. They didn't need Rafe's help. In fact, a third hovering presence, and their father would be bound to object. He should collect Frannie and head home.

But even as he had that thought, he knew he wasn't going anywhere. D'Angelos stuck together. And whether he'd been MIA from this family for years or not, he was still one of them.

Right now, his place was here.

CHAPTER FIFTEEN

SAM SAT IN HIS FAVORITE CHAIR in the living room and fumed. Bendix had just left after about thirty wasted minutes of vague questions and meandering suppositions. It was quite clear that the man felt after all these years there was about as much chance of solving the Accordion Man's murder as nailing Jell-O to a tree.

But it wasn't the sheriff who had Sam so riled. It was his sons. *All* of them.

"Well!" Sam said, slapping his hands down against the arms of his chair. "If it's true that what you don't know can't hurt you, I'd say our sheriff is practically invulnerable."

No one said a thing. They were all too busy pretending they hadn't been listening to every word.

Nick stood across the room, acting as if he had an interest in the kitchen door hinges. Matt sat paging through a magazine on the coffee table. *Cosmo!* What earthly use would he have for that? As for Rafe, he was slouched in a nearby chair, the only one of them not bothering to pretend anything at all.

Sam looked at them in turn. Three grown men. Three *babysitters,* more like it!

"Deck all done?" he asked, cutting into the silence.

Nick looked back over his shoulder. "Not quite."

"No. And do you know why? Because all my sons have been hanging around here looking out for their helpless old poppa when they should have been outside. Working."

"We needed a break, Pop," Matt spoke up.

"Ha! You had a break before Bendix got here. Did you think I was going to be dragged off in handcuffs?" Sam muttered a string of his favorite Italian curses. "Is that what you think of me?"

"Of course not," Nick said, swinging around. "We were just curious to see what the sheriff had to say."

"So now you know. He was just looking for information, and he thought I could fill in some of the blanks. Which I did." Sam shook his head in disgust. "Grown men acting like damned fools."

Across the room, Rafe blew a breath out loudly. "Lay off, Pop. We were just trying to make sure you had support if you needed it."

Sam gritted his teeth. Since his stroke, he should have become used to this—this pact the family had made to keep him wrapped in cotton batting like an invalid child. There was no question that it was done out of love. But didn't they understand that it had bled him of his self-respect, his pride? He glanced down at his clenched hands. They were dense with liver spots and moles. An old man's hands, though he had just turned sixty.

He drew a deep, fortifying breath. By God, he was still the head of this household. In that moment, his will blazed up, stubborn and resistant. "I didn't need protection," he said. "I've been dealing with life since before you boys were in diapers."

Rafe stood suddenly and headed toward the coatrack. "Yeah, you're a tough hombre, all right, and you don't need my help. I think I'll track down Frannie and go home."

"You think the fact that he's the sheriff worried me?" Sam called out to his son's retreating back. "Hell, didn't I get enough visits from the law when you were living here, doing your best to destroy this family?"

Rafe turned on his heel. Sam could see the sudden light of battle in his son's eyes.

"You know what?" Rafe said as he came back into the center of the room. "I'm sick of this. I'm sick of you dredging up my juvenile delinquent days every time I piss you off. Let's do it. Tell me what a rotten son I was. Get everything out, and then maybe we can move on from there. What do you say?"

Matt had risen as well, and he came toward his brother. "Rafe…"

"No, let him spout," Sam said. "It might do him some good."

"You've got that right," Rafe said, nostrils flaring.

On the other side of him, Nick caught Rafe's arm. "Listen, you two…"

Sam silenced him by slicing his hand through the air. He never took his eyes off his youngest son. Rafe was asking for a war that had been brewing for a long time.

"We don't need your help," Sam told Nick and Matt. "And we don't need an audience. Now would be an excellent time to finish the deck."

After a long pause, Matt caught Nick's attention. "Come on, big brother. Let's go hammer something."

Silence descended while the two men left the room. Then Rafe sat down in the chair across from Sam, legs apart, hands between his knees. As though fascinated by the rug beneath his feet, he dropped his head.

Sam waited, feeling bleached with fatigue. It had been a tiring day, but the scarred-over wounds that had been sleeping for years had been ripped open now, and he would not let them return to hiding.

At last, Rafe straightened, as though it were a triumph over gravity. He spread his hands wide. "What do you want from me, Pop? How many more hoops do I have to jump through before you finally get over the past?"

Sam felt his facial muscles tighten. Might as well get to the heart of it. "Do you know what it's like to get a call in the middle of the night from the police telling you that your son is in the emergency room? You're a father now. Someday you'll have to tell me how you feel when Frannie does something that stops your heart."

"Do you think I did it on purpose?"

"I think back in those days you did whatever you damned well pleased. With total disregard to anyone but yourself."

"I know I wasn't an easy kid to raise," Rafe acknowledged. "I know I wasn't dependable like Nick or a charmer like Matt. I was always aware that no competition between the three of us could ever be won by me. But I didn't want to be just another little D'Angelo soldier, taking orders from you all the time."

Sam let his brows soar as disbelief eclipsed everything else. "Your brothers had plenty of independence. I guided them, and they never resented me for it. They got into trouble. They weren't perfect. But they lived and learned. You just lived."

"They never got thrown out of this house."

"Because they never brought drugs into our lives."

The silence seemed to quiver suddenly. All Sam could see in his son's face was a quiet, precise anger.

Rafe shook his head. "What are you talking about? I never did that. I never would have."

Sam snorted. "It was only a matter of time. You would have."

Rafe stood, looking startled. "Wait a minute! Are you telling me that when you came to the hospital and told me I wasn't welcome in this house any longer…" He broke off for a moment, as though unable to find the words. "Are you telling me that was based on something you *thought* I might do?"

"I will tell you what I *know*. The police said you had been involved in a knife fight. That fool Christopher said the two of you went into that alley to buy cocaine. You tried to cheat a drug dealer, and that's how you ended up with twenty-three stitches in your leg. A back-alley skirmish in the dead of night. Over drugs! *Dio!*"

Rafe came closer, standing over him. His son's eyes, so dark a brown that they were almost black, held the stillness of a hurricane's eye, and its menace. "I never bought drugs." Rafe snapped the words out like brittle tree branches. "I never used them."

Sam wasn't about to crumble in the face of his son's anger. "How could I believe that? You had been headed down the wrong path for years. Skipping school, little brushes with the law. Your choice in friends certainly didn't reassure me."

"That didn't make me a druggie."

"I couldn't know that. You certainly had some of the signs of drug use. Nick and Matt were nearly grown, and I wasn't worried about your influence on them. But your sister was only a child. She worshipped you, she'd have done anything you said, and that includes taking drugs."

"For God's sake, what kind of monster did you think I was? I would never have hurt Addy."

"I couldn't take that chance."

Rafe blew a short breath and raked his hand through his hair. "Why didn't you ask me for the truth?"

"The police told me—"

"Forget the police, why didn't you ask *me*?"

"Because I could not be sure you would tell me the truth. If you remember correctly, you and I were not exactly communicating."

"No," Rafe said as though suddenly weary. "That's certainly true."

Sam turned his memories over like stones, recalling all the ways they'd been at cross purposes throughout Rafe's growing-up years. "So where was I supposed to get such faith, Rafe?" he asked, letting his incredulity show in his voice. "That boy you hung out with, that hooligan Christopher, he wasn't fit to sleep with pigs, but you let him lead you into a situation that could have gotten you killed."

Uttering a low sound, Rafe stalked away to stand in front of the fireplace. He stared into the grate, filled with cold ashes. Sam could see the finest tremor in his son's arms, and his own hands were shaking.

"This is pointless," Rafe said in a tired voice. "Why should I bother to explain?"

A shudder of regret, deep and obliterating, moved through Sam's body. He wanted Rafe to make sense of this. To find some way to make it right. Surely if he met Rafe halfway…

"So explain it to me now," he said in a quieter tone. "I promise to listen."

For several long moments, Rafe did nothing but continue to stare into the grate. Then he drew a deep breath, straightened and swung around. "Chris wanted to go down to Idaho Springs to celebrate his birthday.

Get drunk, check out the girls. Maybe buy some drugs. He wanted to try coke. I said no. I was reckless as hell in those days, but I wasn't stupid. So we agreed to disagree, and I came home for the night."

Sam remained silent, waiting. He had loved this boy with all his heart. How could they have come to such an impasse?

"Only I couldn't sleep for worrying about Chris," Rafe went on. "So I snuck out and went after him."

"I assume you found him and proceeded to get drunk together. The police said your alcohol level was past the legal limit."

"I drank, but I wasn't drunk." He paused, then shook his head as though disgusted by the memory. "Eventually a dealer offered to sell us coke. I thought I could talk Chris out of that nonsense, but he began complaining about the price. He started yelling about getting ripped off. He was too drunk to know you don't mess with guys like that. About the time I thought I'd just have to deck him to get him home, he snatched the bag and started running."

"*Cafone!*" Sam had disliked Rafe's friend from the moment he'd set eyes on him. "Did I not tell you that boy was no smarter than a soap dish?"

His son ignored that. "The dealer took off after Chris, and I took off after him. By the time I caught up, he had a knife at Chris's throat. I didn't know what else to do except tackle him. We fought. I got cut. The next thing I knew, the cops were there."

"Thank God for that," Sam muttered. Even after all these years, goose bumps rose along his arms to think what might have happened had the police not come along.

"I know it wasn't the smartest thing I ever did. But they didn't find any drugs on me, and there were none in my system. They weren't going to arrest me. Then in you stormed, telling me I couldn't come home until I cleaned up my act."

Sam gazed at his son in silence, feeling shaky inside and out all of a sudden. "I didn't mean you could *never* come home. The hospital had a addiction treatment center. Professionals you could talk to. I wanted you to get help."

"That isn't the message I got from you, Pop. And you never once asked me for my side of the story."

"So you ran away," he declared, determined not to think about how he might have behaved differently that night.

Rafe stared at him grimly. "I left because there was no point in sticking around. You wouldn't believe me. You never did. I was eighteen, so I knew you couldn't stop me. I snuck out of the hospital and caught a bus to Reno."

Remembering what it had been like to walk into Rafe's emergency-room cubicle and find him gone, Sam's jaw went so tight his teeth ached. "Do you know how difficult it was to come home and tell your mother that not only had you been injured, nearly arrested, but that you had disappeared off the face of the earth as well?"

"I called the next day. You know I've always let Mom and Addy know where I was, that I was all right."

"Do you think that was enough for us? Your mother and I did everything to track you down, but nothing worked."

"I moved around a lot. Picked up odd jobs to pay for the next bus ticket. I steered clear of trouble for the most part."

"That did not keep your mother from crying in the middle of the night."

"I'm sorry about that. I never wanted anyone to worry, but there was no way I was ever coming back here."

"Because of me."

"Yes. Returning home was hopeless. You made sure of that."

The words stung. Sam lowered his head, like a creature at bay. Could he have been wrong all this time?

No! It couldn't be. He had been a good father. He was not a man who rammed through life with so little understanding of his own children. The weight of his shared history with Rafe settled over him once more, years of arguments and punishments and defiance. "I only did what I thought was best," he said, almost to himself.

"You think you know…you always know, don't you?"

"If you had just listened—"

"No, Pop. If you had just stopped *lecturing* long

enough to hear what I was saying. But you never did. Right now I'm learning how tough it is to be a father. But I hope to God that when Frannie and I go head-to-head, I have the good sense to listen to what she's trying to tell me. I know one thing. I'll never just assume the worst of her because it's easier than accepting *I* might have done something wrong."

They looked at one another for a long moment. Then suddenly Rafe was moving across the room. Still trying to make sense of the senseless, Sam shouted after him, "Where are you going? We haven't sorted this out yet."

Rafe slipped into his jacket. "I have. You were right—getting this off my chest does feel good. You've got the truth now. Do with it what you want."

When he started for the door, fresh anger flowed through Sam. "Rafe! Don't you walk out on me!"

His son turned back to face him. "Sorry. Now that I think about it, there's someone else who needs to be set straight, too. I'm tired of getting accused of things I didn't do. When I was eighteen, it was exciting to be considered a badass. Now it's just a *pain* in the ass."

THE BUREAU OFFICE WAS CLOSED by the time Rafe drove down to Broken Yoke. That didn't diminish his resolve to find Dani. They were going to talk.

Now.

It took him a few minutes to find her home address at his construction office. Rafe examined Dani's neat, block handwriting on the back of her business card. Her newspaper had rented a place for her less than a mile out of town.

He made it to her apartment easily enough, a small complex that catered to temporary business tenants and boasted a nautical theme that was completely out of place here in the mountains. Halfway down a long corridor of doors, he found her number and knocked.

It took a long time for her to answer, but at least she opened the door, though she didn't swing it wide. He didn't expect her to.

She blinked against the fading sunlight. The tan she'd gotten the day of the festival had already begun to fade. Or maybe he was the reason she looked pale.

"Rafe," she said carefully.

Now that he was standing in front of her, all the words he'd rehearsed felt inadequate. She looked uncertain, almost fearful. He hadn't come here to bully her into seeing things his way.

Her bottom lip disappeared as she bit it. His voice still felt frozen in his throat, but the leftover memory of that lush mouth against his was enough to melt his vocal cords.

"We need to talk," he said. "About that night in Vegas."

She shook her head so sharply that dark hair danced along her shoulders. "Don't do this to me," she said, and her voice sounded harassed already. "I can't talk to you about it."

Rafe studied her with narrowed eyes. "Now who's

dodging the truth? Until we get this sorted out, we can't talk about anything else." When she made a move to shut the door in his face, he placed his hand against it. "Let me in, Danielle. Let me explain." He turned his head to look up and down the corridor. "If you don't, I'll stand out here and yell my side of the story for everyone to hear. You want to share that with your neighbors?"

She stared at him, a flicker of annoyance replacing the distraction that had been in her eyes only moments before. For a long time, Dani said nothing.

Did nothing.

Rafe stood there, waiting, feeling as though he'd been holding his breath for years.

CHAPTER SIXTEEN

AT LAST DANI STEPPED ASIDE and opened the door wider.

She crossed her arms over one another, hugging her elbows as though she were freezing. He could see misery in her eyes as well, and wished that one word, one touch could change all that. But she needed time. She needed the truth. And he wasn't going to leave here until she got them.

She moved back into the center of the room while Rafe closed the door behind himself. "Say what you have to say, and then please leave," she told him. "I have…work to do."

He cast a glance around the living room, noticing the pile of books on the dining-room table, the stack of mail, a yellow legal pad that no doubt held plenty of notes. A laptop computer—closed. Those were the only personal items he could spot.

The room held the generic perfection of a rental property. It came to him suddenly that Dani would go back to Denver someday, where her life really lay.

Denver was only an hour a way, not the moon. But the knowledge displeased him anyway.

He pivoted. "Sit down," he said, and seeing her resistance, he added, "please."

She took the middle of the couch, her posture ramrod straight. Knowing that he had to measure every word and gesture carefully, Rafe exhaled a deep breath. "I suppose there's no delicate way to put this," he said at last. "The next morning in Vegas, when you woke up. Were you sore? Bruised in any way?" When she looked down at her arms, he went on, "I'm not talking about your arms. Other than that, did you have any reason to think you'd had rough sex?"

"No," she admitted. "But if I'd been given something like Ecstasy, something to make me a more willing partner, I might not have." Her eyes met his in an unblinking challenge. "That still didn't give you the right—"

"Hang on," Rafe said, raising one hand to stop her. "So if there was no physical discomfort, what makes you so sure you had sex against your will?"

"I already told you. At one point, I woke up enough to realize I was naked. In bed with you. You've admitted that. Who do you want to blame for it? Aliens?"

"No. You."

"Me!" She was on her feet suddenly, flashing him a look that was dangerous. "I want you to leave."

She made a move for the door, but he stopped her by blocking her path. "I don't want to force you to listen. But you had your say down at the spring. Don't you think it's my turn now?"

He watched her face, the little quivers of stress that flitted across it, but eventually she sat once more, her hands clasped in front of her in prim submission, shoulders hunched inward. Her thick lashes lowered. Rafe felt his insides squeeze with spontaneous empathy. This was not the way he'd intended this meeting to go.

He dropped to his heels in front of her. "Dani, look at me."

She lifted her head. He thought he saw a mist of tears in her eyes, but in the next moment, she blinked away that telltale weakness, lifting her chin higher. "This is a waste of time," she told him. "Can't you just leave me alone?"

"No. I'm not willing to let this nonsense get in our way any longer. It's too important to me. To us."

She frowned. "What are you saying?"

"I'm saying that I just tried to show a stubborn old man that there are two sides to every story. Whether it worked with him or not, I don't know. But there's not a chance in hell for my father and me if he won't try to see it. It's the same for you and me, Dani. We have to try to sort this out."

"Why?"

Rafe gave her a small smile. When he caught her chin between two fingers, she didn't pull away. "You know why," he said softly. "Because there's something between us. There always has been. But we're never going to have the chance to explore whatever it is unless you meet me halfway."

She gave him a mutinous stare, debating, then she slipped her chin out of his grasp and looked away. For a long moment, she said nothing. Finally she drew in a desperate breath and turned back to him. "Start at the beginning," she said.

Relieved, Rafe felt the jump of his pulse at her sudden willingness to listen.

Deliberately, he put distance between them again, finding a spot on the other side of the living room where he could perch on the arm of a club chair. "What's the last thing you really remember about that night?" he asked.

"The craps table. I remember standing there wishing Gil would take his hand off my butt. No, the elevator! Someone else coming up beside me and taking my arm. It must have been Frank Wescott. They ended up in adjoining jail cells."

Rafe snorted. "Good. I'd like to think of them being used as piñatas in some prison."

"They both claimed they'd never touched me, and I couldn't prove otherwise. There was so little I remembered."

"They had you between them, on the way to a room. They were practically pissing their pants with excitement at the idea of sharing you."

The bluntness of his words made her blink. He

could see the terrible memories trying to take shape in her head. "How do you know that?" she asked in a quiet voice.

"Because I'm the one who shut them down. I took you away from them."

"How?"

"I flashed my casino security badge and said you were suspected of cheating at one of the tables. They were too stunned to stop me. So I hustled you off, and left them standing there in the hallway."

She tilted her head at him, obviously bewildered. "Then how did I end up in that room? Room 226. I'll never forget that number."

"I put you there. One of the maids owed me a favor."

"I don't remember that."

"You wouldn't," he said shaking his head. "By that time you were pretty well out of it. Trying to tear off your clothes. Putting the moves on me. You tried to—" He stopped, realizing that she didn't need to hear all the innovative, sexy ways she'd struggled to engage his interest that night. Better to leave some things unsaid. He rubbed his jaw. "Let's just say you were out of control."

Dani blushed and Rafe watched her hands ball into fists in her lap. "I definitely don't remember any of that," she told him. She tried to make the comment sound offhanded, unimportant, but failed miserably.

He crossed the room to sit beside her on the couch. He took one of her hands, finding the fingers cold and unresponsive. "Don't think about that part," he said. "It wasn't you. It was the drugs."

She nodded. "Go on."

"I tried to get you to settle down, but you kept trying to get out of bed. You wanted to leave the room, and that I knew we couldn't do. So I held you down, and kept holding you down until you fell asleep. That's how you got the bruises on your arms."

She looked him in the eyes. "But I remember what you said. About dreaming of us being together in bed."

He reached up and stroked her cheek with the back of one hand. "Hell, Dani. I probably *did* say that. It was the truth. I'd been wanting you for weeks." He grinned. "It wasn't exactly the way I'd envisioned it, but I have to admit, having you struggling naked against me wasn't the worst thing that happened to me that night." He shook his head. "But that's as far as it went."

"So then you left. And I woke up the next morning, thinking I'd had sex I couldn't remember."

"That's not what I intended. I would have stayed the night with you. I would have made sure you were all right come morning."

"Then why didn't you?"

"Because I was in the hospital in Laughlin," he said, speaking the words slowly because, even now, they were difficult to utter and so hard to believe. "Trying to stay alive."

"What?"

"After you finally went to sleep, I locked you in and

went downstairs. I figured coffee might help. The next thing I knew, your old buddies from Phoenix stuck a gun in my side and were escorting me out to the parking garage. They wanted to know where I'd stashed you."

Her features were written in disbelief. "Gil Rodgers and Frank Wescott are white-collar criminals. Not murderers."

"Yeah, that's what I figured, too," he said with a light laugh. "Back in those days I thought I could read people pretty well. But I underestimated them. I didn't think they were desperate or stupid enough to go to the wall over a little attempted date rape. I thought that, given enough time, we could sort things out, man to man."

"Only...?"

He shrugged, remembering the simple, stupid arrogance with which he'd mishandled the situation. He was lucky he hadn't been killed, after all. "Only before I knew it, one of them clocked me over the head and tossed me in a car trunk. When they finally stopped driving around and opened it up, we were out in the desert. And we'd picked up some badass—local talent, I imagine—who'd been paid to knuckle me up if I continued to be so unwilling to talk." He arched his brow. "You think you can't forget that room number? Hell, I can still see that guy's fists coming at me."

"But you never told where I was."

He gave her a close look. "No."

She stared at him, a strange look, slightly lost, as

though she didn't recognize him for an instant. Then it was gone in the next moment. "How did you get to the hospital?"

"Two boys shooting up cactus found me the next day. Naked as a jaybird and out of my head. I imagine it could have been funny, if it hadn't hurt so badly. Not that I remember much of it."

Dani shook her head, as though in distressed confusion. Before he could stop her, she rose and stalked across the room, her back to him. He had no idea what she was thinking. "This is so hard to believe," she said, her voice so muffled that Rafe barely understood it. "If what you say is true, you could have been killed."

"I nearly was," he admitted.

She swung around, searching his features, as though she could see evidence of what had been done to him in his face even after all these years.

She came back to the couch. "How bad was it?"

"It doesn't matter now."

"Tell me."

He stood. Catching the hem of his shirt, Rafe pulled it over his head and tossed it on the couch. He fingered the surgical scar that still stood out against his flesh. "Ruptured spleen. Busted ribs and collarbone. Collapsed lung. But I guess I was too stubborn to die."

She frowned. "Don't joke about it."

"Don't get too worked up. I'm not proud of it, but in reality, Gil and Frank were just the latest in a long line of ugly, dangerous characters who were part of my life back then."

"They should pay for what they did to you," Dani said with sudden and fierce determination. "Why didn't you help the police find them? Surely a report was filed."

"It was. But I couldn't give them much to go on. And by the time I got out of the hospital and went back to Native Sun, you were long gone. They said you'd quit."

"I thought you'd left me after having gotten what you wanted. Rodgers and Wescott had returned to Phoenix, so I came back as well. We found another way to go after them, and we won eventually. I had no idea you were in a hospital."

"No reason you should have known, I suppose. You know how people come and go in Vegas. I figured you didn't want any reminders of what happened. I sure didn't need any. Figured I was better off just letting it go, considering it a lucky break that I made it out in one piece. In those days, I didn't want too much attention focused on my own past. So Oz just disappeared."

She remained silent, staring down at his bare chest, as though memorizing every curve and muscle. He didn't know if she believed his story or not, but one thing for sure. It was like drowning, to be this close. He was afraid he was going to reach for her, and he wasn't certain what she would do if he did.

"It's over," he said firmly. "You don't have to think of it anymore. You just have to believe me. That's the only thing I really care about, Dani." He smiled a little as she gave him a closer look. "That you believe me."

She shook her head slowly back and forth. "I want to believe you," she said. Her voice was husky, fractured. "It scares me how much I want to believe you."

It wasn't as much as he'd hoped for, but it was enough. For now. When she met his eyes, he knew the extent of his courage. His body had already become excited to have her so near. He was dazzled by her, everything about her. That little upward tilt of the chin, the slight parting of the lips…

He caught the ends of a dangling dark curl that lay against her shoulder, tugging gently until the space of a breath separated his mouth from hers. "Then do it," he whispered. "Let yourself believe me. Can't you feel the truth in your heart?"

She made no answer. But she didn't pull away. A peculiar sound escaped her, a soft moan of despair. In astonishment, he saw that she was shaking.

"What is it?" he asked quickly. "What's wrong?"

She studied his face the way a lost man reads a map to find the quickest way home. "I need you to be with me," she said, as if the words hurt. "Please. Just for a little while."

Without thinking, he drew her into his arms. She went easily against the length of his body, as though he were the only secure warmth in a shifting world. He held her steadily, stroking her hair and back. Pressed so near, she had to know the state of his desire, but to his immense pleasure she didn't seem at all uncertain or hesitant.

"Whatever you want, Dani," he soothed. He bent his head, nuzzling her ear. "Frannie's with Kari and Nick for the evening. She's crazy about the baby. So right now there's no place else I need to be. No place else I'd *rather* be than here."

She burrowed even harder against him, as though she could hide in his embrace.

He was suddenly afraid that he might ruin this somehow. *I have to get this right. Mustn't spoil this.*

But even as he had that thought, he knew that this was not his day for subtlety and he dropped his head to rake his mouth over hers with rough, hungry strokes. She surprised him by returning them with open-mouthed welcome.

He felt her fingers in his hair, light at first, then tugging him toward her as she made soft, throaty sounds that sank all the way through him. His control teetered.

The tantalizing crush of her breasts rubbed against his bare chest, and he realized she wore no bra. The fact that all that separated his flesh from hers was the thin layer of her cotton T-shirt sent his senses into overdrive, and he thought the sooner he persuaded her to take it off, the better.

"This," he murmured, pulling at the edges of her T-shirt. "Why is this still here?"

"I don't know," she said in a whispered caress. "Take it off."

She lifted her arms, and Rafe whipped it over her head so quickly that her hair, barely held in place by a lavender ribbon, fell down her back like a flock of blackbirds. She stepped out of her jeans with his help. Soon there was nothing between them but bikini panties cut so high they almost weren't there.

In very little time, that small scrap of lace and silk had joined the rest of her clothes on the floor. At last he was free to feel her the way he'd always wanted to, with nothing between them. He had imagined all of this, every single day since she'd come back into his life. Her body felt spectacular, satiny, and he was not sure he could ever stop touching her.

All he could think about was being lost inside her and never wanting to leave. He wanted technique and finesse for her, but he was nearly mindless with need now. Lifting his head from her naked breast, he unleashed a slow, sexy smile. "I want to be gentle, Dani," he said in a rueful tone. "But God help me, you make it difficult."

She moved against him in such a pointedly sexual way that he sucked in a harsh breath. She shook her head vigorously. "I don't want gentle. I just want…" She nipped at the flesh along his shoulder, then stroked it with her tongue. "Show me that you want me, too."

Groaning against unbelievable pleasure, Rafe lifted her in his arms. He carried her into what he guessed was her bedroom. As though she were made of the finest china, he laid her on the wide bed. His mind registered the deep red comforter beneath her, but only because it provided such a vivid contrast to her dark hair and the flawless ivory of her skin.

He levered himself over her and looked down into her eyes. "Do I want you?" he asked. He kissed her again, his tongue surged into her mouth, searching, promising. When he pulled back at last, he heard the breathy gasp that caught in her throat. "Direct enough for you?" he asked with a grin.

"Yes…" she said on a husky little laugh, her face exquisitely flushed with passion. "Oh, yes…"

It was time to end this. Impatiently, he rose up enough to skim out of his pants and underwear, his arms trembling for control. He meant what he'd told her—he was never careless these days. When Rafe slipped the foil package of protection out of his wallet, Dani helped him, her eyes never wavering from his.

Chest to breast, thigh to thigh, he lowered himself over her again, and immediately the warm, moist heat of her body sent fire through his veins. For days, for weeks, he had wanted her this way, dreamed of her this way, and now suddenly all the barriers were gone.

Easing himself between her legs, Rafe lay against her, fighting his body's demand that he bury himself in her tight warmth. He wanted to please her, but this was sweet torture, and when Dani's hips rose upward, wanting more, he felt control slip from his grasp completely. He surged forward with one sure thrust. Dani moaned and twisted under his hands. He felt her tighten and squeeze him, a glorious sexy miracle that left him panting.

His movements quickened. Dani pushed back against him. Some tiny part of his brain recognized that she was moving with the rhythm he'd established; he could hear her small gasps of helpless delight. He knew the instant her body began to disintegrate, the tiny convulsions that shook her, the unmistakable feeling of her shattering in his arms, even as he went hurtling toward the same destiny.

And then everything shut down for him. His world tilted. Reality vanished. He shuddered, pulled deeper and deeper into sensation until from a long way off he heard his own rough voice calling her name.

Afterward he lay limp and drained, sprawled across her. He gathered her in his arms, and she settled against him with a soft sigh of contentment. His entire body felt weak and watery. He drew his fingers down the hot, damp skin behind Dani's ear, pushed her hair away, then kissed her forehead. She smiled up at him. He wished for some clever remark, but he couldn't speak.

Gradually he floated, swinging in and out of consciousness. His body felt content, satiated. Beneath him Dani's soft, shaky breaths fanned warmth across his shoulder. He tightened his hold on her, unwilling to let her go even for a instant. His mind knew only that this was where he belonged. Where he had always belonged.

WHEN DANI AWOKE, it was black in the bedroom except for moonlight throwing ghostly stripes across the bedsheets. She turned her head and saw that the green glow of the alarm clock said it was a little after nine o'clock. She and Rafe had been in her bed for hours.

With a silly grin of pleasure on her face, she reached out into the darkness, eager to snuggle against him once more. Her hands encountered nothing but cool linen, the fluffy lump of an abandoned pillow.

Rafe was gone.

Her heart beating insanely, Dani stretched to snap on the bedside lamp. She blinked against the light, but saw instantly that she was alone.

"Rafe," she called out in a sleep-mussed voice, coming up on one elbow.

A few moments later, her heart settled a bit when she heard his voice coming from her living room. From the sound of it, he was talking to someone on his cell phone.

Tucking the sheet around her bare breasts, Dani wiggled upward in bed. She plumped the pillows behind her, then plumped Rafe's as well. It carried the scent of him, and she couldn't help smiling as she plunged her nose into it.

In this moment, she did not believe she could have been any happier. Nothing had changed, and yet everything had. The truth washed over her with a profound sense of inevitability and rightness.

She had fallen in love with Rafe D'Angelo.

How had this happened to her? How had *he* happened to her?

But she knew how, of course. Closing her eyes, she relived every caress and smile and kiss that had passed between them in this bed. Even the quiet lulls between irresistible desires had been sheer heaven in Rafe's arms. The sound of his laughter that she could feel in her knees, the wicked sparkle in his eyes, the glossy thickness of his hair between her fingers—all of it lured her, seduced her. Until she could barely think. She felt as though he were inside her still—but within every cell, every pore.

But it was more than just a physical response. More than just games of passion. She couldn't imagine what had happened to that man she'd known in Las Vegas, but Oz seemed to no longer exist. She only knew how she felt, and she knew when something felt right. And being with Rafe seemed as right to her as breathing.

The question was— How did the man who had stolen her heart feel about *her?*

She wanted to believe that he treasured this time the same way she did, that they had shared something special, something unique. But there had been no declarations of love tonight, no promises made. Building castles in the air out of nothing more than a few hours of great, earth-shattering sex would be a huge mistake. Dangerous, even.

What if he—

The bed dipped a little, and Dani opened her eyes

to find that Rafe had returned. He sat on the side of the bed, his back to her, that wonderfully sculpted expanse of muscle and sinew that even now her fingers longed to stroke.

He turned his head to look at her. "I'm sorry. I didn't mean to wake you."

She swiped hair out of her eyes. "Everything all right?"

"Fine. I just called Kari to ask if they would keep Frannie overnight."

"Did you tell Kari where you were?"

"No." He gave her a lopsided grin. "I didn't have to. Somehow she knew."

"How could she? What did she say?"

"She said, 'Finally! A D'Angelo showing some sense for a change. Tell Dani I said hello.'"

Dani laughed, and Rafe reached out for her. In one easy movement, she lay on top of him. "And *are* you showing some sense?" she asked, tilting her head back to find his eyes.

His hands, which had been wrapped around her back, slid down to stroke her hips. He thrust upward with his pelvis, using his hold to show her that fresh desire stirred within him already. "I'd like to think so, but where you're concerned, I never know."

He kissed her thoroughly, sending luxuriant shivers down her spine. For a long time they lay that way, savoring every touch, every tiny movement, wildly letting desire take them where it would. Dani had never experienced anything like this before. The feeling of completeness, the sensation of being emotionally united with another person, was astonishing.

Finally, she slipped to his side, laying her head against his shoulder. Exhausted, relaxed, and yet, tingling all over. She blinked up at the ceiling, thinking that there was nothing more perfect than this.

"So we have the whole night," she said when she could draw breath at last. "Lovely."

"Yes. I thought so."

She turned her head to find his eyes on her, soft, his expression gentle, filled with the frank, dark promise of the hours ahead of them.

"In the morning, I'll fix breakfast for us," she told him as she brushed a kiss across one of his nipples. His flesh responded with a small quiver. "My specialty—eggs Benedict."

"Umm, can't wait," he replied. He lifted her head up by weaving his hands into her hair, then touched his lips to the corner of her mouth. "I'm hungry now." When she sat up suddenly, he caught her wrist. "Where do you think you're going?"

She sent a teasing glance back at him. "To the kitchen. You said you were hungry."

"I am," he said. Then his smile broadened wickedly. "But not for eggs."

CHAPTER SEVENTEEN

SAM WOKE UP LATER than usual.

It was his habit to make the rounds of the lodge very early in the morning, checking that nothing unexpected had happened during the night, that all the help had shown up as scheduled, that another day would go as planned. He liked the service at Lightning River to appear seamless to the guests, their every whim catered to with what looked like very little effort.

But he didn't know how he was supposed to make that happen when he could hardly keep his eyes open. He had not slept well, tossing and turning until even Rosa had been kept awake. His mind had felt weighted down by a thousand unanswered questions. Frankly, he wanted nothing more than to crawl back into bed and pull the covers over his head like a spoiled child.

Unthinkable, of course, but he could long for the blissful numbness of sleep all the same.

It was still early. Not a soul was downstairs in the lobby area except the front-desk help. He passed his sister-in-law Sofia on her way to the lodge's laundry room with a trio of giggly maids in her wake. In the kitchen, Renata, his other sister-in-law, was issuing orders to the wait staff and barely looked up at him. Rosa sat at the big butcher-block table, paging through books of table settings she was considering for a wedding reception they had coming up in a few weeks.

She gave him a speculative look.

Rosa always fretted over him like a mother hen with her favorite chick. Tenderness for the woman he had loved at first glance warmed his heart, but he ignored her eyes and poured himself a cup of coffee from the large urn that sat near the exit to the dining room. Pretending an interest in the new deck, Sam let himself out the back door.

They'd done good work yesterday, and he'd enjoyed it, though physically it had cost him dearly in new aches and pains. Nick and Matthew, and even Rafe had worked together as a team. Rosa was going to love this little oasis away from everyday stresses. Perhaps he'd put flower boxes around the railing to cheer her even more.

They'd chosen just the right spot, too. From the edge of the deck, the land sloped off toward the lake, and in between the tall grandeur of pines and white-trunked aspen, you could see the diamond-sparkle of the water. This early, the property looked like a charmed world, washed in the last pink shadows of dawn.

Sam breathed in deeply. He could hear a wood-pecker hard at work in the trees. He loved the wild industry of that sound. Overhead the clouds were like stretched cotton candy. He was a fool—and worse, an old fool—to allow his black mood to sour such a beautiful morning.

What was he to do about Rafe?

He heard the door behind him open, and after years of sensing his wife's presence, he knew it was Rosa. The smell of bacon and rich coffee from the kitchen mingled in the air as she came toward him.

She went to the railing. He would not look at her, kept his focus on the trees. He knew what was on her mind. The same thing that was on his. But he didn't want to talk about it.

"You didn't sleep well last night," she remarked softly.

"Neither did you."

"Is there some problem?"

There's a problem all right, and his name is Rafe D'Angelo. But what he said was "No."

His wife turned. The morning light caught the streaks of gray in her hair, and for just a moment he wondered how many of them he had put there. He was not an easy man to live with.

She tilted her head, the look on her features stern, yet loving. "How long do you intend to keep this up?"

"What?"

"This unpleasantness with Rafe. I know you fought yesterday."

He shrugged. "So? What's new about that? We always fight—eventually. That boy pushes all my buttons."

A faint scowl marred Rosa's forehead. "He's not a boy anymore. He's a man." Her voice rose a little. "And he's tried very hard to make things right between the two of you."

He looked down at her, his brows lifting. A spurt of pure annoyance flared through him that she should desert him like this. "Taking his side, are you?"

She stepped close to him and curled her fingers along his arm. "The only side I'm taking is this family's. Hot heads and cold hearts never solved anything. It's time to put old disagreements to rest. They mustn't continue to have such power over you."

"What am I to do, Rosa? If I believe what Rafe told me yesterday, then I was wrong that night in the emergency room."

"You have been wrong before. And will be again, no doubt."

"I can't bear to think of all the wasted years. I thought I knew the truth of it...."

"I think you did what you thought was best for this family. If it was the wrong decision, then it's too late for that now. All you can do is fix the present. Why would you let the opportunity to start fresh slip through your fingers?"

He sighed, feeling put-upon. "After yesterday, he might not be willing to. Your son—"

"He's your son, too," she told him, squeezing his arm. "He'll listen if you handle it right. You raised our children to be kind and strong and to stand on their own two feet. To have good hearts and level heads." She lifted her hand to his cheek, so that he had no choice but to look in her eyes. "You raised them to be like you, Samuel," she said softly. "Don't forget that."

They stared at one another for a long moment. Then Rosa gave him a sweet smile, patted his arm and left him alone once more.

"Damned interfering woman," Sam muttered.

She didn't understand. She couldn't possibly. He ought to go back into the kitchen and tell her all the ways she had it wrong. All those years ago, he might have handled things differently, salvaged something. Was it too late now? Could he and Rafe ever have a normal father-son relationship? Wasn't there too much bad water under the bridge? Rosa had to learn to accept that. He would go in there and make it clear to her, once and for all.

But he looked out into the brisk morning sunlight and did not move.

THE SMELL OF FRESH COFFEE teased Rafe's nostrils, pulling him from sleep. The morning had come faster than he'd expected. Definitely faster than he *wanted*. He knew he could easily have spent several days in bed with Dani, and he couldn't suppress a smile as he gave free rein to his thoughts. In this warm nest of exhausted contentment, wouldn't it be wonderful to do nothing more than learn and relearn each other's bodies?

Hell, maybe he'd suggest it. See what she said.

He yawned and stretched, knowing the impossibility of that. It was time to get up, face the real world once more. Life had a way of getting in your face, making demands. He was a man with responsibilities now. Commitments.

Retrieving his jeans from the floor, he slipped into them. Then he followed his nose to the kitchen.

Dani was there, her back to him as she stood at the counter. She wore a T-shirt in the cool turquoise of swimming-pool water, panties, and nothing but long legs from there on down.

She was humming—surely a good sign—so she didn't hear him come up behind her to push her hair aside. He nuzzled the back of her neck. She smelled like flowers.

"Morning," he said, planting a light kiss against the knob of her spine.

She glanced back over her shoulder. "Good morning. Did you sleep well?"

"No. I slept great. Better than I have in years." He brought his hands around her, cupping her breasts through the T-shirt, kneading gently. "Must have been the bed."

"Must have," she agreed in a teasing tone, then gave him a quick, bold kiss.

Some time during the night, he'd had the stray thought that what had happened between the two of them had to be handled delicately. Keep it nice. Keep it friendly. Give her space if she needed it.

But now that he was holding her again, he realized that finding a real woman with a hunger to match his own put him in danger of losing control entirely. Forget nice. Forget friendly. Being with her like this made an amazing array of fantasies play out in his mind, some of them downright shocking.

When they stopped kissing, Dani relaxed against him. He peered over her shoulder, seeing that she was slicing fresh strawberries into two bowls. She lifted one so that he could nibble it off her fingertips. He made an appropriate sound of appreciation as he let the sweet juice slip down his throat.

When he tried to steal a second one, however, she slapped his hand playfully. "Stop that!" She withdrew two glasses from the dish drainer. "Here. There's orange juice in the fridge. Make yourself useful."

Growing up in the lodge's kitchen, he knew enough not to mess with a woman who had a knife and a mission. He went to the refrigerator and poured the juice. Dani had set a little mountain of plates, napkins and silverware on the breakfast bar. He scooped up everything and took it to the dining area next to the living room.

The table was still cluttered. Carefully he stacked things so he could make space for the dishes. As he pushed mail to one side, a piece of paper that had been folded over itself fluttered to the carpet. He picked it up, intent on adding it to the stack.

And then his breath caught in his throat.

In large, crude letters that had obviously been cut out of various magazines, it contained a very clear message: FORGET THE ACCORDION MAN. DO YOU REALLY WANT TO DIE?

For several long moments, Rafe could do nothing but stare at the words. He felt the banging of his heart in his chest, and had to inhale several deep breaths before the red haze of anger in front of his eyes settled. He couldn't imagine what cowardly SOB would send this, but he knew of only one way to find out.

He went back to the kitchen, stood in the doorway and watched for a few moments as Dani worked. Everything looked so normal. Wooden spoons stood at attention in a small jar on the counter. Crisp, lemon sunlight filtered in through the small window. He could smell the strawberries even from here.

And all the while, this malevolent threat had been here, waiting like a sniper hidden in tall trees.

"When did you get this?" he asked.

She turned, smiling. The smile faded when she saw his expression, becoming a frown as she recognized the note he held in his hand. She bit her lip, as though deciding whether or not she would answer. At last she said, "The day before yesterday. It turned up in my mail at the office."

The day before yesterday? Had she been dealing with this hateful reality on her own for that long?

He tossed the note on the breakfast bar, trying to

keep from showing the alarm that had him by the throat. "It's not very original, is it?"

"No. It's probably just a prank. Some high-school kid with nothing better to do."

"Did you call Bendix?"

"Of course. He's promised to look into it."

Like his father, Rafe didn't put a lot of faith in the sheriff's investigative talents, but Dani's indifferent tone irritated him for reasons he could not fully define. When he spoke, his voice rose, and he was helpless to stop it. "Why didn't you call me?"

"As I recall, we weren't exactly seeing eye to eye about anything at the time."

She dried her hands on a dish towel. Her lips were pressed into a straight line. He knew he'd annoyed her, and frankly, he didn't care.

"I can handle it, Rafe," she told him. "Don't go all caveman on me. I'm a big girl, and most of the time I can take care of myself."

"When I got here yesterday you didn't seem yourself. I thought it was me, but now I see…"

"It *was* you." She came toward him, and when he opened his arms, she slid into his hold like a kitten curled up in familiar hands. "You've always unnerved me. From the day I first met you."

He kissed the top of her head. "This isn't a joke, Dani."

"Maybe not. But look at the way it was put together.

A child could do better. When whoever is doing these things sees that they have no effect—"

"Things?" The word burst from him. He held her at arm's length so he could see her face. "You've had more than one?"

"For heaven's sake, stop acting like the Hillside Strangler has me in his sights."

"Danielle."

Her mouth tightened, and she must have heard the determination in his tone. She was silent for a long time, but his gaze stayed fixed on her. Then her resistance seemed to evaporate because she exhaled a huge sigh and slipped out of his arms to go to the breakfast bar. She picked up the note, studied it for a moment, then turned back to him.

"Just before you showed up yesterday I got a phone call," she said. "Nothing but heavy breathing. I suppose it could have been the same person who sent this and broke into my office."

"Broke into— When?"

"A couple of nights ago. Before the note. I was going back to the office to get something and the door was unlocked. Somebody was inside and he knocked me down before he ran out. I never saw—"

"Wait a minute," Rafe said, holding up one hand. "Someone actually attacked you?"

"Not exactly. I mean, if he meant me real harm, wouldn't they have finished the job? Instead, they just ran off. Thoroughly trashed my office, unfortunately, but it was no worse than that."

The idea that someone would do such a thing sent a fresh jolt of anger through Rafe. Things like this didn't happen in towns like Broken Yoke. "Did he hurt you?"

She grimaced. "Yeah. Bruised my pride."

Rafe pinched the bridge of his nose. "Please tell me you found the nearest phone and called the sheriff."

"I guess that would have been the sensible thing to do," Dani admitted. "But it made me mad. So I jumped up and started off down the alley beside the office to see if I could catch whoever it was trying to scare me."

Rafe look at her, stunned. "What were you thinking?"

She crossed her arms, scowling at his tone of voice. "I guess I was thinking that no cowardly bastard was going to play games like that with me. I had a can of Mace. But then I realized that I wasn't—"

Rafe's hand came up. "Stop!"

"I'm just trying to explain—"

He crossed the distance that separated them in two quick strides, caught her arm and swung her against his chest. As her lips parted in surprise, he lowered his head and kissed her.

He left her breathing hard and raggedly. She stared up into his eyes. "What was that for?"

"Because you make me insane," he told her over the odd, stifling sensation in his chest that felt uncomfortably close to panic. He could feel the anger still inside him, moving like a living thing now. What if something had happened to her? "We have to go to Bendix. He has to give you protection."

"Oh, I'm sure there's money in the Broken Yoke budget for that sort of thing." She laughed a little, an attempt at humor that fell noticeably flat.

His fingers slipped up the sides of her throat. He bent and touched his forehead to hers. "I'll pay for it. We have to find out who this is. I'm not going to let anyone hurt you, Dani."

He hugged her closer, stroking his hand along the run of her vertebrae. His heart tightened with tenderness.

"I'm sure we're making too much of this," Dani said against his chest, but she didn't sound entirely convinced of that. And she didn't move away.

"We're not going to take any chances. Now tell me again about the note, the phone call and the break-in. Don't leave out any detail."

"Rafe…"

"You were at the office…" he prompted.

She gave in with a resigned look, and together they sat down at the table. Rafe made her go over everything once more, asking questions, pressing for more information when she was too vague. The quiet, steady respect he had for her rose. Dani was calm, analytical. In reality, Rafe thought he was more unsettled by all of this than she was.

Finally, they both sat quietly, thinking.

Plucking a strawberry out of her bowl, Dani inspected it as though it were the Hope Diamond. "I wish I could get a fix on who the Accordion Man was." She frowned. "But I've been over the Three Bs' public records a few more times. I've pestered Burt Beckerman at the historical society to death, checked and rechecked back articles. There's simply no mention of an accordion player or *anyone* who went missing around here in the 1950s." She popped the strawberry in her mouth. "After World War II, this town settled down and turned itself into Disneyland."

The phone beside the couch rang suddenly. They both turned to look at it as though a snake had just slithered into their midst. Before Rafe could suggest that he be the one to answer it, Dani picked it up.

Knowing what Rafe's worry would be, she quickly shook her head at him. No problem. Rafe felt his stomach muscles relax.

She returned to the table in just a few minutes. "That was Cissy. She just wanted to let me know she was going to be a little late today." She cast a glance toward the kitchen, where the makings of one terrific breakfast lay unfinished on the counter. "This was going to be such a beautiful morning," she said wistfully. "I was going to make it so special."

Rafe reached across the table and took her hand. "It can still be special. Stay here. I don't want you to go to the office today."

"I have to go."

"Let me take care of you. At least until I can arrange for someone to be with you at all times."

She shook her head. "There's no reason for that. We both have lives to live. I can't just hide out here forever. Besides, how will we ever find out who's doing this if I don't…keep doing what I'm doing?"

He knew she had a point, but he didn't like it. Trying to think of an alternative, Rafe picked up the note, running one finger along its terrible message as though he could lift the identity of the sender right off the words. There had to be some way to figure out who had done these things….

He looked up at Dani suddenly, frowning. "Where's the envelope?"

She dug through the stack of paperwork on the table. When she retrieved the envelope, Rafe saw that it was unmarked, a plain business type without any writing on the front. Not even Dani's name.

He tapped it against the table, his thoughts flitting around in his brain like a moth repeatedly bumping into the light.

"What's wrong?" Dani asked.

"It isn't postmarked. That means it was hand-delivered to your office. How is your mail handled?"

"Cissy goes through it, takes out anything that I don't need to deal with. Sales flyers, junk catalogs, that sort of thing."

"Is it ever left unattended after she sorts it?"

Dani shrugged. "I suppose so. Sometimes Cissy will take a break. Go on an errand. The basket sits on the corner of her desk for me to pick up."

"So anyone who came into your office that day could probably slip it into the stack."

"It's possible."

"We need to talk to Cissy," Rafe said almost to himself. Then he rose. "Get dressed. We have to go."

Looking confused, Dani stood as well. "Where?"

"To Landquist Computers."

"The electronics place next door to my office? Why?"

Rafe stalked into the bedroom to find his shirt. If what he was thinking was a possibility, there might be a way to at least narrow down the suspects. Maybe even pinpoint *exactly* who'd done this. And if Rafe did find out, God help them.

Dani had moved to her closet, but was still waiting for an explanation. As he pulled his polo shirt over his head, Rafe said, "Just before I came back here to live permanently, I was looking at property to buy downtown. That building—where Landquist is now—was empty. It was way overpriced, so I passed on it."

"So?"

"I remember that one of the things the Realtor tried to sell me on was this high-tech security system the previous owner had in place. Too much for a one-horse town like Broken Yoke, but security cameras, both inside and out. They're probably still there."

Dani paused while buttoning the jeans she'd yanked on. "But Landquist Computers moved in a month ago. I covered the grand opening. They could have taken those cameras down."

"Maybe. Or they could have changed them out for their own equipment. But I'm betting that those cameras are still operational and still up there."

Evidently seeing the possibilities, Dani sat on the edge of the bed, rubbing her fingers across her chin as though lost in thought. "And the front doors of Landquist and my office are less than fifty feet apart."

"Which means that anyone who came to your office from that direction could have passed right under the nose of a security camera and be caught on tape." Rafe sat down beside her as he plunged one foot and then the other into his shoes. "If it was recording."

"They could have come into my office from the other direction," Dani pointed out.

"Yeah. But it's worth checking out."

Dani gave him a worried look. "Even if the cameras are still there, even if they were running, do you know how many people could have just been walking down the street?"

Starting to feel more in control, feeling as though they at least had a game plan, Rafe refused to be disheartened. "That corner isn't Hollywood and Vine. And if this idea is a bust, then we'll think of something else. I'll raise holy hell with Bendix. I don't care if he has to call in every citizen of Broken Yoke and grill them until they crack like an egg." He lifted her fingers and pressed his lips to the center of her palm. "No one is going to get away with doing this to you."

She offered him a small smile. "After all these years, can there really be a murderer out there—"

He stepped on those words, that worry, by placing his hand against her lips. "Don't think about it right now." He let his fingers stroke along her cold cheek. "Just think about all the times we're going to be together in this bed. My bed. Any bed you want. We're not going to have just one night, Dani. I don't think either one of us is willing to settle for that."

"About last night…"

He shook his head. "There is so much we ought to talk about. And we will, I promise. But right now, I think we should get to know your neighbor Landquist. Unless you have a better idea?"

She didn't.

CHAPTER EIGHTEEN

RAFE NUDGED HER as they walked through the front entrance of Landquist Computers. She nodded, spotting the security camera overhead just about the same time he did. She'd never noticed the equipment before, though she'd often passed by it. Funny how you could go about your life every day and never realize that Big Brother was watching.

Manny Landquist wasn't quite as helpful as they might have wished. He didn't feel comfortable showing just anyone the company's security tapes, and to make matters worse, the store was in the middle of a big inventory. The place was a mess.

Dani watched Rafe work his magic. Clapping a hand on the guy's shoulder, he led Landquist down the corridor and they talked briefly. When he came back, Landquist was all smiles and took them directly to his office at the back of the store.

Four hours later, they were seated in Sheriff Bendix's office.

On the desk in front of him they had fanned out

pictures they'd printed of each person caught on tape between the hours of 11:00 a.m. and 1:00 p.m. the day the note had been delivered to Dani's office. After phoning Cissy, they knew that had been the only time the office had been left unattended.

Sixteen possible candidates who might have gone into the newspaper office for one reason or another. Fifteen, if you eliminated—for now, anyway—the FedEx guy.

Bendix applauded them for all the legwork they'd done, but Dani could tell the sheriff really didn't think there was much cause for concern. Watching his reaction as Rafe explained, Dani thought it was even possible he resented the fact they'd inserted themselves into what he kept referring to as "an official police investigation."

When it finally came down to what action to take next, the sheriff looked at the pictures once again. He shook his head and said, "Humph," in consternation.

Seated beside her, Rafe shifted in annoyance. She knew he was as irritated by the man's attitude as she was, but nothing good would come from showing it. She touched his arm, a silent communication urging him to hold on to his temper.

They'd stared at the tapes for hours at Landquist's, trying to put names to faces for so long that Dani had a headache. Now this roadblock. With a sigh, she sat forward in her chair, ready to drive home their point once more.

"So there are fifteen people," she said wearily. "Seven strangers—people neither of us know, anyway. Two who we couldn't make out well enough on the tape. One kid riding his bicycle on the sidewalk—I think he can safely be taken off the list, and five people we recognize."

Bendix withdrew two of the pictures from the pile and held them up. "Make that only five strangers. These two I know. Corey Chambers from the taxidermy place out by the interstate and Lilly Richmond. I think we can eliminate her."

"Why?" Rafe asked. "Who's Lilly Richmond?"

"My mother-in-law. She was here visiting from Utah all last week. She's an old witch, but I've never known her to kill anyone." Bendix grinned. "But hell, let's haul her back here for questioning. Might scare the old biddy into behaving herself for a while."

While the sheriff laughed heartily at his own sense of humor, Rafe got up.

Sensing trouble ahead, Dani said quickly, "Let's go over the ones we do know one more time." She looked down at her list. "Polly Swinburne, Burt Beckerman, Cissy's mother Charlene, Geneva McKay and Leo Waxman."

"Can't see Paranoid Polly doing something like this," Bendix said. "If she killed someone, she'd be bragging about it."

Rafe moved closer to the man's desk, radiating annoyance. "If you're not—"

Knowing he was about to get them tossed out in the street, Dani stepped on Rafe's words. "Sheriff, I don't honestly think Polly Swinburne has been doing this, either. But she should at least be questioned. If she came to the office, perhaps she saw the person who left that note. We need all the help we can get. I was in Carson City, so I saw very few people that day."

"So what's the deal with Cissy?" the sheriff asked them for a second time. "Why didn't she see these people between eleven and one?"

Dani watched Rafe's jaw clench and then unclench. "Since Dani was out for the day, she took an extended lunch hour with her mother," he told him.

The sheriff frowned. "And left the office open?"

Dani tried not to let her impatience show. "The inner office—my office—was locked. There's nothing much of value in the reception area, and in a town like this, everyone is used to leaving doors unlocked. She didn't think anything of it."

"I tell people all the time they can't act like we still live under Eisenhower. When I was a kid you could—"

"What's our next move, Sheriff?" Rafe cut in.

Bendix's eyes narrowed. "What do you mean, *our* next move? *Your* next move is to go on home and let me handle this. It's an official police investigation now and—"

"Well, then start investigating," Rafe snapped, evidently no longer able to contain his anger. "What about the fact that someone broke into Dani's office? How are you handling that?"

"The incident is under investigation as well. According to Ms. Bridgeton, nothing was taken so it's a little difficult—"

Rafe swung his arm back to point to Dani while he scowled at the sheriff. "They trashed her office. They knocked this woman down and could have seriously hurt her. What does it take for you to get off you butt and do your job?"

It only got worse from there.

Ten minutes later, Dani and Rafe were standing on the sidewalk in front of the sheriff's office. She sighed. "Gosh, I sure feel safe *now*."

"My father is right," Rafe said in a disgusted tone. "Bendix couldn't find his way through a maze even if the rats helped him."

"Now what?"

"He says he's going to talk to Leo Waxman since his place is on his way home. I think we should focus on the strangers." He glanced down at the second set of photographs they'd taken off Manny Landquist's printer, sifting through them. "There has to be some way to identify them."

"We could talk to your parents."

He gave her an odd look. "Why?"

"Because your mom and dad have been here forever. They might recognize some of them."

"Mom will help. I'm not sure about Pop."

"Why not?"

"Last time I saw him, he was swearing at me in Italian."

"You two are worse than children," Dani said, shaking her head. Then she snapped her fingers as a new idea came to her. "How about Burt Beckerman with the historical society? He probably knows everyone, and we can ask him why he came by the office at the same time."

"Good idea." Rafe shot a look of contempt over his shoulder toward the sheriff's office. "Let's go. Before I go back in there and end up behind bars myself."

Having poured over so many early newspaper articles at the Historical Society Museum, Dani had been in Burt Beckerman's company often. Only once had she been to his home. He lived alone in a small Victorian cottage—a little wedding cake of a house— near the outskirts of town, a widower who still mourned his wife, according to Geneva McKay.

Dani couldn't honestly say that Burt made much of an impression on a person, but she remembered being awed by his front yard. It was small, but lush and beautifully tended, with a trio of bird feeders under tall aspens and so many flowers—the riches of spring. It looked as if it had been copied from the pages of a gardening magazine.

They climbed the front steps, opened the screened door and knocked. For the longest time there was no answer, then finally the door swung wide.

Burt stood there, an elderly man with wispy, cotton fuzz for hair and watery blue eyes. He nodded his head sharply. "I've been waiting for you."

"You have?" Dani smiled at him, wondering if Sheriff Bendix had warned him to expect a visitor.

"I made a mistake," Burt told them in a quavering voice that sounded as gray as his face looked. "It was bound to catch up with me sooner or later. You've figured it out, haven't you?"

Dani frowned at the old guy. "Figured what out, Mr. Beckerman?"

"That I killed the Accordion Man," he said in a scratchy whisper.

And then, he began to cry.

"I SWEAR TO YOU on my wife's grave. It was an accident."

Burt Beckerman sat in a shabby rocker in his living room, his gnarled hands clutching a plaid throw against his rail-thin body as though he were chilled to the bone. His eyes were red-rimmed and filled with fear.

Dani sat across from him on the couch. Sheriff Bendix, who'd arrived only minutes ago, sat next to her. Rafe was leaning in the nearby door frame with broad-shouldered ease. His face looked composed, but behind the surface placidity of his dark eyes, Dani could see banked fires.

Burt's forehead puckered, and his features were apologetic as he looked at Dani. "I'm sorry for what I did to you. I should have just told the truth. That's always better, isn't it? Connie used to say that truthfulness was the main element of character."

Dani didn't know how to respond. It seemed impossible to believe that this ruined old man could be the Accordion Man's murderer and her tormentor. There was something so helpless and lost about him.

"I think you'd better just start at the beginning, Burt," Sheriff Bendix suggested.

Burt nodded. "I guess that's the right place," After a long minute, he shifted back in his rocking chair and said, "Connie—my wife—and I were raised right here in Broken Yoke, next door to each other. I was crazy about her. I knew she was the one for me, and I'd have married her when she turned sixteen if I could have talked her into it."

His features softened, as though he were already lost to the memory of what it felt like to be young and in love. Dani watched him use his thumb to twist his simple gold wedding band back and forth, and she wondered if he was even aware of that tiny movement.

"But then her father died, and times got hard. Lots of people were moving out, looking for jobs down in Denver. Connie got it into her head that she could make good money for her family if she took a job at the Three Bs. That was about the only place in town making a real go of it in those days."

"A job doing what?" Bendix asked.

Two bright pink spots of color stained Burt's cheeks suddenly. No one in the room needed any further ex-

planation. The Three Bs might have been a great place
to socialize, but they all knew it had a history of
offering other amusements as well. Had Connie really
believed that her family's salvation lay behind one of
those rooms, somewhere along that long corridor of
peepholes? How desperate must she have been?

"Don't think poorly of her," Burt said quickly. "She
wasn't that way. She'd hardly ever even been kissed.
She was just scared for her family. I begged her not
to do it. I told her I'd help her. But she wouldn't listen."

Exhaling a long sigh, Burt reached for a photograph that sat on the end table next to his chair. His
fingers traced over the picture, and he looked like
someone lost inside themselves as he stared down at
it. "Myrtle Culpepper hired her on the spot. Connie
was always so beautiful." He passed the frame to the
sheriff like an eager child seeking validation. "You
remember, Bob?"

"I remember."

When the sheriff finished looking at the picture, he
handed it to Dani. This was no picture-book old lady
shot. The photograph was of a pretty woman of about
twenty-five. Trim, with long legs and blond hair that
was a lovely, windblown tangle. Smiling for the camera,
she struggled to hold her short skirt down in the breeze.

Dani handed the photograph back to Burt. Her
heart cramped with pity for him, and she heard
herself say, "You were a lucky man, Mr. Beckerman.
She was stunning."

The old man seemed to rally a little. "Yes, I was lucky. We were married fifty-some years and every one of them was happy." He glanced around the room—as though taking in a lifetime of memories. "I keep this house just the way she liked it. The yard, too. She had the greenest thumb of anyone in these parts, and I couldn't let it go to ruin."

"What happened after your wife was hired?" Rafe spoke up from the doorway. His tone was quiet, thoughtful.

"Mostly the Three Bs provided a place to hang out. We called it a juke joint in those days. Singing and dancing. Having a few beers with friends."

He replaced Connie's picture on the table, and sighed heavily.

"The first night Connie worked, there was also an accordion player new with the band. A guy named Willie Holt. He was just a drifter who was looking to make a few bucks before moving on."

"How do you know that?" Bendix asked.

"Because he noticed Connie right away, and that's what he told her. Said he was working his way to California to be in the movies."

"Connie told you that?"

"Yeah. After I…" Burt trailed off, bowing his head as though in penitence. His fingers on the arms of the rocker had become no more than claws digging into the wood. At last, he raised his eyes. "I was there that night. I was sure I could talk Connie into coming home." Burt's Adam's apple bobbed wildly. "But I couldn't."

Seconds ticked by. For just a moment, the afternoon sun cast long, harsh shadows across the old man's face, giving him a grim, almost sinister appearance. Dani tried to remember that Burt was a murderer, but it seemed so impossible. "So then what happened?" she prompted him softly.

"The band took a break, and the next thing I knew Connie and this Holt fellow were gone. I went upstairs—that was the only place I figured they could be. I heard voices coming from down at the end of the hall—loud voices.

"It was them. Holt had her down on the floor like some animal. She was trying to get him to turn her loose, but of course, he didn't. I guess I just lost my mind for a few seconds. I picked up the first thing I saw and hit him over the head with it."

"The accordion," Rafe said.

Burt nodded. "He stopped moving, and I knew right away that I'd killed him."

Sheriff Bendix shook his head. "So you decided to hide the body."

For the first time since he'd begun, Burt's face flashed with agitation. "No! I honestly didn't know what to do, but I wasn't going to hide anything because a man has a right—a duty—to protect the woman he loves, doesn't he?"

No one said a word.

"Then Myrtle came in. She said there was no way she was going to get caught in the middle of a murder trial. Bad for business, you know. The next thing I knew, we were carting his body into a storeroom. She said she'd get rid of it. That he wouldn't be missed. Since he was basically a stranger, and she'd been going to fire him anyway, no one would find it odd if he didn't come back from break. Connie and I were just scared teenagers. We didn't argue with her."

"And you just left it at that?" the sheriff asked. "You went home?"

"I took Connie home. Later I saw Myrtle in town and she said that our little problem had been taken care of. That's what she called it. 'Our little problem.'"

Rafe had unwound from the doorway and came to sit beside Dani. He said to Burt, "And you never knew what she did with the body?"

"No, and I never asked. Myrtle was killed in a car accident a year later. Connie and I got married. Neither one of us ever went into the Three Bs again. And we never talked about that night. Not ever."

"Myrtle must have walled him up in that room," Dani said.

Wrapped in his own dark thoughts, Burt took several long seconds to answer. "I guess so. I never really wanted to know." He slid a troubled glance at Rafe. "But then you found him, and everything got stirred up again." His gaze traveled to Dani. "And you wouldn't stop digging into it."

"So you decided to threaten Miss Bridgeton," Rafe stated flatly.

Burt bit his lip and ducked his head. "I'm sorry about that. I would never have hurt you. I just thought I could get you to leave well enough alone." He lifted his eyes, and they seemed to be pleading with Dani. "You have to understand—Connie and I lived here, raised kids here, and grandkids, too. When she died, everyone mourned her." He sent a glance toward the sheriff. "Isn't that right, Bob?"

"She was a very fine woman, Burt."

"I didn't want that one mistake of hers—that one night—to be how people remember her. I know what I did was wrong, and I didn't care about me. But Connie's reputation was at stake."

Dani got up and began to pace. "You broke into my office."

"I did."

"How?"

"It's an old building, with old locks. Turns out it's as easy as what you see on television. And what I didn't know, I learned on the Internet. I wasn't really expecting it to work. But it did."

"What were you looking for in my office?"

"Anything that would tell me you were on to me. But I guess no one keeps stuff like that in paper anymore. I didn't know how to break into your computer."

"No instructions on the Internet I take it," Rafe said.

"None that I could find." Burt gave Dani a look full

of misery. "I'm sorry if I hurt you at all. You surprised me by coming back to the office. I just wanted to get away. Nearly killed myself doing it. I have emphysema, you know. As it was, when I got home, I nearly passed out trying to catch my breath."

"You put that note in with my mail."

"Yes."

She cocked her head at him. It was so difficult to imagine a man Burt's age trying to terrorize her. In fact, it was downright embarrassing. "And you made an obscene phone call to me yesterday afternoon?"

"It wasn't obscene," Burt objected. "Truth was, I was so nervous I couldn't talk. So I just hung up." He looked at Dani with resignation. "You know, truthfully, I'm kind of glad to finally have it all out in the open."

A long silence followed. Burt sat there somberly, looking straight ahead, as though he were locked inside a prison of very thick glass. Dani moved to the far side of the room.

She didn't know what to think. A man was dead. Murdered and denied a decent burial for so many years. And yet, somewhere down in the depth of her heart, Dani felt she could understand how it all could have happened. How Burt had been driven to it in horrific moments that had been irretrievable.

Rafe came up beside her. "Are you going to press charges?" he asked.

Dani swung around, watching silently as Sheriff

Bendix began reading Burt his rights. "I don't think that would serve any purpose."

Burt stood, moving in a wooden sort of way as though against his will. Dani and Rafe followed them out of the house. It felt good to be out in the open air again, as though the house had been weighted in shadows.

She watched Bendix help Burt into the back of the patrol car. "Kind of sad, don't you think? A crime of passion that's haunted him for all these years."

Rafe tucked her into his arms. She went willingly, finding his touch so life-affirming in its complete absence of barriers and pretenses. "The judge will take the circumstances into consideration," Rafe said. "He's been a trusted member of the community. And how much jail time can he reasonably be expected to serve, given his age and his health problems?"

Dani lifted her head as inspiration came to her. "The town needs to get behind him. I know people who could help—"

He kissed her, and when she looked at him in surprise, he said, "You are such a soft touch."

Bendix joined them on the sidewalk. "I'm going to need a statement from you," he told Dani. "Can you ride down to the station with me?"

She nodded.

As she tucked her notepad into her purse, Rafe slipped his hand to the back of her neck and rubbed gently. "Can you manage by yourself? I need to pick up Frannie and spend a little daddy time with her since I've hardly seen her in the last twenty-four hours. She has a ballet recital coming up. Her first. How would you feel about seeing it with me?"

The invitation pleased her, but Dani hesitated, not sure just what he was offering. They still needed to talk about last night. Was that the plan? Surely not, with Frannie present. Afterward, maybe?

Why was he the kind of guy whose face seldom gave away what he was thinking? It was maddening. The fact that she was in love with this man didn't mean a thing if he was just looking for company.

She settled for giving Rafe a tentative smile. "Sounds like fun."

"Good." He kissed her lightly on the lips. "I'll call you."

CHAPTER NINETEEN

"COME ON, FRANNIE," Rafe said, knocking on his own bedroom door. "Open up."

"Not yet," his daughter's muffled voice came back. "Just wait, Daddy."

Exhaling heavily, Rafe stepped back and sat cross-legged on the hall carpet. He'd picked up Frannie from Kari and Nick's place thirty minutes ago, and from the moment he'd shown up she'd bounced around him like a silly puppy. Something to do with the ballet costume his mother had finished sewing for her. Some pink, gauzy thing with enormous wings.

Her excitement was infectious. It made him feel good to see her so involved with the family, eager to spend time with new friends, finding her place here in Broken Yoke. Big brother Matt had been right. His suggestion that they get professional help from a child psychologist had been a good one. The sessions the two of them had been going to had made all the difference in the world.

Frannie had chattered excitedly all the way home,

and now he'd agreed to a private showing of her ballet outfit. Because his room had the only floor-length mirror in the house, she'd run awkwardly up the stairs with her costume, closed his bedroom door in his face and insisted that he wait patiently outside while she changed.

He knew Frannie was crazy about playacting, but were all little girls this nuts about dressing up? God, he still had so much to learn.

He glanced down at his watch. It was only five in the afternoon, but he was starving. Neither he nor Dani had stopped for lunch today, and now his stomach growled every few minutes.

He rapped on his door, trying to hurry this along. "I've already seen your costume, Frannie. You're going to be the prettiest ballerina there."

"Not a ballerina!" Frannie yelled in a put-upon voice. "A *fairy*. With wings."

"Oh. Sorry."

The sound of several drawers opening and slamming shut came through the door. "Why don't you have any makeup in here?"

"I'm coming in." Rafe rattled the doorknob for emphasis.

"No! Don't come in. It's a surprise. Just wait."

"Aren't you hungry? I'm making your favorite for dinner. Mac and cheese."

"With hot dogs in it?"

Rafe grinned, drew his legs up and tipped his head back against the opposite wall. He could have predicted that request. Maybe he was getting better at this daddy stuff after all. "Sure. Just hurry up and come out."

"In a minute."

He sat there and tried to keep his mind off his stomach. Had Dani grabbed something to eat yet, or was she still at Bendix's office? He'd call her in a little while to see if they were done. Did she like macaroni and cheese with hot dogs? There was still so much he didn't know about her. And so much he wanted to learn.

"Hey, Frannie!" he called. "What do you think of Dani Bridgeton?"

"She has pretty feet" came his daughter's quick response.

"There's a high recommendation," Rafe muttered. To Frannie, he said, "That's all she's got going for her?"

"She's nice. She doesn't talk to me like I'm stupid."

"Good. Do you mind if she comes to your recital?"

"No." More muffled sounds of drawers banging shut. "Okay," Frannie said at last. "You can come in now."

He rose and entered his bedroom, prepared to look enthusiastic and charmed. Not such a stretch, really. When Frannie chose to act like a typical little girl, he found it almost impossible to keep from smiling, inside and out.

"What's this all about? What's so important—"

His words died in his throat.

Across the bedroom, the balcony doors were open. He was suddenly aware of small details—the way the thin curtains billowed outward and then sucked inward with a snap, the slant of afternoon sunlight lying in stripes across the carpet, how sweet the air smelled.

But the only reality he could really focus on, the only thing that stopped his heart and turned his belly into a cold, slimy hollow was the sight of Frannie.

Dressed in her fairy outfit, she was balanced on the edge of the balcony railing, smiling back at him with the giveaway sparkle of anticipation in her eyes. There seemed to be an ocean of space between them.

Rafe stopped dead in his tracks, but the burning need to do something, *anything,* rose inside him. He wanted to be calm, controlled, not frighten her in any way, but his brain didn't get the message in time to warn his tongue. "What the hell are you doing?" he shouted at her.

Thank God Frannie was not a child who had ever been easily intimidated. She just continued smiling. "I'm gonna show you. I'm gonna fly off the balcony." She wiggled a little on the railing, sending Rafe's blood pumping through his veins even faster. "Watch. I have wings."

"No!" Rafe yelled, and this time his daughter frowned. Trying to get a grasp on panic, he said more evenly, "Frannie, don't move."

"Why?"

"You might fall."

She looked like that idea was completely inconceivable. "No, I won't. But if I do, I put pillows down there just in case. From your bed. So I won't get squished." She scooted forward a little and those ridiculous wings attached to the back of her costume bounced up and down. "I just want to show you."

"Please, sweetie," Rafe stumbled on. His hand stretched out. "Just sit still."

"Why? Aunt Addy said you jumped off the roof of the stable once when you tried to fly."

He took a few paces forward, praying, inventing and rejecting excuses and ideas one right after the other. Finally, he said, "Did she tell you I broke my arm in three places?"

"You did?" Frannie asked, a ghoulish, sudden interest in her voice.

Quickly Rafe rolled up the left sleeve of his shirt, shortening the distance between them. He was at the balcony entrance now. "Look, I'll show you the scars I got." He extended his arm, though there was nothing unusual about it at all. "See this mark?"

"No."

"Right here. Look closer."

She cocked her head and squinted down at Rafe's arm. "I still don't— Hey!"

The moment she stopped looking at him, Rafe had jumped forward to catch the back of her outfit. He heard the flimsy material rip as he yanked hard. Her feet flew up over the railing as she landed in a pink, wiggling heap on the balcony tile.

He grabbed her up, setting her on her feet. His heart

reeled with the sweetness of her body crushed against his. He couldn't help it. Holding her in the hard, possessive circle of his arms, all he could say was "Oh God. Oh God."

Frannie, of course, had a different reaction. She scowled fiercely at him. "No fair, Daddy! I was just trying—"

With his fear subsiding, with his adrenaline settling, Rafe couldn't control his anger. He gave her a firm shake. "You little idiot! What in the name of all that's holy am I supposed to do with you? Why would you think you can fly? You could have been killed!"

"But—"

He took her hand in his, marching her toward the door. "Come with me."

"Where are we going?"

Frannie had to run to keep up with him as he stalked to her room. He opened the door and swung her inside. She stared up at him through a prism of tears, but he wasn't going to let that sway him. "You stay in here and think about the scare you just gave me. You think about using your head for something besides a hat rack."

"What does that mean?"

"Never mind. Take that costume off. Get into your pajamas."

Although tears continued to leak from the corners of her eyes, Frannie's features were brightly defiant. "Why are you yelling at me?"

"I'm taking your accordion away from you."

"But you gave it to me. That makes you an Indian giver."

"I don't care. And no supper. You're grounded for... for I don't know how long yet."

"Why?"

"Because I said so," Rafe heard himself say.

"That's a stupid reason." Her hands were folded over her thin chest now. She had stiffened into a stony image of resentment. "I hate you!"

"Yeah, well right now I don't care about that either. You stay in here until I come to let you out. Is that clear? In fact, I'm locking you in."

"You can't do that," Frannie yelled back, but Rafe was already at her door, fumbling with the lock. He slammed it shut, listened for a minute to the sound of silence coming from within, then went downstairs.

He felt old suddenly, and exhausted.

He went over to the telephone, flipping through his address book. He clutched at his anxiety, but all he could think about was how devastating that little stunt might have been. And he'd let it happen. Who was he kidding? He wasn't getting better at being a father. He was getting worse.

Finding the number he wanted, he dialed quickly and was relieved when the call was picked up on the first ring. "It's me, Rafe," he said without preliminary. "Can you come up to my place? I need help. And I need it now."

DANI SWORE AND SHUT DOWN her computer.

She'd been trying for fifteen minutes to compose an e-mail to Gary about the discovery of the Accordion Man's killer. But it was useless. She couldn't seem to focus, couldn't make the words come together right. Couldn't do much of anything, really, except think about poor Burt Beckerman sitting in a jail cell in Bendix's office.

She knew she shouldn't feel sorry for him. After all, he'd killed Willie Holt and helped to hide the evidence. He'd threatened her. It was just that he'd looked so broken sitting in that cell, so completely undone. Maybe justice really had been served. But things hadn't turned out the way she'd hoped at all.

She wished she could talk to Rafe. He'd promised to call her, but no telling when. Tonight? Tomorrow? It was already seven-thirty, and so far she hadn't heard a word. Maybe he'd gotten sidetracked by his family, or tied up taking care of Frannie.

Then suddenly, the outside line rang in the reception area. She punched the right button and snatched up the phone. "Hello?"

"Dani?"

It wasn't Rafe. But it was close enough. "Frannie? Is that you?"

"Uh-huh."

"What's up, kiddo?"

"Can you come get me?"

The child sounded upset. Dani frowned into the receiver. "Where are you?"

"At my house. Daddy says I can't have supper. And he's gonna take away my accordion. And…and I think I'm gonna be sick."

What in the world was this all about? The child wasn't making much sense.

"So will you come?" Frannie asked.

"What did you do to get into such trouble?"

"Nothing. I was just showing Daddy what I could do in my costume, and he got all mad and threw me in my room and locked the door. And now I'm gonna starve 'cause he hates me."

Dani stopped tapping her finger against the receiver and sat up straighter. "You're locked in your room?"

"Uh-huh."

"Where's your father right now?"

"Downstairs. With a lady."

That surprised her. "How do you know there's a lady with him?" she asked.

"I saw her from my window when she got out of her car. She's always with him. Her name is Heather."

Oh. *That* lady. The one everyone in town talked about. The blonde she'd seen him with at the festival.

Dani couldn't help it. She felt a little spurt of jealousy that Rafe would invite Heather to his place so quickly after the two of them had parted this afternoon. Back in Vegas, she'd always known that Rafe wasn't the kind of man to want for female companionship, though even for him this seemed a bit sudden. But really, hadn't she learned yet that things that appeared to be too good to be true usually were? It was like trying to hold on to magic. It was given, it arrived. And when it was gone, you called for it in vain.

She told herself to stop feeling sorry for herself. There'd been no commitments, no strings, between the two of them. He had a perfect right to see anyone he wished. She'd never been the jealous type. Her main concern right now should be helping Frannie.

"Frannie, why didn't you call your aunt, or your grandparents?"

"I don't know their number. Besides, they probably like Daddy better than me."

"How did you find mine?"

The child sighed in annoyance. "I called 4-1-1 for the newspaper phone number, silly. I'm not a baby."

"No, you're not. You're such a clever girl."

"Daddy doesn't think so," Frannie complained, and it sounded as if she was on the verge of tears. "He says my head is just for hats."

"Don't cry," Dani said quickly when she heard Frannie give a soggy sigh. "I'll try to help you."

"Will you just come, please? I'm locked up just like Princess Fiona."

"Who?" Dani asked, then remembered the make-believe castle she'd seen in Rafe's living room. "Never mind. I remember."

How could a man who would play those kinds of

games with his little girl end up treating her so shabbily? He'd seemed to be making real headway with her. But then, maybe Rafe didn't mind a kid hanging around as long as he didn't have other plans. More enjoyable plans. Like the lovely Heather.

"Hurry up, okay? I'm hungry."

"All right, Princess," Dani promised. "I'll see what I can do to get you freed."

But as soon as she hung up, Dani knew she wasn't going to be the one to go over to Rafe's place to spring his daughter out of her dungeon. It was none of her business, really. And how could it keep from being embarrassing if this other woman really *was* there? She'd call Addy D'Angelo. Or maybe Rose, who had always impressed Dani as the kind of person who knew the best way to handle any uncomfortable situation.

She picked up the receiver again, then replaced it. Rafe's place was only a few blocks away. She could make a quick stop and be on her way. It didn't have to be awkward.

All the way over to the Three Bs, she kept telling herself that. It didn't matter how Rafe's interest in this Heather person affected their relationship. She should have known that last night had meant far more to her than it had to him. It had been a dream, a phantom structure that would have been built on a very shaky foundation. Oz had a gift for making every woman his slave. But he wasn't going to do that to her. She wasn't willing to be just another female conquest for the Wizard of Women.

Frannie was all that mattered now. Frannie. Locked in her tower like a pint-sized Rapunzel.

What kind of father did that?

She parked in Rafe's driveway, behind a hot little sports car that crouched in the moonlight like a caged beast. Feeling ridiculous, trying hard to ignore the small, sad drop her heart gave at the sight of this other woman's vehicle, Dani rapped on the front door sharply.

Rafe answered. "Hi," he said, looking a little surprised to see her. "I was going to call you later."

"And now you don't have to."

He held a wineglass in his hand, half-empty. He frowned a little, like someone at the start of a headache. "Everything all right?"

"You mean at the police station? Yes. But with you, I don't know. You're daughter called me."

"Frannie?"

She couldn't help it. It was just so irritating to come face- to-face with the realization that she'd probably been chasing illusions for the past twenty-four hours. "Do you have any others I don't know about?" she asked.

He caught her mood instantly. In a gently curious tone, he opened the door wider and said, "Why don't you come in?"

"I'm not sure that's such a good idea. I hear you have company."

In the next moment, a woman with a smile as lovely as a toothpaste ad came up beside him. Heather, Dani supposed. She had only seen her from a distance, but she was as beautiful as gossip said. Dressed casually in shorts and a silky blouse, her long blond hair caught up in a ponytail, it was clear she was here socially.

She smiled a greeting at Dani, then touched Rafe's arm. "I'm going to go upstairs and talk to Frannie."

Dani watched her walk away, all long legs and graceful curves. A sharp pang went through Dani's body. Clearing her throat, she swallowed the faint sensation of shock and yanked her mind back to the reason she had come. "Frannie said you locked her in her room," she said. "Is that true?"

"Yes."

She nodded. "Could I ask why?"

"Because at the moment, that's the best place for her." He set his wineglass down on the hall table. "What's this all about, Dani?" he asked, looking confused.

"I don't want to tell you how to live your life, Rafe. But if you want to entertain women here, you can't just lock your child in her room because she's an inconvenience. There are laws against that sort of thing."

His eyes met hers for an instant before she looked away awkwardly. "What the hell are you talking about? I'm not entertaining women. I'm not entertaining anyone." He tipped his head sideways, as though he'd never seen her before. "Are you talking about Heather?"

Dani shook her head violently. "No. Whatever your relationship is with Heather, it's definitely none of my business. I just came by to see that Frannie is all right. She doesn't deserve to be treated this way."

"Dani—"

She made a gesture of finality when he stretched out a hand to her. *Don't listen. Don't let him touch you. You fall off the wagon just once, and you're a goner.* If she could just get away now, maybe her life could get back on that neat, tidy track she could barely remember. She turned quickly and headed for her car.

"Dani. Wait a minute—" Rafe said behind her.

She kept walking, hoping he wouldn't follow, desperate and filled with the claustrophobic need to escape. She made it to her car, but the moment she opened the door, Rafe was there, slamming it shut and pinning her against it.

"What's the matter with you?" he demanded.

Her breath moved inward with slow care. He was so close. "Nothing's the matter with me. You're the one who treats your child like chattel."

She saw the glitter of harsh amusement in his eyes. "I've got a lot of vices, but abusing my daughter isn't one of them."

"Then let her out." She pushed against his shoulder, trying to put space between them so she could get in her car. "And let me go," she added, her voice rising. "I agree. You have plenty of vices. But I'm not interested in talking about them."

He was silent for a long moment, looking at her. But though his voice was quiet and controlled when he spoke, his appraisal of her was callous. "You seem to have something else bothering you besides Frannie's welfare," he said quietly. "Care to tell me what it is?"

"No." She looked away, seeing the muscles in his arm flexing tensely. Her throat felt so dry that it hurt to swallow.

"Tell me," he said. "Get it out. Do you want to fight, Dani? Do you *need* to fight for some reason?"

She shook her head. Her mind felt vacant. "It's not you. It's me. I'm mad at myself for daring to think that…last night…" She looked up at him. "It was silly of me to think that one great night of sex could mean anything more to you than that. You can't change. Oz is just who you are. Who you'll—" She had to stop before her voice broke.

The stillness in his body was full of caution. His dark eyes were more severe than she'd ever seen them. "Oz doesn't exist anymore. I've told you that."

"How am I supposed to believe that, when…"

Without thinking, she looked toward the front door. Inside, pretty Heather was probably waiting for Rafe to return.

Rafe frowned and followed the direction of her glance. He stiffened suddenly, and his short laugh lacked the smallest trace of amusement. "So this is about Heather? You think I've already replaced you with another woman? God, I'd be flattered by your jealousy if it wasn't so ridiculous."

"I'm not jealous. I'm…disappointed for—"

"For trusting me?" he snapped. "For believing me when I told you this morning that I wanted more from our relationship than just a few nights of hot sex? You think I'd sleep with you—share what we shared—and then call Heather tonight because I need a different woman to wake up to tomorrow?"

Dani lifted her chin, feeling as though she were drowning in love and grief but determined not to show it.

He made a low, furious sound in his throat, like a growl. "Okay. You want to know what Heather has that you don't?"

"No."

"A degree in child psychology," he went on as though she hadn't spoken. "Heather is Dr. Heather Bransford. My brother Matt put me in touch with her because frankly, if there's one area I am completely hopeless in it's child rearing. I need her help, and she's been working with me for Frannie's sake for weeks. Tonight I locked Frannie in her room because I didn't know what else to do. She scared the hell out of me by deciding she wanted to fly off my bedroom balcony in her fairy costume." He grimaced. "I might have overreacted. Hell, I *know* I did, but you try reasoning with a kid who's about to take a header off a two-story building."

Dani bit the inside of her cheek. She had to concede the possibility that he was telling the truth. Frannie could be a daring little thing, full of as much mischief as her father had probably been as a child.

"I called Heather and asked her to come over," he went on, "to tell me what to do. She was nice enough to drop everything and come." He lifted his brows. "Does that explanation satisfy you? Or do you need to see her credentials before you believe me?"

A coil of shock tightened inside her. She tried to regain her composure, but the knowledge that she could be so misguided was overwhelming. She was embarrassed about reacting so emotionally, embarrassed to have automatically assumed the worst just because she didn't want to get hurt. What was the matter with her?

Before she could say anything, Rafe spoke, and his voice was frosty. "I thought we had a chance, Dani. I know a person can be with a hundred wrong women and not feel a thing, and then suddenly, feel it like *that*." He snapped his fingers. "That's what I thought we'd found. But you and me—it's no use. You'll never trust me."

"Rafe—"

He shook his head sharply. "Just now you were ready to take the word of a five-year-old child before you'd believe me. Yesterday I had to show you a chest full of scars before you'd consider the fact that I might be telling the truth about what happened that night in Vegas. Well, guess what? I'm tired of trying to convince people who I am. I've got nothing to hide, and nowhere to hide it, but I'm not always going to have a boatload of scars to prove what I say is true. The woman I fall in love with will have to take some things on faith."

He backed away, releasing her.

"That isn't you, Dani," he said in a colorless tone. "Go home."

She stared at him, stunned. She felt like someone stabbed, but not yet bleeding. Numb before the promised pain. Before she could think of anything to say, Rafe had turned and walked away.

She watched him go, wondering how the best moments of her life and the worst moments of her life could happen in less than twenty-four hours.

CHAPTER TWENTY

SAM SAT IN THE THIRD ROW of Broken Yoke's elementary-school auditorium. He watched his granddaughter take little, prancing steps across the stage while her ballet teacher banged out some silly song on the piano. The kid was good, better than the other three up there, but those Pepto-Bismol–pink outfits were all wrong.

He leaned to his left to whisper to Rosa. "Polka dots would have been prettier and made more of a statement."

"Yes," Rosa agreed. "And the statement it would have made is that the instructor is as nutty as a fruitcake. Now hush."

With a disgusted sigh, he settled back once more. He supposed he'd better stay quiet. He was lucky he'd gotten invited to this thing at all, considering that he and Rafe were still on the outs. His son sat strategically placed on the other side of Rosa, recording the whole show. Though they'd all ridden together in the lodge van, Rafe had yet to say more than two words to Sam.

The recital ended. Bows were taken. There was a

ridiculous amount of wild applause for the children and roses for their ballet teacher, who looked like she hadn't been in slippers in about twenty years. Then everyone filed out of the auditorium and headed backstage to pick up their kids.

Francesca ran up to them, her eyes sparkling, her pink tutu waving up and down with every step. "What did you think? Did you see me step on Rhonda's foot? I thought I'd fall down, but I didn't."

Rafe pulled her to his side, bent down and planted a kiss on the top of her dark hair. "I thought you were wonderful, sweetheart. The very best."

"Enchanting!" Rosa added.

"*Bellissima,* Francesca," Sam said. "Do you remember what I told you that means?"

The child went nearly as pink as her costume. "Uh-huh. Beautiful."

"You looked like you could take flight at any moment," Rosa said.

Rafe made a face. "Don't tell her that. I'll be yanking her off the balcony railing again."

Francesca giggled and looked up at her father. "No, you won't, Daddy. I promised. No more scaring you."

Rafe had told his mother what had happened at his place two nights ago, and of course, Rosa had told Sam. How close he'd come to real tragedy. The girl was such a little devil. Perhaps that was God's practical joke, giving Rafe a child who was as strong-willed as he had been.

Francesca began to squirm in her outfit. Rosa motioned to the girl to take her hand. "Come along," she said. "We'll get you changed."

They trooped off together, leaving Rafe and Sam to stand alone in the corridor. The crowd around them was disappearing fast. Rafe leaned back against the wall, crossed his arms and stared down at his camera as though it fascinated him. Sam slipped one arm out of his crutch cuff and wiggled it back and forth, waiting.

The moments dripped away.

After a time, Rafe said, "It was nice of you to come. You didn't have to."

Sam's heart lifted in his chest. Actual conversation. Was it still possible between them? "I wanted to," he said.

More time slipped by while neither of them looked at one another or said anything. The lights blinked in the auditorium, signaling that the room would soon be closed.

Sam cleared his throat. "I suppose I'll have to brush up on all the little-girl things again. I liked it when you boys were in Little League, but I was always lost when Addy tried to teach me how to tap dance." Rafe exhaled an amused breath and Sam added, "You laugh, but just wait until that little monkey wants you to spring for lessons. Your house will sound like a family of woodpeckers have taken up residence."

Rafe shook his head. "It can't be worse than that damned accordion."

"Ah, yes." Sam lifted his fingers. "A word of advice. *Earplugs*. They got me through many a practice of Nick's saxophone and Matthew's drums."

They subsided again. Each into memories of years past, perhaps? Sam swallowed, his heart bumping uncomfortably. Rosa had been nattering at him to make peace, *real* peace, and he wasn't adverse to the idea. It was just that years of *not* communicating with Rafe had rendered him ill-equipped for the task. Where to start? *Where?*

"Rafe," he began hesitantly. "I've given some thought to what you said the other day. About that night in the emergency room."

His son's head came up, his eyes filled with wary discomfort. "Let's not get into it again, Pop. I don't want to fight. I'm tired of fighting."

"Just hear me out," Sam said, lifting his hand as though he could physically hold off a rejection. "Please."

Rafe looked at him for a long moment, then nodded, though Sam could sense how little he wanted to have anything to do with this discussion.

Sam swallowed a lump of uncertainty. Before he could lose his nerve, he said, "After you were born, your mother and I knew right away that you were going to be very different from Nick or Matthew. You were a demanding baby. As a child, your favorite word was *why?* You took unthinkable risks, and when I disciplined you, you never cried. It was unnerving to have a son who seemed so incapable of being reached."

Rafe straightened restlessly. "If this is supposed to—"

"Wait. I'm getting to my point." He spread his hands. "No parent likes to think they make mistakes. But you do. Horrible ones. I was at a loss—feeling as though I was failing you, terrified, really. And I am not a man who accepts defeat easily. Or gracefully."

"You didn't fail me," Rafe said in a quiet voice. "We just didn't…connect."

"I know. When I think about it, you probably ended up feeling that you'd found more of a father in that Wendall Crews fellow—that man who took you under his wing—than you did me. I've heard you talk about him. The relationship the two of you had, that should have been you and me."

"Wendall taught me a lot," Rafe admitted. "He made me realize that I was getting too old to continue acting like a jackass. He was a good business role model."

"I'm sure he was," Sam said, unable to keep the little tinge of resentment from his voice.

"But I never thought of him as a father, Pop."

Sam started. Was his face that transparent? He straightened, determined to get everything out in the open. "Anyway," he said gruffly. "The more you pulled away, the angrier I got. When I came down to the hospital, all of it spilled out. I was angry at myself for not being able to control the situation. But most of all, I was frightened. There was so much blood…."

"It looked worse than it was."

Sam gave a dismissive shrug, then favored Rafe with a close look. "Let me ask you something. When you first saw Francesca perched on that balcony railing, what image flashed in your mind?"

"Frannie lying on the pavement below. Broken into about a million pieces."

"You are discovering what it feels like to be a real parent, then," Sam said. "You want your child to be an individual, to experience all the wonderful things life has to offer. But another part of you wants to protect them forever, so that they are never hurt. And when you can't do that…sometimes you feel as though it's all your fault. When I saw you that night, that's all I could think. *My* fault. *My* failure as a father. I shouldn't have taken it out on you, but I did."

Rafe sighed and raked a hand through his hair. Then he looked straight at Sam. "I'm sorry. I got myself in that situation, and I didn't want to face you—see one more disappointment in your eyes. My pride was hurt. I felt like a damned fool."

Sam's mouth went dry. His son was not a man who apologized easily, Sam thought, and then he had to laugh inside. Neither was he.

He smiled. "Your mother says we are a lot alike. I fear she might be right. But I know that I cannot continue to make our situation intolerable by refusing to move an inch. Do you think we could accept that we both made mistakes and put the past behind us?"

He extended his hand.

Rafe gave him a hard, straight look, one with respect and reconciliation in it. He took Sam's hand. "I'd like that. I really want to live here, Pop. Raise a family the way you and Mom did. There's so much I have to learn, and I can't think of any better teachers than the two of you. If you'll just let me back in the family."

Sam's mouth parted in surprise. "Let you back in? *Dio!* There is no need. In spite of everything that has happened, you have always been a member of this family. You always will be."

He felt choked with emotion, and seeing his son's face, he couldn't help himself. He pulled on Rafe's hand until his son was close, and then Sam captured him in a hug. He didn't care who saw. It didn't feel at all awkward or unwanted. It felt right.

Rosa was suddenly coming toward them with Francesca in tow. The two men broke apart. "Sorry to take so long," Rosa said. "Trouble with the zipper."

"Are we going to get ice cream now?" his granddaughter asked.

"Yes, we are," Rafe replied.

"Good. 'Cause Rhonda asked if I wanted to spend the night at her house, and I said no. I told her I wanted to go out with you guys. With my family."

The child skipped ahead of them. Rosa followed. Rafe waited for Sam to fall in step in front of him, and before he did, Rafe gave him a quick, small smile.

With my family, Francesca had said. *With my family.* Yes, Sam thought. It felt that way at last.

THAT SAME EVENING, Gary Newsome sat in the chair in front of Dani's desk. Her editor had come up from Denver. They'd had dinner, and now it was just the two of them. Cissy was long gone for the day. The office lay in quiet shadows.

"Very nice work, Dani," Gary said for the second time since he'd arrived.

"Thank you."

She'd sent him the story she'd done on the discovery of the Accordion Man's killer, as well as what she'd unearthed about the dead man's identity. All the facts that the paper would print in their next issue. In the back of her mind, she was already thinking of ways to help with Burt's defense, the angle she could use for a story about how love could make you do things you might never consider under normal circumstances. After her last conversation with Rafe, she thought she knew all about that.

Gary looked down at the notes he'd made. "So your Accordion Man was actually Willie Holt from St. Louis. A drifter, just like Beckerman said, and an ex-con to boot. Breaking and entering. Assault. It was probably just a matter of time before he got into real trouble that he couldn't shake."

"That doesn't excuse what Burt did, of course."

"No. But what's this about you getting Broken Yoke to start a defense fund?"

"Well, why not? He's been a model citizen for years.

Nearly everyone speaks highly of him. Shouldn't we try to help him?"

Gary gave her a speculative glance. *"We?"*

"You know what I mean. *We.* As in concerned citizens."

"Don't get too wrapped up in his defense. You have work to do."

From his briefcase he took out a file folder and slapped it on her desk. Dani frowned down at it. "What's this?"

"Your next assignment, if you want it. I'm springing you from this one-horse town. Pack your bags."

She felt a rush of sudden excitement. She picked up the folder and scanned it. Some plastic surgeon in Arvada was taking advantage of good-looking female patients when they were under anesthesia. She glanced back up at Gary. "But I thought my name was still mud—"

"It is. You owe me. I've convinced the right people that I need you down in Denver. So you can work on this—" He tapped the folder. "Or you can consider taking on new responsibilities. Either way, you're out of here."

"What new responsibilities?"

"You can write your own column. All the little stories that you do so well about us crazy Coloradoans. Sort of your own Lake Wobegon. What do you say?"

Dani frowned. As exciting as having her own byline would be, what about what she'd been trained for? "What about serious, investigative journalism?"

"Let me ask you something. Last year you did that piece on that real-estate scam in Glenwood Springs. Which did you like better? Poking through a bunch of musty county tax records, or talking to that old geezer about his war with that James Bond wolf?"

"I admit that the wolf was more fun," Dani conceded. "But it wasn't real news."

"No, it wasn't," Gary agreed. "But think about some of the other stories you've done since you've been up here. The people. It's what you do best." He lifted his hand and began ticking off his fingers. "Human interest. Drama. Comedy. The little daily dose of promise that can make you believe it's not so bad living on this great big blue ball. People want it. They need it. I've been in this business a long time. Take my advice, Dani. Play to your strengths."

She was silent for a long while, considering his words. She tried to picture herself in the role of columnist, and was surprised to discover that she succeeded with very little effort. The truth was, in the weeks she'd been here, she'd grown to love covering the kind of stories she'd been sending Gary.

Without thinking, she asked, "Does it have to be done from Denver? Can't I continue to do it from here?"

"I suppose so," her boss agreed. "But why? Is this town such a terrific place to live that it's worth sticking around?"

She grimaced. "Some parts of it are."

He reached out and snagged the newspaper off the

corner of her desk. It was coverage she'd done for the Accordion Man Festival. Lots of colorful pictures. Lots of people having fun. And right in the middle, a picture of Rafe D'Angelo and his daughter smiling as they held up that red accordion.

Gary turned the paper so that the picture of Rafe was facing her. "Is he one of those parts?"

"Not anymore." Dani pressed her lips together, mortified that he had guessed the truth. Then she looked at him in surprise. "How did you know?"

"Because I am an extraordinary investigative journalist," Gary said in an ego-driven tone. Then he grinned. "And because your receptionist has loose lips. She says you've been moping around here for two days because she thinks you had a fight with the town stud." He flipped the picture around so he could see it, then frowned. "I don't know… Can you be the town stud and still love the accordion?"

She made a face at him. "Accordion music isn't that bad."

Gary laughed. "If you think that, it *must* be love!" He rubbed his stomach, where about half a pound of the Sun Dial's baby back ribs had found a home earlier. "Question is, what are you going to do about him?"

"Nothing I can do," Dani said, settling her chin in her hand. She felt coldly despondent saying it out loud. Had, in fact, felt that way for two whole days now. The death of hope was hard to face. "I blew it big-time."

"So un-blow it."

"How?"

Gary made a gesture of pure impatience. "Dani, you're a smart girl. You know how to get people to talk to you. Figure something out."

CHAPTER TWENTY-ONE

YEARS AGO, DANI HAD ONCE complained impatiently that college was just too hard, that it was going to take too long to get her degree in journalism. He mother had whisked her over to the kitchen table, sat her down and explained in a brisk, matter-of-fact tone that there were no easy answers in life, no shortcuts to anyplace worth going.

It was a lecture that Dani never forgot.

And right now, it was one she had to keep uppermost in her mind.

She sat parked in front of the Three Bs, watching a gold-powdered sunset sift over the Front Range. The mountains were turning purple in the distance, and here in Broken Yoke, twilight had already ignited the street lamps. The night would be like velvet, lush with fragrance from the earthy perfume of flowers that had been planted for the Accordion Man Festival.

Rafe's place was quiet. The curtains were drawn, but there were lights in the upstairs windows and in the living room. Every so often, Dani saw a shadow pass in front of them. Her heart thudded and she could not make it slow down.

She had come here tonight simply because there was nothing else she could do. For days she had tried to put her relationship with Rafe behind her, forget everything. Last night she had told Gary that she'd blown it, and she honestly believed that.

But after another sleepless night, she'd finally come to one, undeniable conclusion. She did not *want* to put the past behind her. She did not *want* to forget. She loved Rafe D'Angelo. Here it was at last, what might be the key to everything she'd ever wanted, shining and golden, if she could just find the courage to face her fears.

She had to.

Because every day without Rafe in her life, happiness moved further and further away.

Grabbing up the newspaper she'd brought with her, Dani got out of the car before she could change her mind. The closer she got to Rafe's front door, the more uncertain she began to feel. *Keep going. Don't stop. Don't stop.* Those words were in her ears like a refrain.

She rapped sharply on the door. From inside she could hear the sound of an accordion wheezing out a song, but it wasn't identifiable. Then suddenly Rafe was standing in front of her, his dark hair furrowed by restless fingers, a day's worth of beard along his jaw. He had never looked more wonderful to her, though she could sense no welcome in him.

"Hi," she said, trying for a light tone.

He looked cautious, noncommittal. "Hi."

"I just stopped by to drop this off for Frannie. I thought she might like to keep it. Start a scrapbook or something."

Conquering the fear that threatened to destroy her poise completely, Dani held out the paper she had brought, the section with Rafe and Frannie's festival picture. An excuse, really, for coming here tonight. He'd see through it in a minute, she thought suddenly.

He took the newspaper and placed it on the hall table. "Thanks. I'm sure she'll be glad to get it."

The wail of the accordion continued to cut the air, little runs along the keyboard that made no sense at all. "I guess you've still got your houseguest."

"Looks like it might be a permanent fixture after all. Frannie wants to take lessons."

Silence then. Unbearable silence between them.

"Well…that's all, really," she said. "Except…" She gave him a hard, determined look. "Damn it, Rafe. I've done some stupid things in my life, but I'm not going to leave here without making sure we get a few things straight. The other day you threatened to shout everything out in the hallway so my neighbors could hear. Well, I'm prepared to do the same thing if you aren't willing to listen."

Rafe looked at her for a long moment. "Then I guess I'd better invite you in."

He stepped aside. She felt a sweet sense of expansion in her breast. Surely no invitation would have been made if they were beyond salvaging, would it? She nodded and walked over the threshold.

They stood in the living room, looking at one another. Now that she had his attention, Dani didn't know where to start, and Rafe seemed uncomfortable, as though he already regretted inviting her in. He slipped his hands into the back pockets of his jeans.

"So how are you?" he asked, but it sounded so polite, so stilted that Dani took no encouragement from it.

"Fine. Busy."

"What's the latest with Burt?"

She told him about her plans to help him. How Geneva McKay and his aunt Sofia were already beating the bushes for support. Since they only had Burt's word about how Willie Holt had died, it wouldn't be easy, but the attorney she'd talked to from Denver had seemed hopeful.

When that topic had been exhausted, Dani said, "So how are you doing with Frannie? Are the two of you making progress?"

"Every day is a challenge. But it's getting better. Heather actually thinks there's hope for me."

She nodded, as though he'd care whether she agreed or not. And then, because she could not imagine what else she could do, she said, "How about us? Is there hope for us?"

Rafe stiffened. "Dani, don't."

"I can't help it. I'm hopelessly in love with you, and

I just don't want to give up on that until you tell me that there's nothing else we can do."

His brow lifted. "So suddenly I'm the man of your dreams?"

"No. Suddenly I'm a woman who's figured out what she's been doing wrong all her life. With men, I mean."

"And what's that?"

She bit her lip, knowing that she had to plunge in, heart and soul. Everything was at stake now. If she failed, it couldn't be because she hadn't tried. In spite of all the wrong turns and lousy odds, she couldn't give up now.

"I've only had a handful of relationships with men," she said. "But with every one of them, I've ended it first. My father left my mother before I was born. He didn't want anything to do with us. My mother mistrusted men all her life, and she had an enormous influence on my life. I think that deep down I've never truly believed that a man will stay. So before they could ditch me, I always ended it with them."

"Good way to protect yourself. If you want to go through life alone."

"I know. But then you came along, and it felt so different."

"How?"

Well, at least he hadn't told her to get out. That had to mean something, didn't it? "At first, it was easy to tell myself I wasn't interested. Back in Vegas…" She stumbled on that word, not wanting to have any reminders of the past between them. "Well, you know how I felt about you back then. But here things seemed so different, and I couldn't help it. I fell in love with you. I was in love with you long before we ever slept together."

"You make that sound like a bad thing."

She shook her head vigorously. "Not at all. But I was constantly wondering what the hell I was thinking—falling in love with a man who had a proven track record as a womanizer, a man who had a history of not staying in one place for very long, a man who couldn't seem to get along with even his own father." She ran her hands up and down her arms as though chilled. "It seemed impossible."

"Aren't you lucky to have escaped all that?" He had a steely look about him, and Dani knew she'd lost a little ground.

"For God's sake, Rafe. You used to be Oz—the Wizard of Women. What was I supposed to think?"

"You could have judged me for who I am today. Not who I used to be."

"I know. I know. I'm not saying you didn't prove me wrong. I'm just telling you that it scared the hell out of me. And I think that's when I started looking for…a way out. A way to end it before you up and left me. I've never been the jealous type. But when I saw you here with Heather, it was so easy to turn it into something awful. It didn't have anything to do with not trusting you. It was just a way to keep from being more hurt by you than I could stand."

"So did it work?"

"No. Without you, I'm more miserable than I've ever been in my life. Please tell me we can make this right."

"Dani—"

"I want to ask you something. The other night you said that the woman you fall in love with had to take some things on faith. *Are* you in love with me?"

"Oh, God," Rafe said, scrubbing a hand over his face for a moment. "I want so badly to say no."

The words warmed her like a blazing fire. He hadn't said no.

He walked up to her, and the flicker of hope she saw in his eyes nearly defeated her. "At first, I just wanted to believe you were an itch I needed to scratch. Every time I was around you I thought I had a handle on it, but then you'd look at me a certain way, or laugh that throaty little laugh of yours, and I felt like I was drowning. The truth is more than skin deep. I could feel it in my bones, even when I was ignoring it on the surface." He caught her arms. "I've never said this to another woman. I'm in love with you. I want to marry you and live together in this crazy town and raise a bunch of kids who can make good brothers and sisters to Frannie."

She stared at him, unable to believe his words. Love put you in such grave danger. And yet, it could come out right. It could all come out right if you just didn't give up. If you worked at it. "I think that can be arranged," she said.

She saw the tiny leap of wonder in his eyes. "Do you think so? I'm not used to this, Dani. I'm not sure I'll know how to do it right. But I know this. Anything I've learned about love, you've taught me."

He gathered her in his arms. He kissed her, so deeply that she thought she would never surface. From here on out, her life would be on a strange and unknown course, but as long as they were together, anything was possible.

In the background, Dani heard a heavy thump, thump, thump from the stairs. "Hey!" a voice called out. "Why are you kissing her?"

Dani lifted her head to discover that Frannie was making her way down the stairs. The red accordion, which was almost as big as she was, was being dragged behind her like a boat anchor, squealing an occasional protest the entire way.

Rafe saw his daughter and laughed. "I'm kissing Dani because I like it."

Frannie abandoned the accordion at the bottom of the stairs and ran toward them like a human tornado. She latched on to her father's pant leg and looked up at him with mischief-filled eyes. "I thought you weren't going to kiss her until *after* you played your song?"

"Frannie..." Rafe said.

"What are you talking about?" Dani asked with a frown. "What song?"

"Daddy said he was gonna ask you to marry him, and that you were a sucker for accordion music. So we've been practicing all day, but now, what's the use if you're gonna kiss anyway?"

Rafe shook his head and lightly clapped his hand over his daughter's mouth. "This child would not know discretion if it bit her on the nose."

Dani tilted a confused look at him. "You were going to ask me to marry you?"

"Yes."

"When?"

"I figured I'd come by your place this evening," Rafe admitted.

"And you were going to play the accordion?"

"I thought it would put you in a receptive mood." He lifted his hands, grinning. "Who doesn't like accordion music?"

"You," Dani said.

Rafe looked sheepish, but amused. "Well, that was before Pop showed me how to play an Italian love song. Want to hear it?"

Dani laughed and snuggled closer against his chest. "Maybe later. Much later."

From between them, Frannie spoke up, "Want to hear me play 'Lady of Spain'? I know the first four notes."

"No!" Rafe and Dani said at the same time.

Frannie pouted prettily. Dani knew she was going to have her hands full with this child, but what a challenging delight it would be. "Well…" the girl said in determination. "Then what *can* I play?"

Never taking his eyes off Dani, Rafe said to his

daughter, "Do you know how to play 'Here Comes the Bride'?"

"No. But I'll bet I can learn it."

"Good," he said, nibbling a kiss against Dani's lips until an eerie wave of warmth touched her, flooded through her. "Because I think we're going to need it very soon."

Don't miss The Return of David McKay
the next book from Ann Evans
coming in October 2008
from Mills & Boon® Superromance.

Bedding His Virgin Mistress

Ricardo Salvatore planned to take over Carly's company, so why not have her as well? But Ricardo was stunned when in the heat of passion he learned of Carly's innocence…

Expecting the Playboy's Heir

American billionaire and heir to an earldom, Silas Carter is one of the world's most eligible men. Beautiful Julia Fellowes is perfect wife material. And she's pregnant!

Blackmailing the Society Bride

When millionaire banker Marcus Canning decides it's time to get an heir, debt-ridden Lucy becomes a convenient wife. Their sexual chemistry is purely a bonus…

Available 5th September 2008

Collect all 10 superb books in the collection!

Queens of Romance

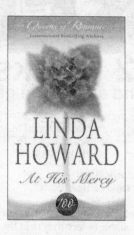

LINDA HOWARD

At His Mercy

Mackenzie's Magic

Maris Mackenzie woke up to sexy stranger
Alex MacNeil in her bed – and she'd lost all recollection
of their night together...

Heartbreaker

Michelle was deeply in debt to sexy John Rafferty, the
tough-talking, hard-loving rancher. Yet out of self-
preservation she still refused to become his mistress!

Overload

Stranded with him in a Dallas skyscraper during a power cut,
Elizabeth Major thought Tom Quinlan was too much for
her to handle. So now he was changing her mind...

Available 3rd October 2008

Collect all 10 superb books in the collection!

FREE!

2 Books
and a surprise gift!

We would like to take this opportunity to thank you for reading this Mills & Boon® book by offering you the chance to take TWO more specially selected titles from the Superromance series absolutely FREE! We're also making this offer to introduce you to the benefits of the Mills & Boon® Book Club—

- ★ FREE home delivery
- ★ FREE gifts and competitions
- ★ FREE monthly Newsletter
- ★ Exclusive Mills & Boon Book Club offers
- ★ Books available before they're in the shops

Accepting these FREE books and gift places you under no obligation to buy, you may cancel at any time, even after receiving your free shipment. Simply complete your details below and return the entire page to the address below. You don't even need a stamp!

YES! Please send me 2 free Superromance books and a surprise gift. I understand that unless you hear from me, I will receive 4 superb new titles every month for just £3.69 each, postage and packing free. I am under no obligation to purchase any books and may cancel my subscription at any time. The free books and gift will be mine to keep in any case.

U8ZEF

Ms/Mrs/Miss/Mr ....Initials............................
BLOCK CAPITALS PLEASE
Surname ....
Address ....

....
....Postcode ....

Send this whole page to:
UK: FREEPOST CN81, Croydon, CR9 3WZ